mo

CW01597811

GR

Leeds Library and Information Service
24 hour renewals
http://www.leeds.gov.uk/librarycatalogue
or phone 0845 1207271
Overdue charges may apply

LD 4979270 9

THE 'Lavender Lady' CASEFILE

THE 'Lavender Lady' CASEFILE

Jessie Daniels

ROBERT HALE

First published in 2017 by
Robert Hale, an imprint of
The Crowood Press Ltd,
Ramsbury, Marlborough
Wiltshire SN8 2HR

www. crowood.com

© Jessie Daniels 2017

All rights reserved. No part of this publication may be reproduced or transmitted in any form or by any means, electronic or mechanical, including photocopy, recording or any information storage and retrieval system, without permission in writing from the publishers.

British Library Cataloguing-in-Publication Data
A catalogue record for this book is available from the British Library.

ISBN 978 0 7198 2477 7

The right of Jessie Daniels to be identified as author of this work has been asserted by her in accordance with the Copyright, Designs and Patents Act 1988.

Typeset by Chapter One Book Production, Knebworth

Printed and bound in India by Parkson's Graphics

CHAPTER ONE

Effie James always rode the Park 'n' Ride bus whenever she went into Oxford's city centre, since parking in the fabled city of dreaming spires was, as every native knew, a total nightmare. And as she rang the bell to alight at the top end of St Giles, an old man sitting on one of the seats near the doors drew back his legs a little to let her pass, looking appreciatively at hers as she did so.

Effie pretended not to notice, but wouldn't have been human if she didn't feel slightly pleased with the compliment. After all, after having reached the huge milestone of her fortieth birthday just last summer, a woman needed all the ego boosting that she could get. And if her legs were still deemed to be noteworthy, perhaps she should make a mental check to wear skirts or dresses more often?

And so with a smile, she alighted from the large and rather grubby double decker bus into a beautiful spring morning in mid April. All down the Woodstock Road, she had noted that the cherry trees were frothing with their particular shade of eye-catching pink and that the gardens fronting the busy road were bursting with the yellow blooms of daffodils, forsythia bushes, primroses and tulips.

It made you feel glad to be alive on such a day, when the sky was a cloudless expanse of azure blue, and all around the blackbirds and sparrows were busy nest-building or feeding early broods. But the moment the thought entered her head, she felt herself tense with a familiar sense of guilt.

Her smile fading now, she gave a mental shake of her head and pushed the thought aside, refusing to let any pall of black gloom settle over her. Instead, she set off resolutely down the busy pavement, just the dozen or so yards that were needed to bring her to Browns, one of her favourite eating places in the city.

As she paused outside the windows of the famous establishment, she caught sight of her reflection in the glass, mainly because the spring sunshine had caught her short, silvery-blonde hair, and had given it a very flattering highlight. Styled in an elfin-like feather-cut, it clung slightly to her high cheekbones and tapered stylishly to the nape of her neck. And so what if her temples were now more silver than blonde? At least it was natural – her ash-blonde colouring coming courtesy of her mother's inherited Swedish genes. Her large, hazel-grey eyes, slightly stubborn-looking chin and wide mouth, however, were all from her father's side of the family.

But as she looked at her reflection in the glass, a niggling sense of doubt began to assail her. Perhaps the outfit had been a mistake after all? Her husband had always preferred her in trouser suits of darker tones – navy, charcoal and deep claret; the neat, impeccably-tailored and sophisticated kinds of outfits that he'd always maintained flattered her the most.

Was she dressed too young?

When she'd looked out of her window this morning, the lovely weather had tempted her into ditching all her tried and trusted outfits, and had lured her into donning something far more frivolous instead. Not that she'd had a wide range of those to choose from – most of her more daring purchases, made over the years in various moments of madness, had been pushed to the back of her wardrobe and had languished there, all but forgotten about.

Now the expression 'mutton dressed as lamb' slid insidiously across her mind, and sent a slight shiver of unease rippling coolly up her spine. She could almost hear Michael's voice saying it.

Well, it was too late to change her mind now, she told herself fatalistically.

And not wanting to be caught preening at her reflection in the glass like some vain schoolgirl, she quickly pushed her doubts to one side, opened the door of the restaurant and walked in. It didn't take her long to spot her lunch companion, since he was already seated and sipping coffee in one of the best tables near the front windows overlooking the pavement.

Her lips, which had been painted a pale raspberry shade barely an hour ago, twisted into a small smile. Trust Duncan to demand the best – and get it.

She nodded at the hostess who'd come to greet her with a questioning smile, discreetly murmured the name of Professor Duncan Fergusson, and was promptly led to her old friend's table. He spotted her approach at once of course, and rose swiftly to his feet.

'Duncan, ever the gentleman,' she said with a smile and gave him a cool kiss on each cheek.

At fifty-two, Duncan was exactly her height (five feet ten inches) with a head of lush and distinguished silver hair, which was echoed in his fine, bushy eyebrows. His neat little goatee beard, however, was a slightly darker grey in tone, and matched the colour of his eyes almost exactly. And even if he had started to grow just slightly podgy in the last few years, with the dreaded middle-age spread claiming yet another victim, he was still a fine figure of a man, and definitely attractive to the opposite sex.

As his long-suffering wife, Margot, could no doubt testify.

'Effie, you look as gorgeous as ever,' he said smoothly in his trademark and pleasing Highland lilt, taking both of her hands in his and spreading them wide, the better to admire her slender figure.

She tried not to shuffle uneasily as he inspected her cream coloured mid-calf length skirt with a matching double-breasted jacket in fine linen, and the pretty honey-gold shot-silk blouse underneath. And once again, couldn't help wondering if she should have stuck with trousers.

But at least she had donned modest black flats to go with the outfit, since she hadn't worn high heels since her teenage years, and the only jewellery she wore was her wedding ring, plus a small stud pearl earring in each lobe.

'It's lovely to see you wearing light colours for a change. I have to say, you brighten up an already sunny day,' Duncan told her reassuringly.

'Flattery before noon might just go to my head,' Effie warned him glibly. She had known Duncan for far too long to ever fall for the psychology professor's easy charm. 'So,' she said, gently but firmly pulling her hands free from his and taking a seat. 'This is nice, even if the invitation came out of the blue.'

She took the chair he pulled out for her, and the hostess chose that moment to ask politely if they'd like a drink. Effie automatically ordered orange juice. Duncan, grimacing at her, ordered a bottle of Chardonnay.

'Yes, I know, but it *is* nearly twelve o'clock,' he said, as if she'd actually chided him aloud for his alcohol-based choice. 'Besides, some of us aren't afraid to live a little,' he added teasingly. 'Oh, and before anything else, I really must apologize for having to ask you out at such a ridiculously early time for lunch, but I have to get back to St Bedes by one thirty for a tutorial. I wish I could just wash my hands of the brats and have done with it, but the Dean will insist that I teach a *few* students now and then. If I had my way, the college would simply pay me handsomely to do my research and then have the courtesy to leave me alone, letting the Junior Fellows do all that tedious tutoring and stuff.'

Effie smiled mildly. 'You know, I'm not at all sure whether to believe you actually mean all that or not. Margot says that it's all for show, and that you really love to have all those adoring undergraduates fawning over you and clinging to your every word.'

'Huh – just goes to show what *she* knows,' he grumbled. 'My nearest and dearest was probably pulling your leg.'

Effie laughed, then moved aside slightly to allow the waiter to deposit her drink in front of her. She also accepted a large menu, and began to scan the choices. This early in the day it had to be something light, of course.

Her eyes dipped instantly to the salads.

'The T-bone steak, with sautéed potatoes, please,' she heard Duncan say, so promptly that he almost certainly couldn't have had time to look at the choices on offer. But then, he probably ate here regularly, whereas for Effie this was much more of a treat.

And the thought gave her pause for a moment. Had it really been so long since she'd eaten out? Then, after thinking about it for a moment, she realized that it probably had been quite a while.

'I'll have the tuna salad, please,' she said. 'No croutons,' she added conscientiously. She had to watch her weight. Then, suddenly and out of nowhere, a thought struck her. *What did it matter if she got fat?* There would be no one at home to criticize her for it, or shoot her disapproving little glances.

For a moment her heart lurched and she felt slightly sick and disorientated. It wasn't an altogether unfamiliar feeling – she'd had odd moments like these for a while now, and she forced herself to take a slow deep breath. Experience had taught her that if she ignored the negativity, it would eventually go away.

The waiter nodded silent acquiescence of her order and elegantly drifted off. It always unnerved her when they did that, and with such aplomb. It made her feel, in contrast, like a country bumpkin let loose in the big city and sure to be found out as a fraud when she committed some gaffe or minor breach of restaurant etiquette.

Not that she'd ever been tempted to become a denizen of the town. She'd lived in the small but pretty village of Hampton Frome, just six miles away, for nearly twenty years now, ever since her marriage to Michael. And Michael had always been happiest in the country, preferring to keep the city relegated strictly to a working environment only.

Before that, she'd been born and raised on a council estate in the local market town of Bicester, but had never felt particularly at home, even there. No, give her a large garden, countryside walks and plenty of fresh clean air, and she was happy. It was one of the many things that she and her husband had always agreed upon.

Which rather begged the question – just why *had* Duncan called her yesterday to invite her out to lunch here in the city? It must have been nearly two years since she'd last seen him and Margot, at some party or other that had been given by his college in aid of a local fundraising event. Of course, Michael had been with her then....

Instantly, she shut the thought off before it could reach its logical conclusion and decided that, instead of sitting here like a lemon wondering why she was here, she should just come out with it and simply ask him.

'So I'm curious as to why you asked me …' she began, and then trailed off as Duncan held up a hand and nodded his head, already making small, conciliatory noises. Since he was in the process of taking a large sip of his wine, she had to wait until he'd swallowed it before her curiosity could be satisfied.

'Yes, of course you are. Sorry, I didn't mean to sound so mysterious over the phone. Or did I?' he added, eyes twinkling.

Effie couldn't help but smile back. This was typical of Duncan. Playful, flirtatious and just a little bit wearing on your patience.

'You did sound just a bit cloak and dagger,' she admitted mildly. Then looked at him in some alarm as a rather hideous thought assailed her. 'Duncan, I hope you aren't going to ask me to become one of your guinea pigs in some sort of awful psychology experiment. Remember, I'm not one of your students needing to up my grades! I don't have to do as you say.'

Years ago, Margot had regaled her with some horrific stories about unknowing, innocent students who agreed to sign up for some university-funded psychological experiments, only to find themselves, like *Alice in Wonderland,* falling down some rabbit hole or other. With the likes of Duncan and his fellow psychology Dons looking on and taking assiduous notes, of course.

'Perish the thought!' Duncan said now, grinning widely. 'I wouldn't dare be so crass. Besides,' he added with a definite twinkle in his eye now, 'if I put you in one of those trials, you'd cause havoc. Half the men in them would—'

'Enough,' Effie said, beginning to laugh. 'Why don't you just tell me what it is that you're after then?'

Duncan smiled, then looked at her rather more closely. She could tell by the way that his eyes darkened that he was about to say something about Michael, and she felt herself freeze. She knew she shouldn't – it had, after all, been nearly a year now, and she should be getting used to it. But she just wasn't. Any mention of her husband threatened to send her into a tailspin, and she felt herself bracing for the impact of his next words.

'Effie, I'm really, really sorry about Michael,' Duncan said gently. 'I had hoped that you'd get in touch with me, you know, just to talk.' He reached across the table and briefly laid his hand over hers. 'You know I'm only a phone call away whenever you need me.'

'Thank you, Duncan,' she said, hoping that her voice didn't sound as stiff as her face felt. 'And thank you for the flowers. I really appreciated them.' She drew her hands carefully free of his, and reached for her glass. She was proud of the steadiness of her hand as she lifted it to her lips, but her small triumph was rather spoilt by the fact that her throat felt so tight that she could only pretend to take a sip.

Duncan nodded, his eyes now looking distinctly professional as they searched her face. 'So, how are you doing?' he asked softly. 'I mean, *really* doing?'

Effie quickly dropped her gaze down to the pink and purple anemones in a tiny glass jar resting in the centre of the table, and laughed gently. 'Duncan, if you think I'm going to sit here and let you psychoanalyse me, you must be … well, mad,' she laughed, 'if you'll pardon the truly awful pun. It's way too nice a day, and I'm far too hungry. Besides, I'm agog with curiosity about what it is that you've got waiting up your sleeve. I'm not so gullible as to think that this is a free lunch, you know.'

Duncan puffed up his chest and looked outrageously offended. 'Effie James! Are you trying to say that I'm one of those people who only get in touch with old friends when they *want something*?' he demanded, his voice reminiscent of a grand actor of the old school, playing some Shakespearean villain on the stage.

'Yes,' Effie said shortly.

'Oh, fair enough then.' Duncan's chest deflated and he went back to his normal speaking voice – soft and deep and with a faint Scottish burr that rested easy on the ear. 'In that case … How do you feel about taking on a bit of an adventure?'

Effie's eyes widened in some alarm and the waiter chose that moment to appear with their food. Ignoring the righteously low-calorific offering that had been arranged attractively on her plate, she studied Duncan suspiciously.

'Ah, lovely. Medium rare, just as I like it,' he muttered, reaching for his steak knife and slicing off a large piece of beef, which he inspected greedily. And it crossed her mind, briefly and somewhat uncharitably, that it was no wonder that he was putting on weight.

Then she sighed and mentally began girding her loins for the tussle to come. She had no doubt, now, that she was in for a fight of some kind, since he'd clearly decided that she needed 'taking out of herself' and had come up with some sort of a project to do just that. And she knew from past experience that when he had his mind set on something, besting him was no easy feat. He had a way of out-thinking you and of sounding so reasonable and logical and helpful about it all, that, before you knew it, you found yourself agreeing to whatever it was that he wanted.

Margot had once confessed to her, many years ago and after one too many martinis, that the only reason she had married Duncan in the first place was because he had bamboozled her into it. Effie had, at the time, thought that she'd just been joking – or perhaps merely exaggerating. A heart surgeon at the John Radcliffe hospital, intelligent, no-nonsense Margot had always struck Effie as being the least malleable woman that she knew. Nowadays, she rather thought that her friend had probably been in deadly earnest.

And perhaps it wasn't so surprising. Duncan had, after all, made it his career to study the human mind, human behaviour, body language and the philosophy of what it meant to be human. And a man like that must find it easier than most to manipulate people. But the fact that he (almost) always had a benign reason for doing so was, of course, his saving grace. Moreover, Duncan made no secret of the fact that he found his fellow human beings fascinating. And if he could make women in particular feel that his fascination was more personal and intimate … well, Effie was sure that he didn't mind that one little bit, either.

Although she did sometimes wonder if Duncan strayed as often as Michael had always maintained that he did. She rather hoped not, for Margot's sake. But then again, Margot seemed to accept her husband as he was, displaying a kind of wry, easy-going aggression towards his philandering that seemed to work well for both of them. Certainly, they couldn't have stayed together for over fifteen years without some kind of an understanding existing between them.

And Effie understood, so very well, that nobody could ever truly understand what went on inside other people's marriages. Indeed, sometimes Effie found herself wondering if she'd ever really known what had gone on inside her own.

'Hello, you still with me, sweetheart?' Her friend's gently rolling voice brought her back out of her reverie with a start and she felt herself flush slightly in embarrassment. She speared an inoffensive little cherry tomato with rather more savagery than it deserved and forced herself to smile.

'Sorry, I sometimes find myself zoning out every now and then,' she admitted wryly.

Duncan nodded gravely. 'It's called grieving, Effie. It affects people in a variety of ways, but everyone who's lost someone dear to them goes through it,' he said gently.

Effie nodded and sought desperately for a way to change the subject. Then remembered that she had a perfect excuse right at hand. 'So, you mentioned something about an adventure. Exactly what kind of an adventure did you have in mind?' she asked cautiously.

'Oh, nothing outlandish,' Duncan promised rapidly, sounding reassuringly soothing. 'So there's no need to look so wary!'

Which, naturally, instantly set Effie's inner alarm bells ringing. Duncan was a lovely man, charming, clever and warm. But he could also be a proper menace at times. And she had the rather uncomfortable feeling that this was going to be one of those occasions.

Definitely time to start putting up the perimeter defences.

'Well, you know I'm volunteering at several charity shops now,' she began quickly. 'Which gets me out of the house quite a bit already. And don't forget, I have the garden,' she pointed out firmly.

Her garden was her pride and joy. Large and lovely, she kept it maintained with the help of Fred, a retired old man in her village.

When she'd first moved into the house after the honeymoon, the garden had terrified her. Extensive and well maintained – if a bit regimented – it had seemed a formidable challenge for her to take on. Her father had always taken care of the tiny garden that had come with the council house that she had grown up in.

And although she had also been initially nervous about taking on the responsibility for a big house, she had quickly come to realize that Michael expected 'the lady that does' to do the bulk of the work. His wife, Effie had been secretly thrilled to discover, wasn't really expected to do anything more than make sure the meals were cooked properly and that fresh flowers were always arranged on the hall table. At the time, she had felt as if she'd begun to live a rather fairy tale existence. The simple secretary who married the boss, and been instantly elevated to 'a lady who lunches'. Not that she'd ever really been one of those, since she'd preferred to carry on working.

However, the garden had been another matter, as it was clear that Michael had expected her to take charge of it and make it her own; he'd made it clear that she should make his house her home.

(Michael had hired an interior decorator that he liked and trusted to help her in the makeover of the house, so that she wouldn't feel overwhelmed, and she had spent a few wonderful months, happily refurbishing the kitchen and bathrooms, and changing the colours of the walls.)

And although she had the services of Old Fred – who knew it like the back of his hand – he had made it known that he would be taking his instructions only from her. And since she couldn't, in the beginning, tell a Canterbury bell from a Michaelmas daisy, it had been a steep learning curve.

But she had surprised herself, and perhaps Old Fred too, by quickly coming to love, and perhaps more importantly, understand and appreciate the plot of land that was all her own. Watching shed-loads of television programmes dedicated to gardening had helped, as did library books. And, from those early, tentative beginnings, Effie had quickly become a passionate gardener. She loved seeing the first snowdrops appear under the apple trees in February, followed by the burst of all the yellow colours of spring – daffodils, forsythia, crocus, primroses.

Rose pergolas and climbing honeysuckle arbours had followed, as had a successful rockery dedicated mostly to succulents.

And Michael had been pleased too, especially when her growing skill and a developing eye for pleasing natural disorder had resulted in their various neighbours complimenting them on their Japanese acers and ornamental wildlife pond.

So perhaps it was not surprising that now her garden was one of the few things that she thought of as actually, truly, belonging to her. She'd chosen every plant, overseen the careful placing of each of the three seating areas, and lovingly pruned every plum, cherry and apple tree. In her garden she could feel the weight of the world slip off her shoulders.

Odd, really, when growing up, she'd never given a garden a single thought.

'With just Fred to help, that takes up the bulk of my time as you can imagine. Fred won't admit it, but he can't do as much as he once could. And what with that, and walking Toad twice a day,' she mentioned her Yorkshire Terrier with a fond smile, 'I don't have much spare time left.'

She'd got the four-year-old dog from a rescue shelter just six weeks after losing her husband. Michael had not been an animal lover, but Effie had always loved them. Growing up as an only child, her mum and dad (perhaps out of a sense of guilt) had spoilt her by letting her have a veritable menagerie of animals for playmates that included dogs, cats, guinea pigs, rabbits and even a white rat.

So when she'd suddenly found herself living alone, and the cold numbness of loss had begun to wear off, it didn't take her long to realize that she really needed another warm presence in her house to keep her company. And taking on a rescue dog had been something of a no-brainer – she'd not only get to stroke warm fur and look into appealing big brown eyes whenever she needed to sit and cry, but she'd also be giving a previously unlucky animal a new, loving home.

'So you can see, I don't have as much spare time as you might think,' she ploughed on. She could feel herself burbling now, but couldn't seem to stop. 'I know everyone thinks that a recent widow, living alone in a big modern house, must have hours and hours on her hands—'

'They must spread out before you like a dessert,' Duncan put in softly, stopping her in manic mid-flow. 'When you lost Michael, you lost your job working at his firm as well, right?' he asked gently.

Effie took another deep breath and did her best to make her shrug look nonchalant.

At nineteen, and fresh from a year at secretarial college, she had found her first job as a secretary at the Oxford architectural firm of James & Fitch. It had seemed to her then, a simple working class girl from Bicester, to be the epitome of hitting it big. Working in the glamorous and beautiful university city for a firm that designed spectacular houses and public buildings for the rich and discerning. It had always been a dream job.

And when, after just six months, she'd been promoted to working with Michael James, one of the founding partners himself, she had been over the moon in more ways than just one. For Michael – a good decade older than herself – had been charming, intelligent, and urbane and had quickly swept her off her feet. Before she'd known it, she had accepted his offer of dinner. Which had promptly led to another date. And then another. Which in turn led to weekends away, a holiday abroad and, barely a year later, an official engagement.

She still had the diamond ring he'd given her at home. She rarely wore it nowadays because it had a tendency to pinch her finger in a certain spot and make it sore.

And after their wedding, Effie had carried on working at her husband's side – not because she continued to need the income, of course. Michael, as well as being one of the senior partners, had also been born into a wealthy family, and had always had a large stock portfolio and real estate purchases to cushion his lifestyle.

No, she'd carried on working simply because she'd loved it. She loved seeing the blueprints of fine houses and public buildings become reality. She loved the way people gasped and admired the creations of her husband and those of his employees when fine Portland stone, brickwork or cornices became real. And she'd also loved working alongside Michael – anticipating his needs, smoothing the way, being his buffer against all the nit-picking, niggardly little day-to-day worries that distracted and irritated him, leaving him free to create and build his visions.

And later, after the years began to roll by and children failed to make an appearance in their life, it had been even more necessary for her to keep on working. To be useful and needed, and to feel validated, even if only in some small way ….

'I'm sorry, I don't mean to pry. Well, perhaps just a bit,' Duncan said, again making her start just a little.

Good grief, she'd done it again! She really was going to have to watch this tendency to just drift off into her own little universe all willy-nilly, she thought uneasily.

Forcing herself to smile, she took a small sip of orange juice. 'Oh, that's all right. And yes, OK, perhaps I do find that sometimes the hours drag a little bit. But that doesn't mean,' she added hastily, 'that I feel the need to fill them up with some kind of an adventure. I'm not a member of the Famous Five, you know! And like I said, I have no intention of being part of some kind of weird psychology experiment.'

Duncan sighed softly and shook his head mournfully. 'Effie, Effie, Effie,' he said with mock sorrow. 'Anyone would think that you didn't trust me.'

'That's because I don't,' she growled, and not particularly jocularly, either.

Duncan bit back a grin. 'OK, pax,' he held up a hand in surrender. 'What say we talk about my latest project instead?' he proffered, spearing a large piece of sautéed potato and chewing it hedonistically. 'Oh my, that's good. Sure you don't want to pinch one off my plate?' he offered.

Effie eyed the delicious-looking, fluffy, golden fried concoction and sighed. 'I'm sure,' she muttered grimly, spearing a piece of lettuce and telling herself sternly that it would taste just as good.

It didn't of course.

'All right, let's discuss your latest project,' she echoed, still not trusting him one inch. 'It's another book, I take it?'

Duncan, in his spare time, wrote books that were almost best-sellers, designed to appeal to the general public who liked to feel that they were being educated even as they were being entertained.

They always covered some aspects of psychology, obviously, but in a way that anyone could digest and understand. Some of his more envious colleagues and critics called them his 'pop psychology scribblings' but Duncan annoyed them considerably by simply laughing it off and accusing them all of being jealous. And, without doubt, the money he earned from his book sales supplemented his university income very nicely indeed. There were even rumours flying about that one of the independent digital channels was thinking of buying the options on one or two of them for a documentary series about life in modern Britain.

'Of course it's another book,' Duncan said airily. 'Ask me what it's about this time.'

Effie sighed theatrically, her lips twitching. 'Oh, Professor Fergusson,' she said in a parody of a breathy, excited little voice, 'do tell me what your latest book is going to be about. I did so adore the way you wrote last time about the psychology behind the transgender boom of the early twenty-first century.' She finished off the performance by batting her eyelashes shamelessly.

'Oh, that was so last year,' Duncan said reprovingly around a mouthful of fried mushroom, not a whit abashed by her performance of an adoring sycophantic student. 'Right now it's all about the paranormal. That's where the real buzz is.'

Effie nearly choked on a slice of cucumber.

'Ghosts?' she finally managed to squeak, after patting her chest and consuming nearly half her glass of juice.

Duncan watched her antics with a gimlet eye. 'Scoff all you like, but there's no denying that it's always been a popular subject – and right now, it's more popular than ever. Haven't you noticed just how many television programmes are dedicated to it nowadays?'

Effie admitted to noticing a programme called *Most Haunted* but had never watched it.

'Oh, there's all sorts of stuff like that out there,' Duncan promised her with relish. 'Something else called *Paranormal Witness*, for example. Of course, a lot of it comes from America, and, as such, is strictly produced for entertainment value only,' he said, a shade cavalierly, Effie thought. 'But there's also some more serious work going on in the field. And some of it right here in good old Oxford, believe it or not.'

Effie looked genuinely surprised. And, quickly understanding the reason for her scepticism, he quickly waved a dismissive hand in the air.

'Oh, not the serious academics of course – you know how snooty and sniffy that lot can be about subjects like that,' he admitted. 'But talented amateurs, now they're another matter.'

Effie leaned slowly back in her chair, looking at her old friend in puzzlement. 'I never had you down as the type who believed in ghoulies and ghosties, and long-legged beasties and things that went bump in the night, Duncan.'

Her friend grinned wolfishly. 'I'm not. But there are a lot of people who *do*,' he reprimanded her primly. 'But what I think is beside the point. For me, it's the *psychology* behind it that is so fascinating.' He leaned forward in his chair, becoming clearly enthused with his subject matter. 'We all know that in today's society, more and more people are actively searching for something to take the place of the established church. All that really began in the sixties of course, with the hippies and their alternative lifestyles, which led more recently to the wave of New Age philosophies.' He paused for breath and to shrug amiably. 'People will always seek out new ways of defining death, and how to cope with their own mortality – that goes without saying. It's all to do with our deepest fears about dying and what comes afterwards. Or more to the point, what might *not* come afterwards. Before, people have always turned to religion to manage their fears. Nowadays, for a growing number of people, it's the paranormal – which makes sense. After all, if you can prove that ghosts exist, or that there is some kind of afterlife, then death loses a lot of the fearsome grip that it has on your psyche.'

'Hmmm,' Effie said vaguely. As macabre and fascinating as all this undoubtedly was, she was not at all sure where her friend was going with this. Or even whether or not she agreed with Duncan's rather perfunctory analysis of the issue. But still, it seemed a safe enough topic. Unless …

'Duncan, you're not asking me to go to some sort of ghastly

séance or something, are you?' she demanded crossly.

And then went cold all over as yet another, and far more hideous thought hit her. He didn't really think that she would agree to be part of some kind of farce whereby some charlatan of a medium tried to convince her that he or she was in touch with her dead husband, did he?

'Perish the thought!' Duncan said, and with enough acerbity to sound genuinely aggrieved. 'If I wanted to delve into the murky world of so-called psychics and mediums, I'd have a big enough pool of people to study, believe me. Unfortunately, there's no shortage of people willing to prey on the weak and vulnerable. And don't get me started on the way the bereaved can be exploited. Not that I'm not saying that there aren't genuine mediums out there; that is, people who actually believe that they have the gift for speaking to the dead,' he amended hastily. 'But that's a whole different psychopathy altogether and—'

Effie quickly held up a hand. 'Duncan, I'm not one of your students, remember?' she reminded him sharply. 'And this isn't one of your famous lectures.'

Duncan at least had the grace to look a little shamefaced. 'You're right. Sorry. I got a little carried away. You know me. Mind you, that's not to say that the whole Spiritual Movement back in Victorian times isn't fascinating. It gave poor, working class women a way to earn vast fortunes by claiming to communicate with the dead. It became a sort of mini-social revolution for them, in an age when the working class poor were trapped in a vicious cycle of poverty. And the movement took in a lot of prominent and intelligent people, you know, in spite of all that ectoplasm nonsense, and frauds merrily table-tipping away and using all sorts of other tricks with smoke and mirrors. Arthur Conan Doyle, for instance …'

'Duncan?' Effie said softly.

'Yes?'

'Not a student, remember?' she repeated sweetly.

'Yes. Sorry. Really.' He made a pantomime of zipping his mouth shut.

Effie slowly began to count. If he made it to five without speaking she'd …

'But really, that's not what I'm talking about,' Duncan said, two and a half seconds later. 'What I'm really interested in, as I said, is the *psychology* behind this latest modern craze for ghosts and the search for evidence of the paranormal and UFOs. Tell me, Effie, what do *you* think makes your average, rational member of the public believe in ghosts?'

Effie sighed patiently, knowing what her friend was like when he had a bee in his bonnet about something. It was all but impossible to distract him. So she shrugged one shoulder, acknowledging that it was easier just to go along with him. (Besides, she'd finished her salad and was trying to tell herself that she didn't feel hungry enough for a dessert. Not even a partially "good" one like fresh fruit salad with just the merest drizzle of cream.)

'I have no idea,' she said in answer to his question. 'It's not something that I've ever really taken the time to think about.'

'Not seen a ghost yourself then?' he asked casually.

'No.'

'What about a friend? It's an interesting fact, but in my preliminary research, nearly everyone I've interviewed admits to knowing someone who's had some sort of paranormal experience, even if they haven't themselves. One chap I talked to, for instance, is a carpet fitter, and he told me that his mate once went into an empty house to lay a carpet, and "someone" invisible kept moving his coat about from place to place.'

Effie smiled. 'Sorry. None of my friends have had their coats moved by the spirits. Or any other article of clothing, as far as I know.'

'So you're a sceptic then?' Duncan asked craftily. 'You don't believe it's possible that, when we die, our spirit or energy or some part of us gets left behind?'

Effie frowned. 'Now don't go putting words into my mouth,' she said crossly, her mind still half on thoughts of mounds of sweet-tasting pineapple and melon drizzled in cream. 'I have no more idea of what really happens to us after death than anyone else. How could I?'

'Well done, I knew I could rely on you to have a truly open mind,' Duncan congratulated her.

And, much, much too late, Effie realized that she'd fallen straight into one of Duncan's famous traps.

'What?' she asked sharply, berating herself for not paying better attention. It wasn't even as if she'd had the excuse of not knowing that he was up to something! 'I never said I had an open mind,' she said. Then flushed slightly as she heard just how silly that sounded. Damn him, this was typical of Duncan. Already he was tying her up in knots. 'What I mean is, I like to think that I'm not so set in my thinking that I'm not open to reasonable ...'

She broke off and took a deep breath. Wearily, and acknowledging to herself that she had been outfoxed yet again by her wily companion, she slumped back in her chair. 'Duncan, just tell me what it is that you want me to do,' she said, finally admitting defeat. 'What exactly does this little adventure of yours entail?'

'Oh, not much,' Duncan assured her, smiling kindly. 'You'll enjoy it, I'm sure. Well, pretty sure.'

Effie's heart sank even further.

'Duncan,' she said repeated, elongating his name warningly. 'Come on, man, just spit it out!'

'I just wondered if you would be willing to be my independent eyes and ears and sit in on a few ghost hunting sessions, that's all.'

CHAPTER TWO

'*Ghost hunting*? You're going *ghost hunting*!' Penny Harris gasped.

Effie, fighting back the urge to blush and still feeling cross with herself for letting Duncan talk her into it, said a shade too defensively, 'Yes, ghost hunting. And why not? What's wrong with that?'

But even as she said it, she knew how outlandish it must sound – especially to Penny who, having spent the last twenty years or so practising as a local GP, was one of the most practical and down-to-earth people that she knew.

When she had first moved into Michael's large, detached home in Hampton Frome upon her marriage, Penny had been one of the first villagers she'd met. And right away the two women had hit it off, although Effie had decided it would be easier if she remained with her old GP's surgery back in Bicester.

And this decision, as the two women had become firmer and closer friends over the years, had probably been a very good one. As Penny herself had said more than once, being someone's doctor whilst also being their friend, wasn't always easy. And had recited a few pert instances where such a conflict could lead to some rather uncomfortable scenarios that would definitely put a pall on any friendship!

Now Penny turned to look at her in astonishment. And since she was, at that moment, in the process of driving her Range Rover down a rather narrow country lane, Effie pointed quickly at the road ahead. 'Eyes front!'

'Sorry,' Penny said. And meant it. A tall, stick-thin woman with a crop of unruly black hair and dark brown eyes, she was usually a very competent and careful driver. Not surprising, since she knew all too well the devastating effects that careless driving could inflict on the human body. She was also just naturally one of those sorts of people who seemed able to do anything and everything well, with a calm, quiet and sometimes perfunctory ability that left lesser mortals, like Effie, feeling hapless and humble.

Which just went to show how shocking Effie's news had been, if it could inspire even Penny to nearly drive them into a ditch. Which, in turn, only served to reinforce just how stupid she had been to let Duncan talk her into helping him with his latest project.

'It's all Duncan's fault,' Effie heard herself say petulantly, and Penny gave a long slow sigh.

'Ah. Say no more,' she said drolly. 'That explains everything. I didn't think it was something you'd be likely to do, off your own bat.'

But Effie *did* say more, of course, and at some length, indignantly detailing not only her lunch date with Duncan but why she was now accepting Penny's offer of a lift into town in order to meet up with a certain Mr Corwin Fielding.

'So Duncan's writing about the paranormal next, is he?' Penny laughed when she'd finally finished. 'That'll please all those stuffy colleagues of his at his college. You know how they like to mock stuff like that. They'll be calling him 'Spooky Fergusson' before long, you wait and see.'

Effie laughed. 'I doubt he'd care,' she said. 'In fact, knowing Duncan, he'd probably revel in it! And, to be fair, he's not so much interested in the actual ghosts themselves – always supposing that they exist of course – but rather the psychology of why hunting them has become so popular. And that's where having a so-called independent observer will come in handy – or so he says,' Effie grumbled. 'He knows I've never had strong views one way or another about that sort of thing, so in theory, I should make a fairly good, impartial witness. All he wants is to get the average person-in-the-street's take on things, from a social and psychological point of view, which he can then use in his book.'

Penny nodded, indicated to pass a trundling tractor, and accelerated smoothly past it. 'Well, that makes sense, I suppose,' she conceded. 'And it's also very clever of him, because it *is* a subject that interests people. And nearly everyone has an opinion about it – either for or against. So he's bound to get lots of sales.'

'Yes, I suppose so,' Effie said, beginning to grin in spite of herself. Her friend noticed and raised an eyebrow in query, making Effie shake her head helplessly. 'Oh, Pen, it's such a hoot, isn't it?' she finally burst out. 'I mean, actual ghost hunting! Me! It's so outlandish and yet so … I don't know. Appealing in a way. I mean, who could resist the opportunity to do something so off the wall?' Then she sighed heavily. 'Trust Duncan to know what would be guaranteed to peak my interest.'

'Yes. He does tend to know what buttons to press, doesn't he,' Penny agreed wryly. 'And how to get his own way. And like I said, no doubt his latest opus will sell very well indeed.'

'I daresay it will,' Effie said, a shade grimly. 'You can always trust Duncan to come up smelling of roses.'

Penny grinned. 'Do I detect a hint of sour grapes in your voice?'

Effie grunted inelegantly. 'Just a few. Really, Pen, I don't know how it happened. One moment I was just sitting there, innocently eating my salad and determined to absolutely *not* let him rope me in, and the next I was agreeing to at least meet with this ghost hunter character and see for myself what it was all about.' She bit her lip and looked out of the side window of the car, at the passing greenery. 'Michael would have hated the whole idea.'

Her friend drew in a slow breath. 'I dare say he would have,' she said flatly, her voice carefully neutral.

'And he wouldn't have wanted me to do it,' Effie added fretfully.

'No,' Penny said, and took a deep breath. 'Which is why I'm glad that you *are* doing it,' she said firmly. 'It's about time you started taking advantage of the fact that you *are* free now to do more of the kind of things that please *you*. Which is good. And this sounds like it'll be fun. It's about time you bucked yourself up a bit.'

Effie glanced at her quickly, then away again. She knew that

Penny hadn't always got on with Michael. In fact, once or twice they'd argued quite vociferously.

'Well, I'm committed now,' she said mildly. 'Well, at least into meeting with this Mr Fielding person anyway. He's the one who runs these ghost-investigations or whatever you call them. If I don't like him, or I think we can't get on, I can always tell Duncan so. And that will be that.'

'Hmmmm,' Penny said. 'Well, I suppose there's no harm in just trying it. I take it that you just have to sit in on this ghost-watching stuff, watch and listen, then report back what you experience to Duncan?'

'That's the general idea. If Corwin Fielding agrees to me doing it, that is. According to Duncan, he's still considering whether or not he wants to take part in the collaboration.'

'Fielding? That name sounds vaguely familiar,' Penny mused.

'Apparently he's something of a minor local celebrity,' Effie said, looking out of the window again as they negotiated the Kidlington roundabout and headed towards Oxford. 'Duncan's already approached him about the psychology book he wants to write, and what role he'd like me to play in it, but Mr Fielding is reserving judgement on whether or not to co-operate until after we meet. Which should be,' she checked her watch, 'in about half an hour or so.'

'Corwin Fielding … I really feel like I know that name,' Penny said thoughtfully. 'He's not a patient … Oh, now I've got it. I read one of *his* books once. Nothing like the kind of thing Duncan writes, obviously.'

'Really? *You did*?' Effie asked, amazed. Then, 'Was it any good?' she added curiously.

'Yes, I think it was rather, if memory serves.' Penny nodded. 'That is, it was well written, thoughtful, and as far as I could tell, he'd been totally scrupulous in his scientific methods and in reporting them. Well, I say scientific – it involved a lot of temperature readings from thermal sensors and camera recording footage in infra green and UV. Along with devices that registered electromagnetic energy and all that stuff. Not sure that a "proper" scientist wouldn't be rather sniffy about it all,' she admitted with a grin. 'But at least his conclusions were honest and clear cut. And he also freely admitted that something like ninety per cent of "sightings" could be explained in non-paranormal terms. So he certainly didn't come across as a fanatic or die-hard believer. But there were also a few incidences that he went into in depth where he clearly believed something "inexplicable" had occurred.'

Effie frowned, already feeling lost and hopelessly out of her depth. 'It all sounds very technical,' she murmured uneasily.

'Yes. I suppose a lot of it was,' Penny said. 'I didn't buy the book, needless to say, Patrick did,' she explained, mentioning her husband with an airy wave of her hand, 'during one of his more esoterically minded fads. I only read it because I was bored and I was expecting to be amused and entertained by some woolly-headed but basically harmless twit. So I was rather surprised and moderately impressed with the way he approached his research.'

'Oh,' Effie said, not sure whether to feel reassured or worried by her friend's surprising endorsement. In truth, she had been half-expecting (not to mention sincerely hoping) that her meeting with Mr Corwin Fielding would turn out to be a bit of a bust. That the man would turn out to be a harmless but obvious eccentric, that they would meet and then quickly agree that perhaps the project wasn't for her, thus allowing her to slither free from Duncan's manipulations. Although, she had to admit, another part of her was hoping that it would all work out well, because the prospect of doing something different and exciting *was* genuinely appealing.

But from what Duncan had told her about Corwin Fielding, Effie had gained the impression that she would be meeting an enthusiastic, well-meaning but fervent believer. A sort of new-age guru who talked to the dead as a matter of course, and probably saw spirits everywhere, including the shopping aisles at Tesco. But if what Penny was saying was true, then she might need to adjust her mental image of the man.

'So you didn't get the impression that he was a bit … well, kooky then?' she asked now, a shade diffidently.

Instantly, Penny shook her head. 'No, not at all. And I think he's also well respected in his field, as a serious researcher, I mean. At least, if the bio on the back of the book that I read is to be believed.

He's got a degree in ... something or other, from a respectable university. Reading, I think. And he's been invited onto several of the more serious-minded chat shows and semi-educational programmes that go out late at night. You know the kind I mean?'

Effie did. After a hard day's work, Michael often liked to watch such programmes, if only to pooh-pooh or laugh at some of the topics.

But now she was beginning to feel more and more uneasy about her upcoming meeting – and in a way that she hadn't previously even contemplated. When she'd set out this morning, it hadn't occurred to her that she would have to do much more than sit and listen to some enthusiast. She hadn't even given a thought as to what kind of an impression *she* should be trying to make. That *she* might be found wanting in some way. She hadn't even done any preliminary reading on the topic. What if this Corwin Fielding person decided she was lacking in intelligence? Wouldn't it be embarrassing if Duncan got his marching orders just because *she* failed to impress Corwin Fielding at the upcoming interview?

'So, where am I dropping you off again?' Penny asked, thankfully interrupting her now painful train of thought.

'Oh, in Park Town,' Effie said, naming a leafy and prestigious area of Summertown, one of Oxford's more upmarket suburbs. 'Apparently he has an apartment there.'

'Very nice,' Penny said. 'Obviously this ghost hunting malarkey pays well. No wonder Duncan's so anxious to get a piece of the pie.'

Effie sighed, her rising anxiety levels now making her feel cross and edgy. 'I just wish he'd left me out of it,' she muttered. 'I'm beginning to feel hopelessly inadequate to the task.'

Penny shot her a sharp look. 'Stop that,' she admonished flatly. 'You're forever doing yourself down. You're as capable and competent as anyone I know. That husband of yours has a lot to answer—'

'But I haven't even done any research,' Effie said, frantically interrupting her friend in an attempt to distract her. The last thing she wanted to do was get into an argument about Michael. 'What if Mr Fielding asks me stuff and I don't have a clue what to say? Oh, I could really murder Duncan right now!'

Penny laughed, a shade callously, Effie thought. 'So why did you agree to help him out?' she asked.

Effie groaned. 'Oh, I don't know. Perhaps because he made it sound so reasonable. And interesting. And he thought it would do me good to get out of the house more and meet new people ...'

She broke off as she saw Penny was nodding knowingly and smiling.

Since they were now stuck in traffic waiting at a large roundabout at the top end of Oxford's Banbury Road, Penny felt safe in taking her hand off the wheel and reaching over to squeeze her shoulder gently.

'And he's probably right,' she said softly. 'Come on, you said yourself it was going to be a bit of hoot. Don't talk yourself out of it now! Just relax and enjoy yourself for once. You deserve it. And stepping outside of your comfort zone will probably do you the world of good.'

Effie fought back the urge to say crossly, *"Oh not you too!"* and instead glared out of the window. Then, after a moment or two, tried to relax. She really had to get out of the habit of making everything such a big deal. (And just when had she started doing that? She was sure she hadn't done it when she'd been younger.)

'Well, we'll just have to see what happens,' she said philosophically. 'Sitting in with the C-Fits for a session or two of ghost-watching probably won't actually kill me, right?' she added, her lips twisting into a genuine smile now. 'Nobody ever actually died on one of these investigations, did they? I mean, just how ironic would that be?' She laughed.

After all, if you couldn't laugh when the joke was on you, when could you? Not that poor Michael had ever really had much of a sense of humour.

'The C-Fits?' Penny asked curiously.

'The Corwin Fielding Paranormal Investigation Team. Or C-Fits as they call themselves for short,' Effie explained. 'Duncan assures me that they're all very nice, well-adjusted people, strictly volunteers of course, who come from all walks of life, and help Corwin out with his research. There's a retired schoolteacher, a builder, a student and, oh, all sorts apparently. The only thing they have in common is an interest in ghosts and the paranormal.'

'OK. Well, that sounds nice,' Penny said, but with such a touch of forced joviality in her tone that it made Effie smile.

'Yes, doesn't it,' she agreed blandly. 'Care to volunteer yourself? You could always keep me company,' she pointed out with a wicked little chuckle.

'Not on your nellie!' her pal said succinctly – if a shade inelegantly. And both women burst out laughing.

Ten minutes later, Effie found herself walking down Park Town, admiring the avenues of leafy beech trees, the green lushness of a small park opposite and the impressive architecture of mainly Victorian and Edwardian houses that surrounded her.

She checked the note that Duncan had given her, just to be sure that she'd found the right address, and after making sure that the number of the house was the one that she wanted, paused outside and took it all in.

It was a mid-terrace large Edwardian house, which, like a vast number of such residences in the city, had long since been converted into flats. But only four, she noted, which meant that the apartments would be large and spacious. Large sash windows set within pale Cotswold stone looked out over the park. Walking up a flight of wide shallow steps that lead to an attractively painted sage-green front door, her eyes went to the listings above a neat set of doorbells and found that Mr C Fielding had one of the flats on the top floor.

Taking a deep breath, and telling herself not to be such a rabbit, she firmly pressed the bell. Well, she thought fatalistically, here goes nothing.

Today, and in deference to yet another sunny day, she was wearing a powder blue calf-length summer dress with a full skirt under a white jacket. Low-heeled white sandals and white leather handbag completed the ensemble. At the time she'd selected it, she'd felt rather proud of herself for yet again shunning the inevitable dark trouser suit. But now she couldn't help but wonder if she should have worn something more formal? A business suit, maybe?

Then again, just what were you supposed to wear on an occasion like this? Even Michael, who'd always known the proper etiquette for any social or business event, might have struggled to come up with what you were supposed to wear to an interview for a ghost hunting position!

Perhaps …

'Hello?' a male voice floated at her out of the ether, and Effie abruptly lowered her mouth towards the intercom and said firmly, 'Hello? Mrs James to see Mr Fielding. I believe Professor Duncan Fergusson told you to expect me.'

Her voice came out reassuringly calm and assertive. Which was good. If you couldn't actually *feel* in control of any given situation, at least you could sound as if you were. That was a lesson Michael had taught her very early on. And it was sound advice that had often served her well over the years.

'Oh yes. Please, come on up. It's up the main flight of stairs, and then turn left.' The voice was pleasant and Oxonian – that curious blend that was not quite upper class, not quite country-yokel and not easily identifiable.

'Thank you,' Effie said, as the door was buzzed open.

Inside, the communal hallway was painted white, with black and white floor tiles giving way to a large and impressive wooden staircase. She walked up the single flight of stairs and turned left, heading down a corridor with dark moss green carpeting and attractive Manet prints on the walls. And this was still just a communal area. As Penny had observed, clearly Mr Corwin Fielding had done very well for himself in his chosen, unorthodox career.

She was just approaching the door at the end of the corridor when it began to open. And, still mentally cursing a certain professor for getting her into this mess in the first place, Effie stiffened her spine and forced a polite smile onto her face.

And as she did so, a man in his early thirties stepped out of the door and smiled at her. He was a little over six feet in height, Effie estimated, with a lean, but well-muscled frame that looked at home in much-washed, pale coloured, tight-fitting jeans and a plain white shirt. His hair was thick and slightly curly, and so dark brown as to be nearly black, and was worn fairly long – whilst not quite sitting on his shoulders, it was certainly well past collar length. (Michael would definitely not have approved.) But it was his eyes that were the first thing that she noticed about him, being cat-green and almost luminous, followed by a strong, not quite Roman nose and a firm, clean shaven chin.

For some reason, she'd been expecting someone much older, and she hoped her surprise had not shown on her face.

'Mrs James? Hello, I'm Corwin Fielding. How do you do?' He smiled and held out a hand. His fingers were long and sensitive, but his grip was firm as he clasped her hand in a no-nonsense shake. 'So glad you could make it. Please come on in.'

Effie forced the smile that was already on her face to stretch a millimetre or two wider, and dragging in a deep breath, stepped into his home.

The first thing she noticed was that it was open plan, with two enormous sash windows allowing the light to flood in. It illuminated, in one corner, a modern kitchen area with marble-top work surfaces and shining appliances, whilst a large sitting area was arranged opposite. Two black leather settees were grouped around a big square coffee table, which was itself set in front of a large fireplace. The fireplace was clearly an original feature, complete with decorative William Morris tiles and a black-leaded grate. Since the day was so warm, the fire remained unlit, and instead, in the grate, stood a large and beautiful flower arrangement of gladioli and leaves. It looked spectacular.

And instantly Effie knew that they had to be the work of a feminine eye with a taste for luxury.

'What a lovely room,' she complimented, glancing up at original cornices and an intricately carved ceiling rose, beneath which hung a modern, eye-catching glass dome. The main colour scheme was a restful shade of pale mint green with hints of lemon and turquoise accents, mainly in the soft furnishings.

'Thank you,' Corwin said. 'Please, won't you sit down?' He indicated one of the armchairs that matched the sofas. 'Would you like a cup of tea or coffee? Or would you prefer something cold?'

'Oh, fruit juice would be fine, if you have any.'

He smiled, heading towards the kitchen area. 'Apple, cranberry or mango?'

'Apple, please.'

Effie sat, neatly tucking her ankles together and slightly to one side. Michael had always preferred her to be lady-like in her habits, and she felt a swift sense of guilt mingled with defiance as it struck her that he almost certainly wouldn't have approved of her being here. He'd never had much time or patience for the more whimsical side of life, being a man of practicality and common sense.

But Michael was gone, she heard a voice in her head say flatly. *And now you're free to act exactly as you like.*

The thought was utterly unexpected and took her totally by surprise, leaving her feeling almost giddy. As if she'd suddenly looked down when just about to take a step, and discovered that she was standing on the edge of a vast precipice. She felt her heart beat leap, and then jumped almost visibly as a shadow fell across her. Looking up, she saw that her host was now standing beside her, carrying two glasses.

'Oh, thank you.' She gratefully accepted one long tall glass, clinking attractively with ice cubes. The distraction couldn't have come at a better time, and she forced herself to take a sip and pull herself together as Corwin Fielding slid lithely into the chair opposite her.

'So, have you known Professor Fergusson long?' he asked with a smile. 'When he first approached me with his proposal I was both surprised and intrigued.'

'Oh yes, I've known Duncan and Margot for years,' Effie said. 'My husband and I often dined with them,' she added, then could have bit her tongue. She knew why she felt compelled to bring Michael straight into the conversation and only hoped that Corwin hadn't noticed that she'd used the past tense.

'I've read one or two of the professor's books, of course,' Corwin said, when it was clear that she wasn't going to elaborate further, and casually crossed his feet at the ankles. 'They're certainly well written and well researched, but to be honest, I'm not quite sure if the paranormal is a field that would best suit his style.'

Effie shrugged casually. 'I wouldn't know about that. I'm not in the publishing business. Nor do I have any experience in your field of expertise.'

If he thought that she was here to be Duncan's advocate, then it was probably best that she made things clear right from the outset. 'Duncan can be a very charming and persuasive man, but if I were you, I wouldn't let him talk you into doing anything that you're not fully comfortable with,' she added calmly.

Corwin's lips twitched. 'Well, thank you for your honesty.' She could tell that he was clearly doing a mental reassessment about his preconceptions of her, and she felt a distinct and curious sense of triumph that seemed totally out of place. 'The professor certainly put forward a good case for us collaborating,' he continued. 'And I can see how we might both potentially benefit from it. He will be able to add another book to his resumé, and it would be good for us C-Fits to have a man of Professor Fergusson's reputation being seen to endorse our research. And it won't hurt us to be associated, even loosely, with a project that has its roots in Oxford academia, either, if it comes to that. But even so, I'm not totally convinced.'

And Effie, who just an hour ago would probably have felt like singing the 'Hallelujah Chorus' on hearing those words, now felt a distinct sense of disappointment wash over her. 'Oh?'

Corwin shook his head. It had the effect of sending the dark mass of his hair rippling around his head, and Effie abruptly began to study a painting on the wall just behind him. It looked like a minor but original work by one of the lesser known French impressionists, and again she got a distinct sense of that feminine touch in the choice of décor.

It was becoming clear to her that Corwin didn't live in this apartment alone. Or at least, not always alone.

'You see,' he was saying now, 'in my line of work, I'm used to a certain amount of scepticism – sometimes rather a swingeing amount, if I'm being perfectly honest, depending on just who it is that you're talking to. And not long ago, a journalist with his own particular axe to grind did a bit of a hatchet job on us.'

Effie's eyes went back to his and sharpened abruptly. 'That doesn't sound very fair.'

'Oh, it wasn't. I believe a close relative of his had been taken for a ride by a so-called medium. A lot of money had exchanged hands, and even more emotional damage had been done. So when one of our team innocently invited this journalist along to experience a vigil for himself, just to prove that we had nothing to do with that sort of thing …' He sighed and spread his hands graphically.

'He wrote a scathing piece for his paper,' Effie concluded flatly.

'Yes. Of course, he never actually libelled us, he was far too clever and wary for that.' Corwin grimaced. 'Nevertheless, I came across as some kind of Svengali-like figurehead out to make money whilst at the same time indulging in some sort of power trip, and the other members of the team were either gullible dupes, or crack-pots. As you can image, it created a lot of ill feeling with everyone concerned.'

Effie nodded. 'And it's almost impossible to defend yourself against something of that kind, I imagine.'

'Exactly. But, sad to say, it's all part and parcel of what we do. So you can understand why it's left us a touch, shall we say, *wary*, when it comes to strangers approaching us, offering something that sounds too good to be true.'

'And Duncan's offer struck you that way?' she asked curiously.

Corwin gave a laconic shrug and again spread his hands wide in a telling gesture. He was, Effie realized, one of those people who communicated not just with their voices but with their whole being. Hands, eyes, body language, all were viable tools to help him convey his feelings.

'Let's just say I have yet to be convinced,' he agreed dryly.

'Well, in Duncan's defence, I *can* say that I believe him to be basically an honourable sort of man,' Effie began, choosing her words carefully. 'And if he's made promises, then I would be very surprised indeed if he didn't keep them. But perhaps, more to the point, Duncan is rather *proud* of his books. And although he sees them as strictly money making projects, he also has a lot of self-belief and pride in himself. Which means that anything he produces has to meet certain standards. His research has to be thorough and comprehensive and fair. And like I said, he's always honest with the people he works with, even if he can be extremely manipulative at times.'

Here she had to smile wryly. 'And I'm a good example of that. When he invited me to lunch, I had no idea what he was going to ask me to do. And, to be truthful, my first instinct was to say no.'

Corwin's eyes widened at that. 'Really? Funny, I don't know why, but I thought ... perhaps, I misunderstood. Professor Fergusson seemed so sure that you were the right person for the job. I suppose I assumed that you had a deep interest in what we do.'

Effie reached for her glass and took a sip. 'Sorry to disappoint you, but I've never really given the thought of ghosts, or UFOs or anything like that, much attention. Oh, like most people, I might have wondered about such things from time to time. Speculated a bit. Who doesn't? But ...' She shrugged casually.

'You've never seen a ghost yourself?' he asked calmly, his tone so neutral he might have been asking her if she took milk in her tea.

'No. Well, not that I'm aware of,' she corrected herself, determined to be totally fair.

'And yet you agreed to meet up with me to discuss going ghost hunting with us,' he mused softly. She could feel his shrewd green gaze sweeping over her, and had a sudden, hideous thought.

Did he see her as some sort of bored housewife, one of the army of well-off, middle-aged women who were desperate to break out and prove to themselves that they were still young and daring, by doing something different and adventurous? Is that who he'd been expecting to show up on his doorstep?

She felt herself become hot with shame at the thought, and then cold with dread. And realized, a shade belatedly, that he was still waiting for her to respond to his question.

'Well, er ... yes, I did,' honesty forced her to admit, and she just knew that she was probably blushing openly now. 'But only because Duncan has a way of getting what he wants,' she added stiffly.

Corwin again cocked his head to one side, his lips twitching with obvious humour now. They were rather narrow but well-shaped lips, Effie noticed. And they could probably curl up in a rather devastatingly cynical snarl, if so required. 'That's hardly a ringing endorsement for the professor.' He laughed.

Effie took a deep breath and tried to pull herself together. This interview was definitely getting away from her. 'I'm just trying to give you an accurate picture of how things are, so that you can make your own mind up as to whether or not we should join forces. As for myself, Duncan thinks that because I have no set ideas about the existence – or otherwise – of ghosts and other paranormal phenomenon, that I'd make an ideal, impartial observer. Which is what he wants. Also, because I haven't read about the subject, nor yet watched any television programmes about it, he's happy that I'm unlikely to have been contaminated with preconceived ideas about it all.' She paused to take a sip of her drink, and shrugged. 'Apparently, all he wants is just an average sort of person, who can give him an honest opinion about what she experiences. And I've told him straight that, should we all go ahead with this, I will give him my unbiased take on what happens, regardless of what either you – or he – might prefer me to actually say.'

She paused, smiled at him calmly, and added, 'And so it's only fair that I repeat that warning to you.'

Corwin nodded. 'Again, thank you for your honesty,' he said sombrely.

Effie smiled uncertainly. 'I'm not sure if I've actually helped you, or made things worse.'

'Oh, you've definitely helped,' he assured her. 'For a start, you've confirmed one or two things for me regarding Professor Fergusson. And you've put my mind at rest about any of the doubts I might have had about your suitability for the project.'

Effie felt her feathers distinctly ruffle. 'Oh?'

As if sensing it, Corwin grinned. 'Please, Mrs James, don't be offended. But I do need to ask you something. Ninety-nine per cent of the time, nothing actually happens on a vigil. We do nothing but spend a lot of time watching instruments and hoping for some kind of phenomenon to take place. It rarely does. But on occasion things *can* happen. Unsettling things. Disquieting things. And nobody can ever be sure just how they'll react to that sort of thing until it actually happens, if you see what I mean?' He paused, then shrugged gently. 'It isn't always easy to be calm and collected if you're feeling genuinely frightened.'

His gaze focused on her sharply and Effie felt herself tense.

'Are you asking me if I have the nerve needed to do the job?' she asked him bluntly.

He spread his hands in an appeasing gesture and then nodded. 'Yes. I suppose I am,' he admitted simply, his green eyes watching her closely.

Effie nodded and took a long, slow breath. 'Of course, I've thought about that aspect of it. How could I not? And, as you say, I have no real idea of how I would react if something … er … weird happened. I'd like to think that I'd have the wherewithal to take it all in my stride and not get hysterical or anything. But I can only say that I'd try my best not to go to pieces. But it may well turn out that I don't have what it takes,' she said honestly. 'In which case, I can promise you that I'll have the good sense to admit as much, and retire from the project straightaway. No matter what Duncan might have to say about it,' she added defiantly.

Corwin laughed and seemed to relax in his chair a bit. 'Fair enough,' he said casually. 'And to be honest, if you'd come out and said that you had no worries at all, or spouted something about having nerves of steel, I'd have been inclined to drop the whole thing right here and now. But I think, Mrs James, that not only will you be able to give a fair and accurate account of anything you might experience, but I would be prepared to bet a considerable amount of money that your nerves will hold out just fine.'

Effie blinked, totally disconcerted. It had been a long time since anyone had given her such a ringing endorsement. 'Oh. Er … well, thank you. And since it seems we're going to be collaborators after all, call me Effie.'

'Effie? Delighted to. And that's a very unusual name.'

Effie grimaced. 'Short for Euphemia, I'm afraid. I don't know what my mother was thinking of.' She laughed. 'She claims that I was named after some heroine in a book that she loved as a child, but I'm inclined to think that she and my father simply couldn't agree on a name, and so decided on something a little different out of sheer desperation.'

Corwin grinned. 'Well, I'm hardly in a position to pass judgement on anyone's given name, am I? It strikes me that we're in the same boat.'

'Yes, Corwin *is* unusual too,' Effie agreed. 'Is it Gaelic?'

'Yes. It means 'from beyond a hill' of all things. Very enigmatic. I think my mother was born a decade or two too late and always fancied herself as a sixties flower child. At least she didn't call me Moon or Seashell or something equally embarrassing.'

Effie laughed. 'Well, I think Corwin suits you,' she heard herself say, and then froze briefly in horror.

What on earth had possessed her to say *that*?

But before she could start to squirm in mortification, he was already laughing and beginning to rise. 'Thank you. And thank you very much for coming. I'm looking forward to working with you.'

Quickly Effie put down her glass, scrambled to her feet and reached for her bag.

'Obviously, I shall have to talk it over with the others again,' he was saying, 'but I don't see any reason why you shouldn't come out with us on a few vigils. Regardless of whether or not we end up accepting the professor's proposition, I think the C-Fits could benefit from a cool, clear, unbiased second set of eyes. As it happens, we've only just this moment agreed to investigate a new case, so you can be in on it right from the beginning. It'll be less confusing that way.'

'That sounds ideal,' she murmured. And, in a bit of a daze, followed him to the door where, once again, Corwin Fielding shook her hand. 'I'll be in touch within the next few days,' he promised. 'The professor gave me your telephone number.'

Effie managed what she hoped looked like a cool and gracious nod. 'That'll be fine, Mr Fielding.'

'I thought we agreed that we'd be Effie and Corwin?' he chided her with a grin.

Effie nodded. 'Of course,' she swallowed slightly. 'Corwin.'

Once back outside on the warm pavement however, she took a

long, slow breath and began to make her way back towards the bus stop.

She felt utterly bemused.

She still wasn't quite sure just how it had happened, but it seemed that she was going to become a bona fide ghost hunter.

CHAPTER THREE

Effie had her first meeting with the rest of the C-Fits, not on a dark and stormy night in a creepy old mansion bequeathed to them by an ancient and now deceased former member, but on another bright and sunny day in a cricket pavilion in a village near Cumnor.

When Corwin had phoned to tell her that the rest of the gang had agreed to her participation, he'd also given her directions to the sports field. Apparently they rented the pavilion for the meetings simply because it was located in a spot more or less equidistant from everyone's home, and was thus the most convenient spot. And since Corwin did most of his office work and writing at his apartment, they had no real need of a well-equipped office space, either, just somewhere adequate where everyone could meet up.

So after she'd parked her car, a rather smart-looking charcoal grey Mercedes that had once been Michael's pride and joy, she found herself surrounded by nothing more spooky than lush green hedges, a neatly mown playing field and cheerful birdsong.

On the patch of asphalt around her was a large white van with the name of a local builder emblazoned on one side, a small Japanese motorbike of some kind, several mid-range small cars of varying cleanliness and a rather sleek Jaguar XJS in bottle green.

With a small nonchalant shrug that was supposed to bolster her confidence, she set off toward the wooden pavilion, nevertheless still aware that butterflies were fluttering around somewhere just under her sternum.

What if, in spite of Corwin's assurances that the rest of the C-Fits were all happy to have her join them on their vigils, they did in fact resent her and distrust her motives?

Then, as she mounted the deep wooden steps and tapped on the door, she told herself not to have such thoughts. And when had she become a worrier? So what if things didn't work out? It was hardly the end of the world, was it? She was still half-inclined to think that this whole thing was a mistake anyway, so it was hardly going to cause her any real regret if things didn't go well.

As the door opened, Effie forced a smile onto her lips which then froze in place as she found herself, not face to face with Corwin as she'd expected, but with a diminutive woman somewhere in her mid-sixties. Her silver hair was cut in an uncompromisingly short, somewhat mannish cut, and she was wearing dark grey slacks with a grey and white knitted jersey. Blue eyes, behind small, rectangular gold-rimmed glasses observed her keenly.

'Hello. I'm Effie James,' Effie said, a shade uncertainly. 'I do hope I've come to the right place ...'

'Oh yes, you have. Please come in, we're all expecting you. I'm Jean Bossington-Smith. How do you do?' So saying, she thrust out a slightly liver-spotted hand, and shook Effie's own extended appendage vigorously.

'We just all call her the boss for short, for obvious reasons,' a youthful male voice piped up from somewhere inside the room, and Effie turned to survey her immediate surroundings.

The origins of the building were obvious by the wooden benches that lined the walls, along with rows of lockers in which sportsmen and women could store their gear. But a small wooden table had been set up in the centre of the room, and from the various folding wooden chairs that had been set up around it, a group of people watched her curiously.

The young man who had spoken grinned widely, and behind her she heard Jean Bossington-Smith say sharply, 'That'll do, Mickey.' And then, to Effie, 'I'm the group's secretary, I suppose you could call me. I tend to all the admin and keep the records. I'm also the treasurer and co-ordinator.'

'Like I said, we all call her the boss because she sees to everything. Isn't that right, Corwin?'

The youth had to be the owner of the motorbike outside, since a leather jacket hung on the back of the chair, whilst a crash helmet resided underneath it. He had masses of curly light brown hair and curiously golden hazel eyes that Effie suspected would attract young women in droves. A pointed chin and high cheekbones didn't hurt, either, even if his skin was still somewhat prone to the odd spot of acne.

From one side of the table Corwin rose, grinning widely. 'It's all totally true, I'm afraid.' He laughed, coming forward to guide her towards the table and pulling out a chair for her. 'I'm just the head of the C-Fits in name only. Without Jean, our work would just grind to a halt.'

She saw Jean Bossington-Smith flush slightly, but whether with pleasure or in embarrassment at the compliment it was hard to say.

'Behave, Corwin,' the older woman said gruffly but affectionately, and Effie had no trouble in guessing that this woman was the retired schoolteacher that Duncan had mentioned as being one of C-Fit's regular investigators. And had probably once been a rather formidable headmistress as well if the way the others so naturally deferred to her was anything to go by. 'The young man with the attitude is Mickey Urquhart, Mrs James, and I apologize for his tom-foolery.' She shot him a stern glass, and he blew her a kiss.

'I'm studying civil engineering at Wadham,' Mickey said, half-rising and half-bowing, and confirming her guess that he was the student that Duncan had also mentioned. 'Glad to meet you, ma'am.'

'Ignore him,' Jean Bossington-Smith said, clearly enjoying the exchange of banter and leading her to guess that it was probably a regular occurrence. 'He might have the brains but he lacks maturity, alas. We tolerate him simply because he helps us haul the heavier equipment about.'

But Effie was beginning to get the hang of this now, and didn't believe her for one moment.

'Everyone,' Corwin said smoothly, and sweeping a hand around the room, 'this is Mrs Effie James, our latest recruit. As you know, Effie's here as an impartial observer for Professor Fergusson, who's writing a book on the psychological aspects of what we do.'

'It sounds really interesting. I don't suppose I'd understand much of it, but I for one will be interested in reading it when it's finished.' The woman who spoke was very tall and fiery-headed, and looked to be in her late twenties. She had big, friendly brown eyes and an open smiling face, full of freckles.

'This is Gisela,' Corwin introduced them as Effie took her seat and he sat down by her side, casually leaning his bare forearms on the top of the table. Effie noticed several long dark hairs lying flat against his skin below the bright white cuff of his shirt, the sleeves of which had been rolled back to just above his elbow. And being so close to him now, she caught the fragrance of his aftershave – something sharp and with a pleasant tang of citrus. 'Gisela is our "sensitive" and stills photographer,' he added matter-of-factly.

Gisela smiled and waved a large, rather old-style looking camera at her, and grinned. 'Don't look so alarmed. I'm not a medium or anything like that. I don't go around saying "is anybody there?" or stuff like that.'

Effie, who felt ashamed to realize that some of her surprise and unease must have shown in her expression, quickly made demurring noises.

'It's OK, don't worry about it,' Gisela said generously. 'Everyone has that sort of reaction when they find out what I do in my spare time. Most people just assume I'm slightly bonkers, but I'm not, I promise! By day I'm a dental hygienist, believe it or not!' She laughed. 'You'd be hard put to find anybody more average or boring than yours truly.' Her head cocked slightly to one side and her eyes narrowed thoughtfully. 'It's just that I've always been sensitive to atmosphere – any kind of atmosphere. And there's nothing unusual in that. A lot of people can sense, for instance, when they walk into someone's home that the owners have just had a spat, and in spite of them being all sweetness and full of hospitality, they're actually seething inside.'

'Oh yes,' Effie agreed with relief, beginning to feel a little less uneasy now. That kind of thing she could relate to. She had friends who were good at that sort of thing too. But she rather thought that there was nothing in the least otherworldly about it. Surely it only proved that some people were just better at picking up on non-verbal clues and reading body language than others?

'It's just that, over the years, and especially since working with Corwin and doing meditation and yoga and stuff like that, I've managed to hone it,' Gisela swept on. 'Now I can definitely pick up on places that have an atmosphere. You know, sad, angry places where people have died and have left behind some kind of energy. I mean, it's hardly surprising, is it? Death must be such a wrench and shock for some people – especially if they die young, or violently. It's bound to leave a trace, isn't it?' she said appealingly.

'Now you're frightening her, Gisela,' the man seated opposite her said, in a rich, melodious and unmistakably Jamaican accent. In his late forties or maybe early fifties, he was perhaps an inch or so shorter than Effie, and had tight curly black hair which was just turning grey and lovely ebony skin that seemed to almost glow with health. He grinned, revealing slightly nicotine-stained teeth and held out a hand, with the yellowing fingers of a serious nicotine addict.

'Lonny Wrighton, Mrs James.'

'Just call me Effie, please.'

'Effie, pleased to have you with us.'

'Lonny only comes out with us in order to escape from his home life a few nights a week,' Mickey couldn't resist piping up. 'And with eight kids, a nagging wife, and regular visits from his sister-in-law from hell, who can blame him?'

'*Mickey*!' It was, inevitably, the boss who scolded him for this latest outrageous statement, although Effie noticed – with relief – that everyone else was chuckling, including Lonny himself. Obviously they were all immune to his pronouncements.

But by now Effie was beginning to get the feeling that she probably wasn't going to be able to take to Mickey much. She was finding his immaturity annoying, rather than engaging. But she couldn't let that become a problem. In any group of people, there were bound to be some you got on better with than others. It was just one of those things and you simply got on with it and accommodated it as best you could.

'He's only partially right, Effie,' Lonny said now amiably. 'Between us, Mandy and I do have eight children, two each from previous marriages who live with our previous partners, and four of our own. But only the youngest three of those are still living at home with us. And my sister-in-law, who does occasionally come over from Jamaica to stay, is a lovely woman who cooks divinely. So you see, I come out solely in the hope of seeing or discovering something inexplicable and exciting. As does our young friend here.'

'And have you ever done so?' Effie asked, genuinely curious now.

'Not yet, alas,' Lonny answered her question with a sad smile. 'Mind you, there have been occasions which have turned definitely interesting.'

'Now let's not get ahead of ourselves,' the fifth and final stranger in the room finally spoke up. 'If I understand Corwin right, Effie's here to see and observe and make up her own mind about what's what. Not have us bend her ear with our own experiences and hearsay evidence.'

The man speaking was thickset, with a balding head and button black eyes. He was almost a caricature of a working man, since he was wearing dust-imbued denim overalls, and had large muscular arms, peppered with various tattoos. Even this early in the season he had the tan of an outdoorsman, and was almost certainly the owner of the white builder's van, parked outside. And his eyes, regarding Effie steadily, were clearly alive with intelligence and good humour.

'Malc Thornton,' he nodded at her and held out a large, callused hand. He took her own with surprising gentleness and Effie smiled at him with genuine pleasure. There was something gentle about him that immediately appealed to her.

Corwin leaned back in his wooden chair, which creaked a little alarmingly as he twisted around on it, the better to look at her. 'Effie, it's important that you feel comfortable with us and with what we do here in the C-Fits. So I just thought, before we start out, that we'd go through some basic things with you, and make sure that you're aware of some ground rules.'

Effie nodded, straightening up a little and hoping that she looked reasonably intelligent and competent. 'Of course,' she said. Her voice, she was pleased to note, sounded perfectly cool and composed.

'OK. What the C-Fits is all about is investigating cases of suspected paranormal activity – nothing more and nothing less,' he said firmly. 'Mostly, people who've read my books or learned about us from our website get in touch and ask for our help. They believe that they've come across something that may have supernatural overtones, and want our opinion. If it sounds like they have a reasonable concern, we then agree to do a preliminary investigation. And based on how we assess the situation after that, we either agree to do a more thorough investigation, or we bow out.'

'Do you often do that?' she asked quietly.

'More often than not to be honest,' Corwin admitted wryly, as Mickey Urquhart gave a scornful snort. 'Sorry to say, most of the calls we get are either from hoaxers who want a laugh at our expense, or from people who think that it'll be a bit of a laugh to have ghost hunters about, and something amusing to talk about at their next dinner party. Whilst some other calls are from people with serious issues that have nothing to do with the supernatural – sometimes mental, sometimes familial.'

'Yeah, like that whacko out near Witney who wanted us to "exorcise" his sister,' Mickey put in with a hoot of derision and Effie tried not to wince.

'We quickly figured out that he only wanted to put doubts about her in his father's mind so that he'd inherit the bulk of the family money,' Gisela put in sadly.

'Good gracious!' Effie heard herself say faintly.

'Exactly. Not surprisingly, Corwin pretty quickly put him straight on that,' Mickey said with evident satisfaction.

'If we could get back on track, everyone,' Corwin said firmly, and Effie saw Jean Bossington-Smith give a pert nod of approval.

'As I was saying,' Corwin said, but not without shooting a Mickey a swift, repressive look, 'we always have to check everything thoroughly, and make sure of just exactly what it is that we're being asked to do. And if anything about it rings alarm bells, we just back off. But sometimes, things look more promising. And our latest investigation, the one that we're all about to start on right now, is a case in point. I'm just about to bring everyone up to speed on that, since I've only had the chance to tell them the basics so far.'

The others, Effie noticed, all found his words encouraging and shuffled happily on their seats in anticipation. She herself did not feel quite so sanguine.

'I was approached last week by the daughter of an old lady who has recently died,' Corwin said, his voice becoming gradually more eager and excited as he talked. 'Her mother, Claudia Watkins, was in her eighties and had a heart condition, and was found dead in her home beside her bed by the woman who helped out in the house. The family doctor, who'd been in attendance just the day before, signed the death certificate, citing heart failure as cause of death. The lady was duly buried in her local churchyard, and her daughter, Isabel, was named as executor of her Will.'

Effie nodded. So far it all sounded rather clear cut, almost mundane, even.

'Now it seems that Mrs Watkins was a very wealthy woman, who lived in a big house in Adderbury, and Isabel has temporarily moved back into her old family home. This is in order to help the family solicitor make up an inventory of the house's contents, since her mother had requested that most of the furniture and various fittings be sold off at auction, in order to benefit a local charity. And it was then that she began to experience certain phenomenon.'

It was at this point that Effie felt herself tense up slightly. This, she supposed, is where it all got rather weird and extraordinary. And yet, when she stopped to think about it logically, she was being rather silly to feel so anxious. She had just temporarily joined a paranormal investigative team, after all. What else had she been expecting?

'I see. Can I ask what sort of things?' she asked, determined to show some backbone.

Corwin beamed at her. 'Of course you can. You can ask anything you like, at any time,' he told her reassuringly. 'We all remember what it was like to be new at this, so don't feel embarrassed or reluctant to ask if there's something you don't understand,' he encouraged her. 'It seems that as soon as she began staying in the old house, Isabel began to have troubling dreams about her mother. In them, her mother was trying to tell her something, or warn her about something.'

'I see,' Effie said politely, and felt a distinct sense of anti-climax.

Corwin grinned at her. 'And there's absolutely nothing in that, you're thinking,' he guessed accurately. 'As was I, at that point. After all, grief affects different people in different ways, right? And the bereaved often do have dreams about their loved ones. It's only natural. In fact, it might be odd if they didn't. And dreams where someone is trying to warn you about something can be easily explained in other terms. Your psychology professor, for instance,' Corwin pointed out with a smile, 'could probably come up with any number of reasons for it. Unresolved guilt or anxiety,' he shrugged. 'Or insecurity at losing a parent. Anyway, the point is that that was not the only thing that Lady Cadmund told me about.'

'*Lady* Cadmund?' It was Mickey who inevitably butted in again, looking comically stunned. 'Blimey, we're ghost hunters to the gentry now, are we?'

Jean Bossington-Smith sighed elaborately.

Corwin sighed patiently. 'Only minor gentry, I think. From what I've been able to learn about the family for my preliminary research, Isabel married a man with a very obscure title and some farmland. She doesn't even call herself "Lady" as far as I know. Not that that's relevant.'

'No. We help anybody who needs it, no matter who they are,' Gisela put in firmly, smiling at Effie. 'Rich, poor or posh. We don't differentiate.'

'Right on, sister,' Mickey said encouragingly.

'Are you children quite finished?' Corwin laughed. 'Do you want to be briefed or not?'

'All ears, Chief.' Mickey saluted smartly.

Lonny and Malc exchanged elaborate eye rolls. Clearly, they were all used to putting up with his clowning around. But Effie, who thought, frankly, that Mickey was a bit of an idiot, decided to keep her opinions firmly to herself.

'Right. Isabel herself didn't attach much significance to the dreams, either,' Corwin carried on, 'but she then began to feel cold. And by that I mean,' he turned once again to Effie, 'cold in a way that can't be easily explained. Although the house is old and big, she swears that she wasn't standing in any draughts whenever she noticed these cold spells. And since it was a house that she grew up in and was very familiar with, she'd know all of its little peculiarities and foibles well. Furthermore, as you're aware, we've been having an unseasonably warm spring this year. Even more significantly than all of this, however, she came to realize that she only felt cold when going into a certain room.'

'Let me guess,' Effie said. 'The bedroom where her mother died?'

Corwin grinned and wagged an admonitory finger at her. 'And there's your first lesson, Effie. Never assume! Because no, as a matter of fact, it isn't her mother's bedroom, but her bathroom that gives her the chills.'

'Oh,' Effie said, feeling deflated and foolish.

'Don't worry,' Gisela put in kindly. 'I'm sure we all thought the same thing as well, didn't we? I know I did!'

Everyone nodded, and Effie smiled at her gratefully.

'And then, a few nights ago, Isabel swears she could smell lavender,' Corwin said. 'Her mother's favourite scent. Apparently, Claudia Watkins not only favoured eau de cologne in that particular fragrance, but in her soap and shampoo also. Of course, being a sensible sort, the first thing Isabel said that she did was to check and see if there was anything lavender-scented still lying around, but she remembers throwing all of her mother's used personal toiletry items away. And she was right – there was nothing of that nature left in the house to account for the fragrance.'

'But sometimes scent *can* linger,' Effie objected automatically. 'If her mother used talc, for instance, the fine powder could have made its way into the cushions or towels, and then any disturbance of those items could then release the scent.'

She felt no compunction in playing devil's advocate in this way. After all, Duncan had made it clear that he wanted her to use her common sense, whilst retaining a clear head and an open mind. And her own self-respect would not allow her to get lulled into seeing everything the way the rest of the C-Fits did. They might all be very nice and genuine people, but she was not about to forget that they all had a vested interest in seeing things a certain way. A way that tended to validate and confirm their own hopes and beliefs in the paranormal.

'Yes. Good thinking,' Corwin surprised her slightly by saying approvingly. 'That's the kind of thing we're always having to bear in mind. Contrary to popular belief, far from taking even the most flimsy of evidence at face value, proper investigators are all about trying to do the exact opposite. Given any 'evidence', the first thing we do is try to dismantle it,' he informed her flatly. 'But in this case, Isabel was positive that the scent, in her own words, was just "suddenly there" and "very strong." Too strong, she believes, to be any residue of the kind you're talking about, which by its very nature, would tend to be faint. And her mother has been buried for nearly two weeks now and given the warm weather, Isabel has had doors and windows open on a number of occasions to give the rooms a good airing.'

Effie nodded slowly. 'Yes. I see,' she said cautiously. She could now certainly understand why the story had captured Corwin's attention, and given him reason to think that it might be worth checking out. 'So we're going out to the house to do one of those preliminary investigations that you mentioned before?'

'Yes,' Corwin confirmed. 'Primarily, I want to meet Isabel Cadmund face to face and get a better idea of her. Previously, we've only spoken over the telephone. We also need to see the house. I've done some Googling and basic research on the family and on Mrs Claudia Watkins in particular,' he added, reaching down into a smart black leather attaché case nestling against one of the table legs. He brought out a sheaf of papers encased in clear plastic folders, which he quickly handed around.

Effie glanced at her own copy, and saw that it was headed THE LAVENDER LADY CASEFILE, and underneath it a three digit number, presumably referencing some kind of filing system.

'During the course of the investigation we'll add our findings to the file, which we can then take home with us and study,' Corwin explained for her benefit.

'What kind of findings?' Effie asked, trying not to sound nervous.

'Well, that's where mostly Lonny and Malc come in,' Corwin said. 'They are our technical team.'

Malc grinned. 'Sounds grand, doesn't it?'

'Mostly we simply set up the equipment and monitor it,' Lonny put in. 'Microphones that are noise-sensitive and will record throughout the night or day, whenever something sets them off. Then there's cameras in UV, infrared and infragreen that also records digitally and continuously. Later we take it in turns to watch a couple of hours of footage each, on the lookout for anything that seems anomalous.'

'My room-mate especially likes that bit,' Mickey said with a grin. 'The bloke thinks I'm nuts. I spend hours and hours watching in "real" time an empty room, hoping to spot something weird happening. I only stop when I actually start to go cross-eyed.'

Effie laughed obligingly.

'Then there's the EMFs,' Lonny said. And seeing Effie's blank look said quickly, 'Sorry, electromagnetic field meters. They measure any electromagnetic energy that might be about.'

'Ghosts, for some reason, give it off,' Gisela put in matter-of-factly.

OK, Effie thought. Now I'm really beginning to feel like Alice after tumbling down the rabbit hole.

As if sensing that she was beginning to feel rather overwhelmed by it all, Corwin suddenly leaned forward in his chair again and caught her eye.

'Don't worry, it's like everything else. It seems very confusing to begin with, but you'll learn as you go along. Before long it'll all seem normal, believe me. Just follow the rules and you'll be OK.'

'Ah, rules,' Effie said, feeling on firmer ground now. Michael had been a firm believer in those. So she could certainly follow rules, as long as she was sure that she knew what they were. 'And they are?'

'Once a vigil begins, don't move around too much,' Corwin said at once. 'Always remember, our equipment is set up to record sound and movement. So no talking unless absolutely necessary. Keep a small digital camera and a recorder with you at all times – most of us use our mobiles or tablets for that, and if you see or hear anything, try to get some kind of documentary evidence of it.'

Effie took a slow, deep breath, and fought the urge to gulp.

For some reason, the boom in modern technology and in social media in particular, had passed her by. Although she'd been fairly well up on computers in the office when she'd first started work at the architect's office, over the years the technology had changed so fast. Worse still, Michael hadn't been keen on the boom in social media, and hadn't wanted tablets and "all that other paraphernalia" in the house. And he'd stoutly maintained that if he wanted to watch a programme, he had a large-screen television for that, and had no intention of watching something on a laptop computer.

So for years now, their home had been a rather techno-free zone.

As a consequence, she hadn't really had much to do with Twitter or Facebook or any of the other things that most people nowadays took for granted – and Corwin's sweeping assumption that she was *au fait* with all the latest gizmos worried her slightly.

On the other hand, she *had* been half-heartedly thinking of getting a modern mobile phone just lately, with all its cameras, gadgets and bewildering apps. It had just seemed rather silly not to take advantage of all the stuff that everyone else seemed to take for granted.

Clearly it was now time to bite the bullet and launch herself into the twenty-first century. Surely if she bought the latest tablet or phone, someone could teach her how to use it properly? Either Duncan or Margot, or Penny, for instance. They'd know how to digitally record stuff, wouldn't they? After all, she told herself firmly, it can't be *that* difficult – even seven-year-olds could handle their apps with ease!

Whatever an app was.

'It's best if you also keep some kind of written notebook with you as well, and make a note of the time and circumstances surrounding anything that strikes you as being of any interest at all immediately as it happens,' Corwin swept on, thankfully interrupting her wandering attention.

And now Effie couldn't help but smile. An old fashioned notebook and pen was something she *didn't* need to worry about!

'And if you *do* encounter something that worries or alarms you, call for help at once. There will always be one of us within near distance and we'll always come running,' Corwin told her sternly.

'And that's not just because our heroic natures will make us want to come to your aid,' Mickey laughed, 'but because if something *is* happening, we'll all be as jealous as hell and want to see it for ourselves too!'

'But seriously, Effie, remember,' Corwin said gently, reaching out and putting his hand reassuringly over hers, 'the chances are that nothing of any significance *will* happen. But if it does, you only have to keep calm and remain rational. So far as I'm aware, nobody has ever come to any serious harm whilst doing the sort of thing that we at C-Fits do. We don't do so-called "extreme" ghost hunting, OK?'

Extreme ghost hunting, Effie thought with a small gulp that she hoped wasn't actually audible. What in the world was *that?*

'Yeah, we'll see you're all right, Effie,' Gisela promised her warmly. 'And if there *is* a ghost about, I'll feel it first and make sure you're never left alone.'

Effie, not sure whether to feel reassured or insulted by the younger girl's kindness, smiled grimly. 'Well, all right then,' she heard herself say firmly.

Mickey gave her a cheeky thumbs-up, and she hid a weary sigh as she repeated the infantile gesture back at him.

Corwin's fingers tightened briefly over her own, then he stood up.

'OK then. If everyone's happy, we'll get going. I've entered Isabel's address in my sat nav, so everyone can follow me. Effie, we usually car-pool – it saves on petrol and we like to think that we're doing our bit for the environment. Do you want to ride with me?'

Effie blinked, a little taken by surprise, and then forced herself to nod. 'Oh, yes, thank you.'

Mickey laughed. 'Don't let Zoe find out you're giving lifts to beautiful women, Chief.'

'Mickey!' the boss said warningly, whilst Effie wondered just who Zoe might be. But nobody stopped to enlighten her as, in their keen rush to tackle their newest project, everyone made for the door.

Corwin parked the Jaguar under the boughs of an old horse chestnut tree and cut the engine. The pretty village of Adderbury was situated barely a stone's throw from the growing market town of Banbury, and boasted its fair share of picturesque, vernacular architecture, rose-bedecked cottages and gardens set within narrow lanes. It also had a well-frequented village pub on the main road, and was definitely commuter-belt territory, with not only London but also Birmingham being barely an hour away by motorway or train.

The home of the late Claudia Watkins, however, lay further down the hill and into the village on a narrow, leafy lane tucked firmly away from the busy main road with its stream of polluting and noisy traffic. Here, in the gardens visible on one side of the residence, laurels and silver birch gave way to manicured lawns and charming flowerbeds. Red brick walls set still further in the distance and disappearing behind the house, promised that most desirable of things – an old-fashioned country house vegetable garden. And in the very far corner, Effie could even see a lovely little orchard where several apple trees, so ancient they were almost stooped to the ground, were defiantly blooming with pink and white blossom.

As they all clustered around on the pavement, it was clear to everyone, if they hadn't known it already, that the former occupant of such a place must have been very wealthy indeed. The house was attached on one side to another building of similar style, age and size, that had been turned into a lovely-looking country house hotel called The Rollwright Inn. In today's market, and given its desirable location, it must have been worth a small fortune.

Square, uncompromisingly Georgian, and with all of that era's simple but elegant features, the back of the house overlooked a nearby field, where sheep were grazing peacefully. Made of the local reddish-brown ironstone that almost glowed in the sunlight and with a large expanse of blue-grey slate roof, it seemed to watch them hopefully, like a friendly dog just waiting to be acknowledged.

There was nothing in the least foreboding or sinister about it.

Beside her, Mickey whistled through his teeth. 'How the other half live, right? Or rather how they don't, in this case! Let's hope the old girl doesn't disappoint us, hey?'

'I wouldn't even be able to afford to rent a single room here, should the family sell up and turn it all into flats,' Gisela agreed, instantly making Effie feel uncomfortable.

And looking back on her teenage years, Effie found it hard to recognize the girl she had once been. The large, anonymous comprehensive school that she had attended, the hours spent mooning over pop stars with her friends (with whom she had now lost all contact), the usual experiments with make-up and clothes. Her favourite colour had been amethyst, she remembered, and she seemed to dress in nothing but various shades of purple and pink!

It all seemed to have happened to someone else now.

It was harder still to remember how she had thought and felt back then. She seemed to recall that she had wanted to go into business for herself one day and start her own retail empire. Maybe travel the world. All pie-in-the-sky dreams of course, but they had meant a lot to her.

All that had changed, of course, when she'd got a real job and had grown up. And met Michael.

At first, her parents had been a little wary of Michael James – perhaps because he was their daughter's boss, and perhaps also because he was so much older than she was. And Effie could understand why they'd been worried that he might try and take advantage of her. Both of them had grown up in working class families, and felt a certain, understandable wariness, when it came to people who had always had money and privilege.

And certainly Michael, by any standards, had been a wealthy, urbane and well-educated man, with that certain gloss that had been totally alien to the world in which Effie had been raised.

By an unspoken but tacit understanding, everyone had

acknowledged that he'd been well out of her league. Which had made their courtship a rather fraught one!

She'd also been well aware that, before Michael had put an engagement ring on her finger, several of their neighbours and some of her mother's friends with daughters of their own, had barely been able to conceal their envy. And had almost certainly made some spiteful or sneering comments about their relationship behind her back.

But after their marriage, of course, her parents' fears had dissipated, along with all the speculation and gossip that Michael had only been interested in a brief fling with a pretty young girl, and things had quickly settled down.

To Effie, of course, it had all been so new and exciting. Leaving home for the first time, the new job and the unexplored territory that was marriage. And all the undeniable perks that came with marrying a wealthy man.

And one of the things that Effie had now come to take for granted was her home in Hampton Frome. Now, listening to Gisela, she realized, with a real start that made her feel slightly sick, that the younger girl probably regarded her as a wealthy, middle-aged matron.

And she was!

Wasn't she?

Except she didn't feel like one of those at all. Effie suddenly blinked, feeling the absurd desire to cry. Recognizing the onset of mild depression, she sternly told herself to cut it out. Now was not the time to start indulging in self-pity or a bout of contemplating her navel!

'Well, are we going to stand around admiring the scenery all day or are we going to go in?' Jean Bossington-Smith asked crisply, thankfully snapping her out of her painful reverie.

Lonny grinned as Mickey smartly saluted her.

Corwin shook his head and reached for the gate, pushing it open and allowing them all to precede him up the short front path.

'Let's show a little decorum and sensitivity, please,' he said, looking firmly at Mickey, who at least had the grace to blush a little.

And Effie felt a little better that she wasn't the only one who found Mickey rather tiresome. But clearly the others had all learned to cope with his clowning around, so she would too.

'Sorry, Chief,' Mickey said. But to Effie, he didn't sound as if he meant it.

The front garden was relatively small, but was nevertheless packed with spring bulbs and bedding plants and looked well-maintained, with not so much as even a dandelion leaf daring to raise its green head in the mulched earth.

And as they approached the wide wooden door set squarely in the middle of the building, with three large sash windows lining up either side of it like a regiment of soldiers, it began to open.

The gardener in Effie, which had been admiring what must have been a century old wisteria that was climbing the walls, gave way as she firmly transferred her attention to the matter in hand.

The fact that they hadn't had to ring the bell to gain entry told her that the lady of the house must have been watching anxiously for them to arrive, but Isabel Cadmund didn't show any outward signs of nervousness or angst. Instead she looked at them with the beginnings of a warm smile as she stepped outside to greet them.

Dressed in warm-looking black trousers and a cream-coloured Arran sweater knitted in a complicated design, she looked to be in her early sixties. Clearly once a blonde, her hair was now mainly grey but she had made no attempt to dye it. Thick and long, it hung down her back in a functional plait. Her face was free of make-up and her grey-green eyes crinkled in attractive crow's feet as she smiled at them.

'Hello, you must be Mr Fielding,' she said, looking from Lonny to Malcolm and then firmly settling on Corwin.

'Yes. Hello, Lady Cadmund. Thank you for inviting us into your home.' Corwin quickly introduced them all and Isabel stepped to one side.

'Oh, please, everyone, call me Isabel. And won't you all come in? I was just about to put the kettle on. Would everyone like tea?'

And with that prosaic and rather pleasant invitation, Effie James found herself stepping into her very first haunted house.

CHAPTER FOUR

Isabel led the way through a splendidly traditional hall, which came complete with a sweeping wooden staircase, black and white tiled floor, a grandfather clock ticking ponderously in one corner, and a side table, which currently housed a vase of seasonal daffodils that were only just beginning to droop slightly.

It gave Effie the feeling that the late owner had been very much a traditionalist who, like Michael, had preferred to keep her home well away from the upstart invasions of the twenty-first century. This impression was reinforced when Isabel showed them into a long drawing room with an open fireplace and elegant wooden tables, and a slightly worn but still elegant Wilton carpet. There was not a television set in sight.

'Please, sit down, everyone,' Isabel said with a brief smile, indicating the variety of comfortable looking chairs and sofas that were scattered around the room. 'I have to confess to feeling a little nervous. Now that you're all here, I feel like I might have given you a false impression. And I would hate to think that I'd wasted your time. It's not as if I've ever actually *seen* anything.'

Corwin smiled at her, whilst everyone got settled down. Jean, Effie noticed with a smile, had already got out a notebook and was prepared to write – no doubt in extremely efficient shorthand – anything of interest that the lady of the house might have to say. Gisela was sitting quietly with her eyes almost closed, soaking up the atmosphere – or whatever it was that 'sensitives' did, Effie supposed, a shade uneasily. She had a feeling that it was going to take her a little time to feel totally comfortable around the lanky redhead. Lonny was openly admiring a painting of a landscape on one wall, whilst Malc simply sat and watched Isabel Cadmund thoughtfully. Mickey's eyes were darting everywhere, but at least he remained mercifully silent.

'I'm sure you won't have done that,' Corwin reassured their hostess soothingly. 'And there's nothing to feel nervous about. I promise you, we won't do anything without your permission, or explaining clearly what we're doing and why. If you change your mind at any time, or have second thoughts, we will leave immediately. And none of us are interested in talking to the press or seeking publicity for ourselves. In fact, if you don't tell anyone else, there's no reason why anyone should even know that we've been here,' he reassured her. 'We're all very discreet, and it's a policy of ours never to discuss our clients, even with our own family members.'

Isabel nodded, looking visibly more comfortable after that little speech, and Effie found herself becoming more and more impressed by the group's professionalism. They might, in the strictest sense of the word, be amateurs but that clearly didn't mean that they were either inexperienced or clumsy.

Isabel had taken a seat near the fireplace, and was leaning slightly forward in a hard-backed chair with a brocaded seat of pink and grey. Her hands were clenched between her knees, and she looked resolute but pale and rather grim-faced. Underneath it all, Effie had the impression that the older woman felt utterly at sea. Clearly the situation in which she found herself was one that she felt profoundly uncomfortable with. And who, Effie thought a shade wryly, can wonder at that?

What would she do if she ever thought her house was haunted? But who could haunt it except Michael and …

Abruptly and brutally, Effie shut that train of thought down. She really *had* to get out of this habit of letting her mind wander so.

'I suppose I should tell you right away that my family – well, the majority of them anyway, are not … Well, let's just say that they don't agree with me asking you here,' Isabel blurted the confession out all in a rush. Then she laughed slightly, and looked instantly a good decade younger. 'My husband thinks I'm potty, to put it bluntly, but he loves me, and so he's indulging me. But then Jeremy hasn't been staying here. And I have,' she added grimly.

At this, Effie felt the others around her perk up with interest, and simply had to hide a smile. They were like a pack of hunting dogs, amiable and friendly enough, but now that they'd scented their quarry, one or two of them were almost quivering with anticipation.

Needless to say, Jean Bossington-Smith was not one of them. Nor, surprisingly, was Corwin. Effie saw that he was simply watching his hostess with quiet, intense concentration. Today he was dressed in black trousers, with a cream-coloured shirt and a black sleeveless waistcoat glinting with silver embroidery. This unexpected and slightly flamboyant style suited him however, lending him a curiously elegant but raffish sort of appearance, that was made even more striking by his long, untamed dark hair. He looked, Effie thought, a bit like an eighteenth century roué after a hard night's gambling at some scandalous gentleman's club or other.

'And of course my brother Monty doesn't approve, but then he seldom does,' Isabel continued, giving another sudden laugh. 'Growing up, Monty and I always fought like cat and dog – perhaps because I was the oldest, and Monty, as the only boy, thought he had a right to lord it over me.'

Everyone smiled, anxious to put her at ease.

'At least Ros isn't so narrow-minded. That's my daughter. Mind you, she was fond of her grandmother, and was without doubt Mum's favourite,' Isabel confessed. 'That's why my mother left her all her jewellery. And she had quite a bit of it – Mum liked to wear diamonds. And emeralds. They suited her,' Isabel said, a mixture of pride and exasperation in her voice.

Slowly, the personality of the dead woman was becoming apparent, and Effie could feel herself being drawn into the drama. For all her self-inflicted lectures to remain aloof and unbiased, she was beginning to see the allure of what the C-Fits did. And wasn't it something of a privilege, really, to be let into a stranger's family secrets and dramas?

'So at least Ros doesn't altogether dismiss my … What do I call them? Fears? Doubts? Experiences?' Isabel shrugged her shoulders helplessly. 'Well, let's just say that she's not willing to write me off as a hysteric just yet. Besides, she knows her grandmother was one very strong-willed – and some might even say cantankerous – old woman. And if it's possible to, well, come back and haunt a place, I suppose Mother would be an ideal candidate to do just that.' Isabel laughed. 'She would certainly have been very angry about dying, and it would have been just like her to decide that she wasn't going to actually leave the premises until she was good and ready!' Isabel smiled and shook her head.

'She sounds as if she was a formidable lady,' Corwin agreed.

'And it's often people like that who are most reluctant to pass over,' Gisela said softly. 'When they find themselves suddenly dead, it can make them feel very cross and cheated. And I can already feel that a very strong personality indeed lived here.'

Isabel Cadmund looked at the tall redhead with a start of surprise, and then, after a brief hesitation, nodded uncertainly. Like Effie, it was clear that she didn't quite know how to react to Gisela's 'insights'.

'Your mother, she had set ideas, am I right?' Gisela asked, looking towards one of the large windows, where a green leather seat faced the glass, overlooking the pavement outside. 'And once she'd made up her mind to do something, nothing would convince her to change it?'

'Yes,' Isabel said, staring at Gisela with growing fascination. 'And that chair you're looking at was her favourite spot. She'd spend hours reading a book there, or just watching village life go by.'

'Yes, I know,' Gisela said simply.

Effie blinked.

'She could be very old fashioned too, which as you can expect, led to a certain amount of tension,' Isabel carried on. 'And not just in the family, either – although she never approved of Celia, Monty's wife, and made no secret over it. But then, Celia has a hide like a rhinos … Er, she took it all in good part.' As if suddenly aware that she might be letting more slip than she'd meant to, Isabel visibly pulled herself up short. 'But, as I was saying, Mother didn't always restrict her opinions on how things should be done to just the immediate family, unfortunately. Poor Geoff, for instance, was beginning to feel at his wits' end ...' Isabel's voice wavered as it suddenly occurred to her that she had been about to be indiscreet, yet again – and with people she had only just met. Which was a very un-British trait.

'Geoff?' Corwin encouraged her softly. Whilst he might be sympathetic with her instinctive need to guard her privacy, he also obviously needed Isabel to be open and honest. And it made sense that the more he learned about the possible source of the phenomenon, the easier his job would be.

'Mother's head gardener,' Isabel replied automatically to the prompt. 'Well, that sounds much grander than ... I mean, Geoff's worked here for nearly thirty years now, but mostly alone. Although in the spring, he has a few of the older, retired men in the village come in to help him out for a few hours a week.'

'Yes, I noticed the grounds were lovely.' Effie felt she needed to do something to earn her keep, and if she could help Corwin put Isabel at her ease, then she felt she ought to do so. 'Was that a walled garden in the back that I saw?'

'Yes.' Isabel looked at her eagerly, clearly relieved to be talking off-topic, as it were. 'Geoff's marvellous with growing the fruit and vegetables, mowing the lawns and keeping the shrubbery under control. But Mother, right up until she died, would insist on over-seeing the flowers. She always cherished her roses and peonies especially.'

'And did their ideas not match?' Effie asked with a smile. And when Isabel looked at her, a shade puzzled, she added gently, 'You said your mother's strong will caused some friction with him? Did they argue over the begonias?' she added with a grin.

Isabel instantly grinned back. 'Oh! Yes, I see what you mean. No, it wasn't to do with the flowers. I'm afraid it was just another notion that Mother had got into her head. She was prone to having ideas that were set in stone, you see. There seemed to be no rhyme or reason to them – let alone logic. But once it was implanted in her head, she wouldn't be moved on it. And one of them happened to be that, once Geoff had reached his seventieth birthday, he simply had to stop working and fully retire. Of course Geoff, who's as fit as a flea and loves the grounds here like they were his own, had no interest in giving up work. So they argued about it all the time.'

Isabel sighed and shook her head. 'Mother was a wonderful woman, don't get me wrong. She was intelligent and passionate about the things that mattered to her. And generous to those who were in her favour. But she was always strong-willed. As a girl of just seventeen, she ran off and married a man called Walter Watkins, a feed and grain merchant. Her own parents were landowners in Berkshire and had been hoping she'd marry the son of a neighbour who was set to inherit half of the Downs. As you can imagine, her elopement didn't go down too well.'

'Good for her,' Gisela said approvingly, and Jean Bossington-Smith went so far as to nod her head in approbation as well.

Isabel got up and went to a sideboard where she retrieved a silver-framed photograph. 'This is Mother when she was in her thirties. Although her marriage was very successful, and Walter surprised everyone by buying out his bosses and turning the company into a real money making enterprise, thus setting up the bulk of the family fortunes, unfortunately he died young.'

She handed the photograph to Corwin, who studied it intently for a few moments, before passing it around.

'Mother had to raise my brother and myself all alone. She'd been widowed for well over forty years before she died,' Isabel explained.

'She never re-married?' Effie asked quietly.

'Oh no. She was fiercely loyal to Walter's memory.'

Effie nodded. Having defied her family and 'married down' as the saying went, the old lady had probably had too much invested in him to let go of him easily.

Malc leaned across and handed her the photograph, and Effie took it, looking down at the image of a woman dressed in 1940s chic, in a form-fitting skirt and jacket of some dark colour. The photograph, being black and white, probably didn't do justice to the face that gazed implacably back at her. Dark hair had been swept to the back of her head in an elegant and elaborate chignon, whilst a strong jaw and a slightly pugnacious chin stopped her just shy of being truly beautiful. But fine dark eyes captured your gaze, and Effie could well imagine that this woman had probably still been striking to look at, even if age had weakened her heart, turned her hair to silver, and slightly bent that once-rigid looking spine.

She passed the photograph on to Lonny.

'She looks very imposing,' Effie said with a smile.

'Oh, she was. Everyone in the village knew her of course. Even the influx of new people in recent years recognized the fact that she ran the village, even if she never sat on a council committee in her life, and never could be persuaded to join the WI. Still, somehow, nothing ever got done unless Claudia Watkins gave it her seal of approval. Clive said she treated the village like her own personal fiefdom – and that everyone was either too bemused, too busy, or too entertained by it to really care.'

'Clive?' Corwin queried.

'Ros's husband – my son-in-law. He and Mother never really got on. In fairness to Clive, I don't think anyone short of Prince Harry would have been good enough for Ros in Mother's eyes! And a self-made man definitely wasn't looked on favourably. Funny, when you think about it – you'd have thought that she, of all people, wouldn't have looked down on him for that. But she always said that he was no Walter. Perhaps if he'd been in a different business ...'

She sighed and broke off, again aware that she might have been about to say something less than complimentary about her own daughter's husband to comparative strangers.

'I'm sure he's perfectly respectable, Lady Cadmund,' Jean spoke up for the first time.

'Oh, he is! He owns a construction company – you've probably heard of them.' She named a firm that had recently built a vast building estate on the outskirts of Banbury. 'He's currently negotiating with a local farmer to build thirty houses on his land near Bloxham,' she added. 'And that didn't help, of course. Mother said that the countryside would be paved over entirely if people like Clive had their way. Oh, the arguments they had .... But that was just Mother. To be honest, I think she rather liked to argue with people.'

'Yes. I can sense that,' Gisela said. 'And you feel as if she's still here? I can understand why. She's such a strong presence, isn't she?'

Perhaps it was something about the matter of fact way that Gisela spoke, or the ease with which she said it, that made Isabel finally open up.

'I suppose she is,' Claudia Watkins's daughter admitted. 'Would you like to see her room?'

Of course, everyone did. Even Effie. After hearing so much about her, she was curious to see Claudia's private rooms, as well as more of the lovely old house.

Isabel led them back into the hall and up the stairs, which were made of oak and had been worn smooth over the years, as feet had climbed the treads and countless generations of fingers had clutched at the banisters.

At the top of the stairs the landing divided, with a set of doors leading off to the left and the right. Isabel turned right, and led them to the very end of the corridor, where a master suite had obviously been created – complete with a dressing room and walk-in wardrobe.

Quietly looking around, they all stepped into a large, comfortable bedroom, decorated in tones of blue and green, with the odd apricot accent. A large four-poster bed, with sheer white gauzy curtains tied back with tassel-ended ropes of twisted apricot silk, dominated one wall. An unlit fireplace on the far wall bore mute testimony to the days before central heating. Heavy, gilt-framed paintings hung around the walls, depicting various rural landscapes and one or two anonymous people – probably family ancestors.

'The bathroom she always used is directly opposite,' Isabel said, pointing through the still open door, but making no move to go inside herself.

'This is where you've often felt inexplicably cold?' Corwin asked.

Wordlessly Isabel nodded, but her hands went up to the tops of her arms and rubbed briskly, as if she was experiencing the chill all over again.

'Would you mind if Malcolm and Lonny went in there?' Corwin asked, and Isabel smiled and shook her head.

'Please, feel free. That's why you're here, isn't it?'

The two men quickly left, both of them clearly eager to check it out, with Mickey quickly following after them. Gisela drifted towards the bed as if fascinated by it. Jean and Effie, however, both moved to one of the two windows, drawn by the light filtering in from outside and the view over the village.

Because Claudia's bedroom was located at the far side of the house, Effie realized, as she leaned out of the window and looked down, the wall right next to where she was standing didn't actually belong to the house, but to the inn next door. A rather prosaic, black-painted drainpipe marked the demarcation, and as she followed it down with her eyes, she noted that it ended in an unlovely and modern concrete square with an iron grating inside, denoting a drain.

But the inn's front garden was every bit as colourful as Claudia Watkins's own, and beyond the pavement and pretty horse chestnut trees, which were about to burst into candles of white and pink bloom, the village scene could have graced any box of chocolates or jigsaw puzzle.

'Lovely scene, isn't it?' Jean murmured beside her. 'I live in a bungalow in Kidlington with a view of the back of a supermarket car park. Still, it's convenient for the shops.'

Effie, a shade taken aback, didn't quite know how to respond to this abrupt and totally unexpected confidence by the rather remote, former schoolteacher, and found herself grappling for something non-committal to say in response.

'Do you suppose the village has any shops?' she heard herself ask politely. 'Nowadays, they seem to be rather rare, don't they?'

'I think we might have a cold spot in the bathroom, Corwin,' Malc's cheerful and definitely excited voice abruptly brought any small talk to an abrupt end, and both women turned back automatically to the centre of the room.

'You felt the cold in there too?' Isabel asked, her voice understandably hopeful. 'It's not just me then? I'm not imagining things?'

Malc looked at Corwin and nodded. Lonny smiled happily. 'We

both felt that it was definitely colder in one particular spot, but we need to make sure. We should definitely set up some temperature monitors in there, Chief,' he said. 'I recommend at least five – that way we can pinpoint the cold spot very accurately.'

Corwin nodded and turned to Isabel, but as he began to explain what his fellow C-Fit members meant by this, Effie saw his gaze flick her way too, and knew she needed to pay attention as well.

'It's important that our findings are clear and open to outside scrutiny and valuation, Lady Cadmund. Simply taking one temperature reading of a room, even if it does show it to be colder than the rest of the house, doesn't really prove anything. It could be down to ventilation – it is a bathroom, after all, and probably has some form of air filtration going on. Or it could be down to a draught or an ill-fitting window. But if we set up multi-temperature gauges, and it can be demonstratively proved that one small area *within* the room is significantly lower than the rest of the room, then that's a different thing altogether. Because, logically, there is no reason why it should be so.'

'So you *are* interested in looking into things for me?' Isabel said quickly.

'If you're sure you'd like us to, yes,' Corwin said. 'Perhaps now would be a good time to discuss just what that would entail, so you can think it over. It's important that there be no misunderstandings between us.'

'Oh yes. Perhaps we should go back downstairs,' Isabel said, clearly happy to leave her mother's bedroom. 'It was in here that I smelt the lavender so strongly,' she added, aware that her reluctance to remain must be obvious. 'And I have to say, of all the things that have been happening around here, that … er … unsettles me the most. I haven't been in here since … well, since that time.'

'Of course,' Corwin agreed at once.

Back in the elegant lounge and over cups of tea, which Isabel had made herself and brought in on an enormous tray, Corwin laid out the C-Fit's wares, as it were.

'If it's all right with you, Lady Cad—'

'Isabel, please,' she insisted again. 'We never use Jeremy's title.

It's so ancient and, besides, in today's world, it's insignificant as well.'

'Thank you, Isabel.' Corwin smiled at her gently. 'What we do is start off with a series of what we call vigils. Most of these will take place overnight, but not all. Contrary to popular belief,' he paused to grin widely, 'ghosts don't just come out to play at night. We have all experienced some interesting phenomenon in daylight hours too.'

'And what is that you do, exactly, on these vigils?' Isabel asked, beginning to look both genuinely curious and excited for the first time. It was also an excellent question, Effie thought silently, because she was dying to know herself.

'Well, first we'll set up temperature gauges all around the house, not just in the bathroom,' Corwin said. 'Although we'll concentrate more in the bathroom, the others will help provide us with an overall measurement of room temperatures. We'll also set up recording equipment which will capture any sounds, and any EVPs.'

'EVPs?' Isabel echoed, again saving Effie the necessity of having to do so herself and thus showing up her own ignorance about such things.

'Oh, sorry. I get so used to using the jargon, I sometimes forget that I'm doing it,' Corwin apologized at once. 'EVP is short for electronic voice phenomenon. Sometimes the digital recorders pick up noises that people, that is, the human ear, can't always detect. And by using computer-assisted enhancement technology, we can sometimes produce startling results.'

'Oh,' Isabel said, a shade uncertainly. And Effie couldn't help but wonder if, like Effie herself, their client had instantly realized that anything could be faked with a computer. You only had to watch any modern sci-fi blockbuster film to know that any phenomenon could be faked with the help of technology.

Not that Effie had any reason to suppose that either Corwin or any other member of the group would actually condone or commit fraud. But then again, Effie couldn't help but think cynically, it was very hard to take anything on trust nowadays.

But there was little point mentioning any of that just now.

For one thing, she was no IT expert, and wouldn't be able to tell whether anything had been fraudulently produced anyway. And she was hardly likely to insult those around her by pointing out her scepticism.

Still, she made a mental note to voice her misgivings about it to Duncan. That was, after all, the kind of thing he wanted to know about.

Blissfully unaware of her cynicism, Corwin carried on enthusiastically. 'Then we'll set up the night-vision cameras, in ultraviolet and infra green and red,' he explained, his enthusiasm so genuine and infectious that Effie was glad that he hadn't been able to read her mind. 'We'll also concentrate some of these in specific areas – her favourite chair, for instance, and any other spots around the house where you think your mother would have spent most of her time. These digitally record everything that happens in real time, and is again stored on a computer, so that we can watch the feedback any time we want. Again, sometimes the cameras pick up things the human eye misses – especially in the dark.'

In the dark? Effie thought. *We aren't going to have any lights on at all*?

'It all sounds very technical and scientific,' Isabel acknowledged. 'Perhaps even Monty will be forced to admit that things are being done properly. I think he was imagining us all sitting around a table with a single candle burning, our fingers touching whilst strange knocks and bumps came down the chimney!'

'No, we very rarely hold séances,' Corwin said flatly, and Effie distinctly felt her heart flutter at the word 'rarely.'

But before she had time to explore that avenue, Corwin was again speaking. 'We also set up various other pieces of equipment, designed to pick up any other kind of energy that might be present.'

'And what do you want me to do while you're doing all this, exactly?' Isabel asked, looking nervous once more.

'Nothing at all,' Corwin assured her instantly. 'Just go about your usual routine. I take it you're sleeping in one of the other bedrooms?'

'Yes.'

'Then just go to bed as normal. Of course, there will be no cameras or equipment in your room,' Corwin said. 'That would hardly be appropriate. We want to be as unobtrusive as possible.'

'Thank you,' Isabel said with clear relief. 'But what will you do? Patrol the house?'

'Oh no, in fact, we'll do the exact opposite,' Corwin said quickly. 'We tend to all stay put in one place and keep very quiet. Either Malc, Lonny or myself will monitor the equipment and camera feeds. We set it up so that it all feeds back to a set of monitors in, say, this room, which we'll use as our main base of operations. The rest of us will split up and stay in various other rooms in the house and simply sit still and quiet and watch and listen.'

We will? Effie thought with a bit of a gulp. *Alone*?

When she'd agreed to go through with this, she had assumed for some reason that they'd all stick together. Or at least that she'd be partnered with someone else.

But as Corwin caught her eye, she felt her backbone stiffen and was damned if she was going to look like a chicken, so she simply smiled briefly and did her best to look unconcerned.

'Well, that all sounds very fine and reasonable,' Isabel said with a smile. 'When did you want to start?'

'Well, if you're sure you want to go ahead …'

'Oh, I do. It'll be a relief just to know that something's being done,' Isabel admitted. And no doubt the older woman would be relieved to no longer be staying in the house alone.

'How about tomorrow night then?' Corwin asked.

And again Effie blinked. *So soon?* Somehow, until now, the whole ghost hunting thing had been a rather abstract thought in the back of her mind. Something that was there, but something she didn't really need to give any real attention. Now it was suddenly immediate and *real.*

Then she told herself firmly to get a grip. If she was going to do this thing – and it looked very much as if she was – then she couldn't go around being such a scaredy-cat. Clearly, she was going to have to develop a calm, cool-headed detachment about the whole thing. Not to mention grow a bit more of a backbone!

But as they left Isabel, with their reassurances that they'd be back promptly at seven o'clock tomorrow night, Effie had the distinct feeling that it might well be a case of easier said than done.

As they drove back towards the cricket pavilion in Corwin's Jaguar, Effie watched the passing scenery in silence for a while, trying to process all that she'd seen and heard. And to try and sort out exactly what it was that she was going to tell Duncan, when they met up later.

She knew that her old friend was eager to get her first impressions and opinions, and before today, she hadn't even considered the fact that she might find that in the least bit difficult. But now Effie wasn't so sure. Was it really going to be so easy to adequately express her thoughts? Did she even know what they were, come to that?

Duncan was expecting an intelligent and clear report, but just how was she supposed to deliver that? How, for instance, could she adequately describe to a psychology professor her thoughts and feelings about Gisela, for instance? Did she like her? Yes, undoubtedly. She liked all the C-Fit members. (And if she still found Mickey annoying, and could have done without his habit of constantly going out of his way to be deliberately provocative, then at least she was fair-minded enough to admit that he had an eager and genuinely curious mind.)

But did she actually *believe* that Gisela was a 'sensitive?' Did she think that, back at the house, the redhead had actually 'picked up' on the character and spirit of Claudia Watkins? Or had she just made some clever and intuitive guesses? Perhaps without even being consciously aware that she was doing it? Focussing on that chair by the window, for instance, seeming to 'know' that it had been Claudia's favourite spot, could have been merely a lucky guess, or even a reasonable assumption on her part. The chair had clearly been in that position for some time, and old folks often liked to look out on the world through a window from the comfort and warmth of their home. It wasn't much of a leap for your subconscious mind to make the connection, leaving you feeling as if you'd simply 'felt' it.

She certainly didn't believe for one moment that Gisela was an out and out fraud or charlatan, or that she was being deliberately deceitful or even disingenuous. It was perfectly feasible that Gisela herself truly believed in her 'abilities.' But Effie had her doubts. How could she not have? How could any *reasonable* person not have? After all, she'd only just met Gisela, and was relying solely on her own instincts about the girl. But she was not so naïve as to think that she couldn't be conned by a very good actress.

But how could she try to make Duncan adequately understand her ambivalence?

'Penny for them,' Corwin said, his voice bringing her rather abruptly out of her somewhat gloomy thoughts.

'Oh, sorry. I was just thinking … about Isabel,' Effie fudged, unwilling to discuss with this man, of all men, her growing sense of inadequacy. 'She seemed very nice, didn't she?' she heard herself say. And instantly felt dismayed. What an inconsequential, utterly unhelpful thing to say.

'Yes, she did. I liked her,' Corwin said warmly. If he had noticed the inanity of her comment, at least he was too polite to draw notice to it. He changed gear competently and accelerated a little, but Effie felt perfectly safe in the car. Like her late husband, he was clearly a very good and safe driver.

It had taken her three goes to pass her driving test, and although she'd been driving for many years now, she still felt a vague sense of relief whenever she'd reached her destination or arrived home.

Now Effie stirred on her seat. 'About this vigil tomorrow,' she said firmly, determined to be business-like about things. 'I'm slightly worried that I'll do something … I don't know … inappropriate. Something that might ruin your recordings, say. It all sounded so scientific and complicated. What if I sneeze or something?'

Corwin laughed. 'We might all sneeze, Effie,' he teased her gently. 'Try not to tie yourself up in knots about it. You don't have to sit like a statue, you know. At some point you'll need to use the loo, just like everyone else will. We just try to keep movement to a minimum and the noise down as much as we can. Don't worry – you'll soon get used to the routine.'

Effie sighed a little. Right. Sure she would!

'Look, we're all going to go back home and get an early night, OK? If possible, sleep in really late tomorrow morning – as late as you can,' Corwin advised. 'Pulling an all-nighter takes it out of your body clock, and believe me, you need to be as rested as possible.'

Effie blinked. Of course – she hadn't even considered that aspect of things. Tomorrow night she had to stay wide awake and alert for hours at a time. Oh good grief – supposing she fell asleep in the early hours and started snoring! It would probably set off all sorts of Geiger counters or something. Did she snore? Michael had never said that she did, and she was sure that he would have mentioned it if she had.

'Relax, you look petrified.' Corwin's voice, warm and amused, once again cut through her thoughts, and she forced herself to smile back at him.

'Sorry. It's just … this is all so very …' She waved a hand helplessly in the air.

'Crazy? Bonkers? Nuts? A waste of time? Ridiculous?'

'No! None of those things,' she reassured him with a laugh, beginning to smile in earnest now.

Then, as she was looking at him, she saw his face suddenly sober.

'Are you scared? Is that it?' he asked, taking his eyes off the road for a quick look at her. And in that briefest of moments, Effie could sense his concern. 'It's all right to admit it if you are, you know.' He carried on gently. 'We all have our moments. Especially in the beginning, when we're still new to it all. Malc confessed to me, months after his first vigil, that he'd been afraid his chattering teeth would be picked up on one of the monitors.'

'Malc did?' Effie repeated, amazed. The builder had struck her as one of those men who wouldn't back down from anything. Not because he was particularly aggressive, but because he seemed possessed of a laid-back strength of will that would take some shaking.

'Yes – even Malc,' Corwin reassured her. 'We've all felt … I was going to say spooked,' he laughed, 'but under the circumstances, perhaps I should find a better word. Let's just say that each and every one of us can feel frightened sometimes. We don't expect you to be superwoman, you know.'

'Well, that's a relief.' Effie smiled wryly. Because a superwoman she certainly was not.

'You'll be fine,' Corwin predicted, slowing down as they approached the turn off to the narrow lane that bordered their unconventional HQ, and a moment later, turning into the car park. 'Oh good, Zoe's already here,' he said, and Effie looked and saw a tall woman with long blonde hair, leaning against a sporty little car painted an eye-catching shade of tomato red. 'We're heading out to the theatre later,' he added, as he turned off the engine, and quickly checked his watch.

'So, tomorrow night; the routine's simple,' he said, turning his head to look at her once more. 'We all meet up here an hour before a vigil,' he began as Malc's van parked alongside.

The van had a bench behind the front seats, so most of the others tended to use it as their main means of transport. No doubt come tomorrow it would be full of their equipment too.

'I hand out the assignments,' Corwin carried on, putting up a hand and smiling at the blonde woman who had now started walking towards them, 'and when we're all clear on what we'll be doing, we'll head on over to Adderbury. If at any time you're not sure of anything, simply ask one of us. Oh, and be sure to bring your mobile too,' he added, opening the door and climbing out, continuing to talk as Effie also got out of the car.

'Then you can programme all our numbers into it. Before the vigil begins, we set our phones to vibrate, so you can send a text message if you don't want to physically come and find one of us.'

Effie nodded and sighed. One thing was very clear – before coming back to the pavilion, she needed to buy an all-singing, all-dancing mobile phone or tablet! And learn how to text.

As for the rest of his instructions, she wasn't sure what he meant by 'assignments.' It rather implied that she would have to do more than sit and watch and listen. But before she had a chance to ask, the blonde woman stepped up to Corwin, took his face firmly in her hands, and passionately kissed him.

Effie abruptly looked away.

She was still decorously inspecting her shoes when she heard Corwin's voice again a few moments later.

'Effie, this is my girlfriend Zoe. Zoe Younger. Zoe, this is the latest member of our group, Mrs Effie James. You remember, I told you about her.'

'Oh yes. The professor's spy?' Zoe laughed. 'Hello. Welcome to the madhouse.' She thrust out a hand, which had been manicured to perfection with the nails painted a demure shade of peach. A large, complex geometric ring in various shades of gold, matched a bangle on her right wrist.

Effie felt herself stiffen at the reference to Duncan, and forced a smile to her face as she shook hands. 'Hello – the spy, yes, that's me. Just call me James Bond.'

Now where on earth had that riposte come from?

Effie blinked in surprise as behind her, she heard Mickey suddenly roar with laughter. 'Hey, that's good, that is. Effie *James* – *James* Bond, get it? Hey, Eff, I think you've just earned yourself a nickname. From now on I'll just call you double-oh-seven.'

Effie bit her tongue, hoping that she wasn't blushing. She'd already made a fool of herself in front of the younger, attractive woman. She didn't need her folly to be reinforced. Sometimes she wondered if Mickey was ten years old, instead of his (alleged) decade older.

'No, you won't,' Jean Bossington-Smith told him smartly, coming to her rescue.

Then she added amiably, 'Hello, Zoe. I didn't know you were free tonight.' To Effie, Jean turned and said, 'You might recognize Zoe from the television?'

Effie felt herself stiffen even further. Good grief, was the woman famous? She knew that a lot of local popular culture had probably passed her by, since she spent more time gardening than keeping up with things in the 'celebrity' world. Was Zoe Younger some famous fashion model or something? A pop singer even? She could certainly be either. In her early to mid twenties, along with the very noticeable long blonde hair, she also possessed a pair of big blue eyes that were set in a pretty elfin face, and a lean frame that nevertheless had curves in all the right places.

She realized that everyone was waiting for her to respond, especially Zoe, whose sharp eyes were definitely narrowing now in a show of distinct displeasure at her display of ignorance, and Effie felt a momentary sense of panic assail her.

'I'm so sorry, but I'm afraid I don't watch that much television,' she heard herself blurt out apologetically.

Behind her, she was sure she could hear Gisela muffle a sudden snort of laughter. But she might have been mistaken, for Zoe was now laughing and making a show of putting her at her ease.

'Oh, there's no reason why you should recognize me, Mrs James. I'm hardly a celebrity. Jean here tends to flatter me.'

Clearly she was waiting for Corwin to step in and fill the breach. And, not missing his cue, he smoothly did so.

'Zoe forecasts the weather on our local digital station.' He named a channel that Effie had never even heard of, let alone watched. But his voice was rich with pride as he explained, and he was clearly supportive of her career. 'And she's going to be doing the shows for one of the large satellite stations soon,' he added, naming a station that she definitely *had* heard of, and commanded viewers in their millions.

Clearly, Zoe was a woman who was going places.

'Oh, that sounds interesting. Where did you study meteorology?' she asked pleasantly. After her gaffe, she needed to sound at least reasonably intelligent and capable of making social discourse without making a total fool of herself.

'Reading. It was how I came to meet Corwin, actually, when he was a mature student there,' Zoe said, her voice a shade tight now. 'One of my fellow classmates was going out with him, and we double-dated with the boy I was dating at the time.'

'Obviously neither relationship lasted,' Corwin added laconically, 'and after we'd split up, Zoe and I got together.'

Zoe slipped her arm possessively around one of Corwin's and smiled happily up at him. 'And we've been together ever since. Nearly three years now,' she finished, her gaze meeting Effie's coolly.

And Effie, with a start, realized that this woman was definitely, if silently, warning her off. And warning her off Corwin!

And the realization felt utterly bizarre.

Michael had been the only man in her life – ever. For all her adult life, she'd thought of herself as a sexual creature only in regards to him and their marriage. So for another woman to regard her as a threat concerning *her* man, felt distinctly odd and baffling.

What on earth was this beautiful, glamorous woman worried about? It wasn't as if Corwin could possibly ever give her, Effie, a single – even remotely – amorous thought.

The idea was utterly absurd.

With a bit of an effort, Effie smiled stiffly and nodded at her. 'Well, I'm pleased to meet you, Zoe. Will you be coming on our vigil tomorrow?' she asked levelly.

'No, afraid not. I'll be in the television studio. But I do like to come when I can, don't I, Corwin? I do so love what he does. I think it's so sexy.'

'Corwin, I've got to get off,' Malc spoke. 'I've got a job tomorrow in Milton Keynes but I'll be back here in time for the pre-meet briefing, don't worry.'

'OK,' Corwin said, and as the builder turned and walked away it was, thankfully, the prompt for everyone else to split up and head towards their own transport.

Mickey's motorbike roared into noisy action as Effie slipped behind her steering wheel, and he shot off first. But as she carefully manoeuvred her car towards the entrance, she stopped to let Corwin's Jaguar go out in front of her. But with a smile and elaborate hand gesture through the windscreen, he beckoned her to go first.

In her rear view mirror, Effie watched as Zoe Younger turned her head to say something to him.

She drove at a steady thirty miles an hour down the narrow country lane, unaware of how tense she felt until she noticed the Jaguar behind her indicate to turn left at the approaching T-junction, whereas she was turning right.

Once the sports car was out of sight, her whole body seemed to slump in relief.

By the time she reached Hampton Frome, Effie was roundly if silently cursing Duncan Fergusson.

Before that seemingly harmless lunch invitation of his, her life had been quiet, safe and utterly predictable.

Now, given Zoe Younger's inexplicable animosity, and her own doubts about all this ghost hunting business, she couldn't help but wonder just what kind of a mess he'd got her into.

CHAPTER FIVE

Extract from the journal of Corwin Fielding:

12 April: Our first vigil on the Claudia Watkins case starts tonight. Our client, Isabel Cadmund, has agreed to our usual terms and seems to be a creditable witness. Lonny and Malc are sure that there is a cold spot to be found and monitored in Claudia's bathroom, and we're all looking forward to getting some good data on that.

Our newest member, Effie James, strikes me as being an intelligent, capable woman, if a little nervous and unsure about the project. When Professor Fergusson first approached me with his proposal, I had serious doubts. But after having met his candidate for observer, most of my concerns have lessened significantly. Having said that, however, it remains to be seen whether or not Effie is suited for the role. Not everyone can remain impartial or unbiased, and not everyone has the necessary attributes for paranormal research. But I imagine that tonight, and the following weeks, will go a long way towards establishing this.

The rest of the group, I am glad to say, have all told me that they are happy for Effie to be part of the group. Jean, in particular, seems to think that she will be an asset, and all of the others seem to like her and have no objections to working with her – although both Malc and Lonny have made it clear to me that they are still uncertain about Professor Fergusson's work. Like me, they are concerned that the finished book might misrepresent us. But the professor has agreed to let me read all his proofs, whenever the C-Fits are mentioned, before going to the printer, and so far I have no reason to doubt his word. And Effie, a long-time friend of the professor, gave me what I considered to be a very honest portrait of the man, and on that basis I am inclined to go ahead with this collaboration, and hope for the best.

Naturally, should I come to believe that Effie is not suited to her role, I will terminate our arrangement at once. As I will if I see any signs that either she or the professor are in any way starting to renege on our agreement, or otherwise bring the C-Fits and myself into disrepute.

On a more happy and personal note, Zoe …

The next day, Effie and Gisela chose to ride with Jean to Adderbury, since the back bench in Malc's van had been commandeered for large and extra equipment. Effie, sitting in the front passenger seat, was not surprised to find the ex-schoolteacher a proficient and careful driver.

From the back seat, she heard Gisela sigh heavily. 'Do you think this time we might get lucky, finally?' she asked, her question clearly directed at Jean. 'It seems ages since we had anything really promising. Not since the mist at Steeple Aston if my memory isn't playing tricks on me. And between you, me and the bedpost, I think Corwin is beginning to get a bit anxious that he doesn't have much usable stuff for his next book.'

'You know as well as I do that you never can tell,' Jean said patiently. 'But Malcolm seems sure that the cold spot in the client's bathroom is real enough.'

'Well, that's something,' Gisela agreed, watching the passing greenery thoughtfully. 'Having hard solid data always floats Corwin's boat. And I suppose it gives our detractors something solid to chew over. But it's not exactly new, is it? We've had … what, five cold spots so far. It's not like filming actual mist, is it?'

Finally Effie could stand it no more. 'Mist?' she echoed curiously. 'You mean like weather-type mist? Why is fog so interesting?'

Jean smiled but Gisela burst into laughter, then instantly apologized. 'Sorry. No, we're not talking about weather conditions.

When we set up in the cellar at Steeple Aston, it was just a dull overcast day, in fact. No mist or fog in sight.'

'Oh, I see,' Effie said. Although she patently didn't.

Naturally, it was the ex-teacher who took it on herself to explain things. 'Most people think "seeing a ghost" means seeing a recognizable person – or at least, a distinctly human shape,' she said. 'You know, we've all heard the usual stories. A person walks into a room, and sees someone else that they know to be dead, sitting in a favourite chair or reading a book. Or maybe a witness will report seeing someone walking out of the room and into another one, but when they go to look, nobody's in there.'

Effie nodded quickly, having heard such tales herself. It was pretty standard stuff.

'But actually, those sightings, although always interesting, are not as golden as you might think.' Jean paused in her lesson to slow down slightly as a flash sports car zipped past them, before continuing smoothly, 'Since, by their nature, they're open to several interpretations. For a start, they're always second-hand, and hearsay evidence. And most people, on hearing such a tale, immediately think that the witness was either drunk, or imagining things, or was simply a victim of an over-active imagination. What's more, I'm sorry to say, a lot of people simply have a nasty habit of just tending to see what they expect to see, if you get what I mean.'

And on seeing Effie's brow furrow a bit, Jean smiled and obligingly elucidated. 'For instance, if, on entering a room, they were used to seeing a certain person sitting in a certain place, or doing a certain activity, then even if they know that person is now dead and gone, they can still imagine that scene very accurately. And might confuse what they've *actually* seen (which is nothing) with what their memories insist they *should* be seeing – which is their family member or friend or whoever, sitting in their normal chair. The brain can be a tricky thing sometimes.'

'I think I understand what you mean,' Effie said cautiously.

'But mist is very different,' Gisela put in.

'Yes, but what exactly are you talking about?' Effie asked. 'Do you mean actual mist, like steam that causes condensation on a window, or some form of gas?'

'Sometimes, but often, something much less nebulous than that,' Jean said firmly. 'Which can obviously be very exciting! Last year, in Steeple Aston for instance, we were investigating an old house that was being remodelled. Several of the builders were refusing to go down into the cellar, although they'd never give the foreman any real reason for it. Which, as you can imagine, caused the poor man no end of problems, since they needed to get the damp course sorted out. Eventually he persuaded one of the men to talk to him, and he admitted that several of the men had "seen strange stuff" down there. And the more the cellar's reputation for weirdness grew, the more the men made excuses not to go down there. In exasperation, the foreman agreed to call us in to check it out, hoping to placate them. I think several of the workmen thought that we were exorcists or something. Anyway, we set up cameras and left them recording overnight, and when we reviewed the tapes, we saw a definite mist formation form and reform.'

'In a human shape?' Effie asked, still not sure she was getting a clear picture of what they were actually talking about.

'No. In a thick, swirling, moving formation that changed shape as it shifted,' Jean said. 'Think of the way that a flock of starlings moves across the sky, or a small school of fish, trying to avoid a predator. Like that. Remind me, and I'll ask Malcolm to run the recording for you so that you can see it for yourself. It's in infrared, of course, so it's not as clear as it would have been if we'd managed to film it in daylight. But it's certainly clear and conclusive. There was a definite mist formation in that cellar. Corwin covered it very comprehensively in his latest book that's due out next month. Once it hits the shops, he's going to release the footage on the internet. It's bound to have serious investigators clamouring.'

'Oh,' Effie said, a shade blankly. 'So what happened then? After you'd got it on film?'

'Well, of course, we were all very excited, and held some daylight and night-time vigils,' Gisela said, then sighed heavily. 'But it never came back. The builders were convinced it was gone and finally went down and sorted out what needed doing, and the house sold quickly. We asked the new owners to let us know if they ever had any other problems, but so far they haven't been in touch.'

'That's often the way, I'm afraid,' Jean admitted a shade grimly. 'We get some sort of usable data, usually on our very first vigil, or when we leave the equipment unmanned overnight, and then, afterwards, when it's got our attention and we start to seriously investigate, the activity stops. It's as if the phenomenon knows that it's been found out, or is being observed, and is reluctant to continue.'

'That must be frustrating,' Effie said diplomatically. But she couldn't help but feel sceptical. Perhaps the 'phenomenon' didn't want to bear up to proper scrutiny because 'it' knew that it wouldn't pass the test? Although how a prankster would set about reproducing a swirling mist, she wasn't quite sure. But then she wasn't very technically minded. No doubt any reasonably competent chemist or physicist could do it. But why bother?

'I've got a good feeling about this latest case,' Gisela said suddenly and ominously from the back seat.

'Oh?' Jean said sharply, her voice tinged with hope. 'Did you sense something?'

'No. Nothing specific,' Gisela admitted at once. And Effie made a mental note to record the younger woman's innate honesty in her notes for Duncan. 'You know I would have said if I had. But I did get a strong sense of that old lady. And let me tell you, she's really mad about something. Let's just say I've got a real feeling that this case isn't going to just fizzle out on us.'

Jean looked pleased, and, with a little start of surprise, Effie realized that, for all her reserved and prim manner, Jean Bossington-Smith was as excited and committed to ghost hunting as anyone in the group.

Corwin's Jaguar was already parked outside on the street when they arrived. Although the Rollwright Inn almost certainly had a large car park further around the corner for the use of its customers, Corwin probably didn't want to antagonize Isabel's nearest neighbour by taking up spaces there.

Malc's van pulled up behind them, and Mickey jumped out and opened up the back, and Effie watched as the men set about lugging equipment inside, unsure if she was supposed to offer to help. But since neither Jean nor Gisela did so, she supposed that the men considered such work to be their domain.

Instead, the women went inside where Isabel was standing in the hall, looking a little bemused as the piles of cameras, boxes of meters and microphones and other gauges piled up around her.

She offered the three women coffee, which they all accepted, and followed her into the kitchen. As in most historical buildings, the kitchen came as something of a disappointment. Used to vast modern kitchen/diners that were so beloved of property shows on the television, the Georgian builders of this house had clearly considered kitchens to be strictly the domain of servants. So although the ceilings were still high, there was very little light or workspace, and the few modern conveniences that were actually in evidence – the white goods such as the fridge and washing machine – stood out like sore thumbs.

Nevertheless, the room had all that was needed, and soon the four of them were happily sitting around the square kitchen table and sipping coffee from a variety of cheerful mugs.

'I'm really glad that you're here,' Isabel said at once. 'No matter what the others say. I've even had George Dix over here, moaning on about my unorthodox methods. I tell you, I'll be glad when probate is finished and done with, and I can go back home.'

'Who's George Dix?' Gisela asked bluntly. Although both Effie and Jean had been wondering the same thing, neither of them would have dreamed of asking. But Gisela had an infectious, innocent, straightforward way about her that would nearly always fail to annoy. And it certainly didn't discomfit their client.

'Oh sorry, the family solicitor,' Isabel clarified at once. 'Well, Mum's solicitor, anyway. She'd been with the same firm for years. Although that was a near-run thing apparently.'

'Sorry?' Effie felt emboldened enough by Gisela's example to probe delicately.

Isabel gave a sudden laugh, her hands cupped around her mug for warmth. 'It was the usual thing, I'm afraid. Either George had done something to get in her bad books, or else Mum had just got another bee in her bonnet about something. But for the last month or so, she'd been mumbling and rumbling and threatening to take her business to another firm. Apparently there's a new broom in town, and he'd been "courting" her. And Mum, typically, liked to ruffle feathers from time to time. I think it amused her to set George in a bit of a tizzy. Of course, she probably wouldn't have done anything about it really. She was very much a traditionalist at heart, so it was very unlikely that she'd have actually gone so far as to remove her affairs from his hands. But there had definitely been trouble of some sort.' Isabel sighed. 'So I suppose it's no wonder that George is anxious to see that everything is resolved smoothly. The senior partner in the firm has probably warned him to make sure that it does, not that I have anything against the poor man. But then, George has always been a bit of a dry stick anyway. And when he heard about you … he sort of got a funny look in his eye.'

'Oh don't worry about what *he* says.' It was again Gisela who rushed in where angels feared to tread. 'Most people act squirrelly when we're called in. We just learn to ignore it.'

Isabel looked startled for a moment, and then laughed. 'Well, as it happens, I *did* tell George that he'd just have to like it and lump it, since I had no intention of changing my mind about you. Then he went all stiff and proper and reminded me that as executor, it was my responsibility to see the inventory of the house was conducted in a proper and secure manner.'

'Good grief!' Jean Bossington-Smith said sharply. 'Did the man actually intimate that one of us might actually run off with the candlesticks or something?'

Isabel blushed guiltily, a clear admission that the absent Mr Dix may have done just that. And for a moment, there was one of those appalled silences when everyone was too frightened to say anything for fear of making things worse.

But really, Effie thought indignantly, it was a bit thick when someone all but suggested that he thought you might be a thief!

Then Gisela began to giggle and finally laugh out loud, which made Effie and Isabel also began to grin. Finally even Jean managed a stiff smile. Although Effie rather thought that, should the boss ever run into the unfortunate solicitor, the former school-teacher would give the man a rather pithy piece of her mind.

*

As it turned out, it took a few hours for all the equipment to be properly set up and according to Corwin's exacting standards, by which time Effie was beginning to feel slightly bored, if truth be told. Luckily, a vast number of the smaller cameras and recorders would be left in situ throughout the course of the investigation, to save time. But the bigger cameras and meters – and, of course, the computers and laptops – would have to be removed in the morning and then set up again at the next vigil. And so it was nearly nine o'clock before the men finally joined them in the kitchen.

Corwin leaned negligently against one wall and ran a hand through his hair.

'OK, so we're clear that we all know what we're doing,' he began. 'Isabel, please follow your routine as usual. If you like to watch television late into the night, then continue to do so. If you have a bath before you retire, or you like to read in bed, or whatever, please carry on as normal. For our part, we'll be scattered around the house and hopefully won't get in your way. Malc is going to spend the night in the bathroom, monitoring the temperature gauges. Gisela wants to spend the night in your mother's bedroom. I trust you have no problem with that?'

'Oh no,' Isabel said at once. But she was visibly shivering, and Effie would have bet money that she was probably thinking 'rather her than me!'

'Lonny and I are going to take turns monitoring all the feedback in the lounge, where we'll have the images from all the cameras set up. Jean is going to stay here in the kitchen, and Effie in the hall. Mickey is going to do some patrols outside, and watch the gardens nearest the house. We usually like to do an outside survey, at least once, just in case there's any phenomenon occurring outside that nobody has had the opportunity to notice,' he broke off to explain to a clearly fascinated Isabel. 'And since it's such a mild night tonight, we thought we might as well take advantage of it.'

Mickey grinned. 'I bought a thermos and night-vision goggles. I'll be fine,' he reassured Isabel who was looking a shade concerned for him.

'Well, if you're sure,' Isabel said. 'And, actually, I think I'll retire early tonight. I haven't been getting much rest recently, and I feel as if I could sleep for a week. Just knowing I have other people around me will help with that, I'm sure.'

'OK, that's fine. I just need to know – if anything happens, do you want us to come and get you, or would you rather be told about it in the morning?' Corwin asked her with a grin.

'Oh no. Come and get me,' Isabel said at once.

'Fine. Although, as I explained before, the chances of anything happening are quite remote.'

Isabel gave a dry laugh. 'You know, I'm not sure whether to be relieved or disappointed by that.'

It was a sentiment that Effie understood only too well.

The grandfather clock struck midnight. Effie didn't jump, because she'd been watching the minute and hour hand creep to the top of the clock for some time now. For some reason, it had become important to her to mark the midnight hour, and its passing. Perhaps because midnight had the reputation of being the 'witching hour.' Whatever on earth that was.

It was certainly the hour when things started to happen in the old hammer horror films she'd watched as a child.

Or perhaps it was simply because, for some reason, she'd just assumed that nothing would happen until after midnight – as if that hour was some sort of other-worldly starter's bell for any ghouls and ghosts that might be about.

When, back in the cricket pavilion, Corwin had given out her assignment, she had felt relieved that she wasn't being asked to sit vigil alone either in Claudia's bedroom, or the bathroom, or the lounge, where her favourite chair was positioned. And then, after thinking about it on the journey to Adderbury, she became less sure.

Weren't hallways traditionally a hot spot for ghost sightings? Remembering even further back to the old black and white Hollywood movies that her gran had loved to watch, didn't ghosts like to make appearances on the stairs, and sweep across the floor and walk through walls?

Of course, she was aware that her deliberately light-hearted scoffing was designed to give her courage. But now, after two hours of sitting in the very comfortable armchair that Corwin had carried through for her, Effie was beginning to realize that it wasn't courage she needed, so much as a way to control her boredom.

Funny, but it hadn't occurred to her until now just how dull sitting in a chair in the dark with nothing to do could be!

Perhaps that was why she'd been watching the clock so closely.

And now that it had actually struck the hour, and nothing at all had happened, she was beginning to feel a growing sense of panic. Not that something 'spooky' might happen. But at the thought that she still had another six or seven hours of this to get through.

She hadn't even been able to bring a book to read, of course, because she was sitting in the dark. Well, relative dark. (And then, suddenly, wondered if a Kindle or something would provide enough light on its screen to enable you to read at night? If so, she might just get one to go along with her new mobile phone.)

Although Corwin had left her with a pair of night-vision goggles that she could put on if she wanted to, one quick look at the eerie green-tinted vision they produced had been enough to persuade her that she preferred to do without. Besides, a street light outside was filtering in enough light through the windows to keep her happy.

One of the stairs suddenly creaked, but Effie barely noticed it. The first time it had done so, it had made her nearly jump out of her skin, but she quickly discovered that it was just the old boards resettling after Isabel and the others had gone up them. Besides, the stairs in her own home often gave the odd creak. Houses made noises all the time. So what?

So this is ghost hunting, Effie thought wryly. She was getting a slightly numb bum from sitting in one place for so long. And at some point she was going to have to use the loo, as Corwin had predicted. On the plus side, though, she didn't feel tired, nor did she feel in the least bit scared.

She knew that, just through the door into the lounge, Corwin and Lonny were monitoring the cameras and equipment and were within calling distance. Gisela was upstairs and – if she had any sense – was probably sleeping soundly on Claudia's bed. At first, Effie had thought that the tall redhead was being brave, offering to stay there, but now she wondered if the clever girl simply hadn't chosen the most comfortable billet.

As the minutes ticked on towards one o'clock, Effie came to two conclusions.

The first being that she could do this job standing on her head.

And secondly, that she must be out of her mind to consider doing it for even one more night.

Because it was becoming more and more clear that Corwin's prediction that nothing was going to happen had been all too accurate.

That was when her new mobile phone began vibrating in her handbag. And since her bag was resting against her thigh, she almost shot off the chair in shock. OK, so perhaps she wasn't quite so laidback as she'd supposed. She took a calming breath, patted her chest to reassure her heartbeat that it could now return to normal, and reached inside for the phone. The glow from the screen illuminated the text clearly.

It was from Malc, and presumably had been sent to all their phones simultaneously.

The message was short, and clear, and sent her heart once more racing into overtime. COME TO THE BATHROOM. NOW!

'It's there,' Malc hissed, pointing towards the spot in front of the sink, above which a small, white bathroom cabinet had been affixed to the wall.

Effie, standing behind the others, peered through a gap between Mickey and Lonny's shoulders, and saw nothing but a bathroom sink. No mist. No ghostly outline of an old lady, washing her hands. Nothing. What was she supposed to be looking at?

'You sure?' Corwin asked. He wasn't exactly whispering, but his voice was low and held a definite quiver of excitement now.

'Sure, check the gauges yourself. I've been moving the thermometers around in twenty minute sessions ever since I got here, trying to pinpoint it. It's definitely right there.' And again Malc pointed to a spot by the sink.

Corwin nodded and set off on a brief circuit of the room, checking the thermometers that Malc had placed in various locations, whilst the builder handed over a notebook to Jean, who read quietly through a list of temperature readings.

As Corwin reached the thermometers, she would read off the last note Malcolm had made of them, and Corwin confirmed that they were still reading the same – with only a few very minor variations.

And allowing for the door being open, and the presence of human body heat, all the readings were what Effie would have thought of as 'average' room temperature. Until Corwin came to the thermometer that Malcolm had put on the floor nearest the sink. And the reading from that, Corwin confirmed quietly but with evident satisfaction, was that it was a full seven degrees lower.

Effie shifted slightly from one foot to the other. Seven degrees? That was quite a difference, wasn't it? The two other gauges that were on the floor were reading only slightly lower than the others, which made sense. Warm air rises (she remembered that from a long ago science lesson at school) but draughts whistle under doors. So of course those gauges would register a slightly lower temperature than others set higher up.

But just one gauge, reading a full seven degrees lower? What was *that* all about?

'Malc, set up a thermal camera on this spot and record in real-time until it's light,' Corwin ordered.

'No probs.'

'And put our most sensitive microphone on it. Just in case of EVPs.'

'Got it.'

Effie and several of the others took the opportunity to use the other bathrooms for a quick toilet break, whilst Corwin went to fetch Isabel. But when their client finally arrived, having taken the time to hastily pull on some clothes, everyone was back, not wanting to miss any of the action.

Isabel looked bewildered as Corwin explained what was going on, but it was clear that she also felt gratified that the scientific instruments had confirmed her own experiences in there.

'Did your mother ever have a nasty experience in here?' Corwin asked quietly. 'A bad fall maybe, or some other unpleasant episode that would explain why a cold spot should be here, and nowhere else?'

'No, not that I know of,' Isabel said, sounding puzzled. 'At least, she never told me about it if she had,' she amended.

Corwin then deliberately stepped into the cold spot and looked around. As well as possessing a gorgeous roll-top bath on clawed feet, plus a modern shower, the room was large and square, and mainly beige with orange accents. Eventually he looked at the sink, then reached up and opened the cabinet.

'I can feel it's definitely colder standing here,' he said. Inside, the cabinet was totally empty.

'I threw all of Mother's stuff out, like I told you before. Well, her toothpaste and toothbrush and that sort of thing. Her bottle of St John's Wort I gave to Annie. That's the daily woman who came in to "do" for Mother. Mother was a firm believer in St John's Wort, and convinced Annie of its merits too.'

Corwin nodded and sighed. Clearly he was looking for something that would explain the cold spot, and just as clearly, there was nothing there.

He glanced once again at the temperature on the floor.

'It's now nearly ten degrees colder,' he said. 'I can feel goosebumps starting to rise on my arms,' he added matter-of-factly.

And suddenly Effie had to fight the urge to go inside and pull him away from there. Clearly the man was mad!

'And what did you think, when he said it was ten degrees colder?' Duncan asked curiously.

They were sitting in the front room of her house the following evening. Effie sighed gently, shifting Toad, who had been sitting on her lap, onto the sofa seat beside her. The little Yorkie sighed elaborately, but quickly settled down.

Effie shrugged restlessly and walked across to the French windows looking out over her garden. A pair of greenfinches, who had been helping themselves from a birdfeeder, flew off in alarm.

'Honestly?' Effie said, her back still turned to him. 'I suppose the first thought I had was that ten degrees was a hell of a difference, with no clear explanation for it. And then I have to say that it did cross my mind to wonder just how accurate the thermometers were.'

But even as she made the admission, she felt slightly guilty.

Behind her she heard Duncan scribble something down, although, like the other sessions they'd already had, he was also recording the conversation.

'You know, this feels very much like we're having a professional consultation,' Effie complained. 'You'd better not be psychoanalysing me on the sly, Duncan.'

'Of course I'm not. But this *is* just the sort of stuff I need. So, your first reaction was to doubt the evidence. Do you think they'd faked the readings?'

'No!' she said at once, and a shade too sharply, for although she still had her back to him, she could sense her old friend was watching her curiously. But even as she felt the desire to defend both Malc's and Corwin's integrity, she had to remind herself that she hardly knew either man.

And yet why should they bother trying to deceive her?

As she thought about it, the answer became obvious. Corwin Fielding made a good living from writing books about ghosts. And the others were all heavily invested in proving their beliefs to be valid. Even Jean Bossington-Smith, who Effie was increasingly coming to see as a ferociously honest and forthright person, was obviously emotionally invested in the project.

'So if you don't think that the reading was fraudulent – what then?' she heard Duncan ask mildly, and Effie's lips twisted into a brief smile. Duncan might say he wasn't playing the psychologist with her, but she knew shrink-speak when she heard it.

'Don't be all reasonable and rational with me, Duncan,' she warned him succinctly, coming back to the sofa and sitting back down beside her dog. Absently she reached out to stroke his silky fur. 'I suppose I thought the thermometer might be faulty,' she finally said, cautiously.

'Which would be a bit of a coincidence, don't you think?' Duncan pressed, but still in that annoyingly mild and reasonable voice. 'One of their many temperature gauges just happens to give a faulty reading, right in the room where Isabel told you she always felt cold.'

Effie eyed her friend with a sour smile. 'So just what are you saying, Duncan?' she turned the tables neatly on him.

Her friend raised one innocent eyebrow. 'Me? I'm not saying anything. It's what you're saying that counts. *You're* the one doing the vigils, *you're* my observer. What I'm interested in is what *you* think. It's clear that you're becoming intrigued and interested. And it's clear that you like all your fellow ghost hunters. And why not? I liked them all well enough when we met up too. And there's nothing wrong in any of that, you know – they're probably all very likeable people, so why shouldn't you make friends of them? It's what I more or less expected,' Duncan encouraged. 'Just don't be scared to tell the truth about how you feel. If you're going to do this thing, you need to do it honestly and whole-heartedly, or else what's the point?'

Effie sighed. 'Duncan, I don't know what I thought, all right?' she finally snapped. 'Perhaps the temperature readings were wrong. Or maybe there's a rational explanation for the temperature drop. Or maybe they are conning me or playing me, and I'm too naïve or stupid to spot it. Maybe only Malc on his own, or Malc in collusion with … someone else … is conning not only me, but the rest of the group as well. Or maybe there *is* something going on that I simply don't understand. The possibilities are endless, and I just don't know. All right?' she finished, feeling exasperated and thoroughly out of sorts.

Duncan grinned widely and began scribbling furiously. 'Well, that's just fine. This is good stuff, Effie, really – it's psychologically fascinating. Which is what the book is going to be all about, after all. You're doing great!'

Effie eyed him with an unkindly eye, and only just managed to refrain from throwing a cushion at him.

CHAPTER SIX

The next day dawned with some low and scudding clouds that played tag with the sun, dipping the unseasonably warm temperatures abruptly, and casting the day from brightness to gloom and then back again.

And for some reason, Effie felt the need to go to Adderbury on her own and just take stock. As a child, she'd always been something of a loner and happy with her own company, and could spend hours reading or drawing. And perhaps because she'd grown up as an only child, she'd come to rely on her own judgement fairly early on in life. And right now, she needed some time without the other C-Fit members around her, for although she found their company lively and friendly, they also had the tendency to confuse her.

What she needed was some quiet time alone in order to process recent happenings, and without Duncan and his constant, annoying probing into how she felt and what she was thinking.

In short, it was time to take a step back and try and get some perspective.

And the more she thought about what she might like to do, the more she felt compelled to visit Claudia's grave. She knew from Isabel that her mother was buried in the local churchyard and so after breakfast – which had consisted of her usual bowl of oat granola and a glass of orange juice – she headed out that way.

With Toad beside her on the passenger seat, happily barking

away excitedly at passing motorbikes and noisy tractors, she experienced a curious feeling of lightness. And it took her a few seconds to recognize it for what it was.

She felt happy and optimistic about the future, for the first time in what felt like a decade.

Once in Adderbury, she drove slowly around until she found the church and then parked outside, careful to keep Toad on a lead as she went inside to explore the churchyard. She'd made sure to take him for his usual morning walk before setting off, so that he didn't need to cock his leg disrespectfully on anyone's final resting place. And for a few moments she lingered idly among the older gravestones, pausing now and then to read the names and dates on them, and speculate.

She knew that a lot of people, like herself, found it fascinating to wander around gravestones, especially the older ones, with their evocative, old-fashioned names, and their sometimes heartbreaking messages. Was it just being maudlin? Or was it human nature to be merely curious? Did it evoke a feeling of general human kinship with strangers she would now never be able to meet, or was there something darker and more atavistic at work? Did it make you feel somehow better to be alive and well and breathing, when all those around you weren't?

Frowning at the uncomfortable direction her thoughts were taking her, Effie told herself to get on with it, and looked around for the newer interments, eventually finding them at the farthest end from the church. As she approached, with the stones around her getting straighter and cleaner as she went, her eyes became fixed on a patch of recently moved earth that now had grass turf unevenly patched together on top of it. And sure enough, as she reached it, a small temporary plaque set at one end bore the name of CLAUDIA WATKINS, with her date of birth and death.

She knew, from the experience of burying her own husband, that a carved gravestone could take anything up to eight months to arrive and be fitted. And since Michael's parents had long since died, it had been left to her to choose the wording for it. For some time she'd agonized with that, wondering if a quote from the Bible might be appropriate. Although not a regular church-goer, her husband had always attended their local Church of England church at Christmas and Easter, and she knew Michael had respect for tradition.

In the end, exhausted by the whole process of trying to think what she should opt for, she'd simply settled for his name and the stark dates of his life and death.

Uneasily now, she wondered if Michael would have preferred something a little more – not flamboyant, certainly, but more personal?

With a sigh, she firmly pushed the thought aside. Here she was, uselessly wool-gathering again, when she'd so recently promised herself that she'd make a concerted effort not to let her mind drift so often. The trouble was, since losing Michael, it had somehow became a habit. And it left her feeling like a piece of mindless flotsam or jetsam, simply floating wherever the tide took her. And it had to stop, damn it!

With a scowl, Effie forced herself back to the task at hand, and looking down at the old lady's grave, she realized that someone, almost certainly Isabel, had laid fresh flowers recently; a bunch of bright and cheerful daffodils with forsythia sprays. At that moment, the sun went behind a cloud and, as it nearly always did on a still brisk spring day, an instant cold breeze seemed to spring up to replace it. Smiling at the cliché, Effie turned up the collar of her caramel-coloured suede coat with its warm sheepskin lining, and continued staring down thoughtfully.

Not that the patch of disturbed earth was being particularly helpful. But then, what had she expected? Unlike Gisela, she was certainly no 'sensitive'. No ghostly voice talked to her. Amused at the idea, Effie sighed and glanced around, vaguely seeking some kind of distraction from her introspection.

Beyond the stone walls, the village seemed determined to be unhelpful, as it remained silent and seemingly empty. But from her experiences of living in her own small village for so long, that didn't particularly surprise her. Often there would be a flurry of activity from her neighbours in the morning and evening rush hours, leaving the streets empty during the day. Occasionally Effie would see another dog walker, like herself, and they'd exchange the usual pleasantries about the weather and each other's canines, but mostly she could walk for miles and not meet another soul.

Perhaps, because Adderbury was by far a much bigger village than her own, and so very near to a large and popular market town, she'd expected a little more from it.

With a last brooding look at the final resting place of the lavender lady of Corwin's latest casefile, she turned away, her little dog bounding eagerly in front of her, joyously exploring the new sniffs and sights around him. He paused to bark maniacally at a grey squirrel that was bounding along the low stone wall surrounding the churchyard before leaping up into an adjacent tree, and she had to pull hard on the lead to tug him away from it.

Back out on the lane, she randomly chose to turn right, and found herself wandering down pretty little side streets and lanes filled with attractive cottages and other prime real estate before finding herself in a little square that housed, surprisingly, a handful of small and bespoke shops.

A tiny butcher shop that specialized in local game had a hare and a brace of pheasant hanging in the window. A cheese shop that, from its odd and meagre opening hours had to be someone's hobby rather than a money-making concern, boasted a selection of hand-crafted cheeses, including a goat's cheese with milk sourced from a local farm. Attached to it, in a tiny lean-to, a baker had set up another business, offering intricately flavoured, homemade breads. (Effie suspected the wife of the cheese-maker had taken up bread making as another hobby.)

The butcher's shop was open, as was a second-hand vintage clothes boutique. And sited next door to that was a delightfully quaint little herbalist's shop, bearing the enchanting name of JASMINE'S APOTHECARY, and which instantly drew her eye. Like the other shops, it had clearly once been a large cottage built solely as living premises, but now one large display window in what must have formerly been the parlour, was packed with enticing wares. Intriguing lotions in a variety of jewel-coloured jars warred for attention with attractively shaped and unwrapped soaps in more pastel shades.

The floor above, Effie guessed, had probably been remodelled into a small flat, which was either rented out or provided accommodation for the business owner.

Effie nervously eyed the hand lotions and face creams. Clearly the herbalist made all her own stuff since there were none of the generic, high-street brands on offer, only pretty, good quality glass jars with hand-written labels. They looked, she had to admit, very bespoke and attractive. But she had always used the high-end, well-known commercial products herself, since they were the kind that Michael had always bought for her on her birthday. And the thought of buying something that had been made in the back room of what was, literally, a little cottage industry like this, worried her. What if the herbalist didn't know his or her job very well? What if she bought some hand lotion and found herself coming out in a rash?

Just as she was contemplating such a hideous fate and deciding that it was probably best not to risk it, the door opened and the old-fashioned bell situated in the opening, tinkled merrily. And an old lady came through the aperture, followed by a large, heavy-set younger woman with a mass of dark brown hair and big brown eyes.

'Now, you be sure to soak your feet in warm water and one dash of that every night, and I guarantee … Oh, hello,' the younger woman broke off abruptly as she spotted Effie.

The old woman blushed a little, and clearly not liking to discuss her podiatry problems in public, mumbled something about knowing how to use the tincture, and hurried away.

Effie smiled to cover the slight awkwardness that followed and, to cover the silence, nodded towards the window. 'The, er, lily of the valley hand cream. Is it for sensitive skin?' she asked. Not that she had particularly sensitive skin.

'Yes, I'm always very careful to get the PH balance right,' the younger woman said, thrusting out a friendly hand, which was as big as that of a man. 'Jasmine Carteret. I'm the apothecary. Or herbalist. Or village wise-woman, or whatever you want to call me.' She laughed.

'Oh, hello. Effie James. I'm a …' Effie suddenly stumbled. How exactly did she go about introducing herself nowadays? 'Er, a friend of Isabel Cadmund's,' she selected finally. After all, she could hardly introduce herself as your local friendly ghost hunter, could she? Not that she believed that this woman would probably bat so much as an eyelid if she did.

Large, pleasantly overweight, and wearing a long floral skirt and gypsy-style white blouse that had a ruffle at the top of each arm and left her fast-bronzing shoulders bare, Jasmine wore her 'alternative lifestyle' attitude like a badge of honour.

'Oh, Izzie. Isn't she a pet?' she said with a grin.

Effie blinked, rather taken by surprise. She knew, of course, that in this day and age, having a title meant little to nothing, but she still felt rather wrong-footed to hear Isabel Cadmund being referred to so casually, and seeing it, Jasmine laughed.

'Sorry, don't mind me. But Izzie's family. Well, sort of. That is, by marriage.' Jasmine laughed again and took another huge breath. 'Sorry, that all sounded rather scatty. A thing I'm often accused of, sadly.' But she grinned widely, showing rather uneven, but very white teeth. A good advertisement, presumably, for her own homemade toothpaste? 'Let me start again. Clive, my brother, is married to Izzie's daughter, Ros.'

Effie nodded. 'All right, I think I've got it!' she said with a smile.

'Oh sorry, come on in. Here I am keeping you chatting on the doorstep. When the sun goes in it still gets quite chilly, doesn't it?' Jasmine said, standing to one side.

'Oh, I don't want to …' Effie looked down to where Toad was standing patiently by her feet, 'bring a dog inside your lovely shop.'

'Oh, isn't he gorgeous!' Jasmine said, spotting him for the first time and instantly bending down to stroke him. Naturally Toad agreed with her – he was gorgeous, as nearly every human he met seemed to tell him. He did his usual tail-wagging dance as Jasmine ruffled his ears. 'Don't you worry about bringing him in,' she said, looking up at her. 'He's such a cutie, I'm sure he'll be fine. You were asking about the hand lotion?'

Effie, even less sure than ever that she could trust anything that was produced by this woman, followed her a shade reluctantly into the shop and promptly felt a little ashamed of herself. For not only was the interior scrupulously clean and well kept, the walls also housed several reassuring certificates and licences that proclaimed her to be a well-educated and fully, legally qualified herbalist.

Dried flowers hung appealingly from the ceiling, and several small pots of sweet-smelling herbs grew on the window sills. And inside a large and clearly old glass display cabinet – one that would have had an *Antiques Roadshow* expert salivating – were several jars of pills and potions, all neatly labelled with a brief explanation of what herbs they contained, and what use they should be put to.

One bottle in particular, with a pretty label showing a sketch of a rather nondescript little yellow flower, caught her eye. St John's Wort. Effie had heard of it, of course, since it was a fairly common and well-known product, but for a moment couldn't figure out why it was ringing such a loud bell in the back of her head. And then suddenly she remembered.

Isabel had said that her mother had been a regular taker of it.

'Do you suffer from depression?' Both the voice and the question made her jump slightly, and Effie turned quickly to look at Jasmine.

'What? No. Why?' she instantly responded defensively. Did she look depressed? She knew she hadn't been sleeping as well as she might, but the black hole that had seemed to swallow her after losing Michael had begun to recede at last, and even in her darkest hour, she'd never taken anti-depressants. Surely it wasn't so obvious that she still sometimes found life rather overwhelming?

'It's just that I saw you looking at the St John's Wort,' Jasmine said, with a small smile. 'Sorry, I didn't mean to sound as if I was prying. Or judging. Believe me, that's the last thing I'd ever do,' she assured her warmly. 'I suppose I just assumed that, because you were so interested in it, that that's what you'd come in for.'

'Oh, I see,' Effie said with some relief. And ruefully told herself that that's what came of allowing herself to be so paranoid. 'It's just that Isabel told me just the other day that her mother used to take it, so ...' She trailed off, not willing to discuss either Isabel or her family's private business.

'Oh, Claudia. Yes, she did,' Jasmine nodded vigorously. 'In fact, I was the one who put her on to it, actually. The Grand Dame saw it as her duty to patronise all of our village shops, bless her, and she started coming in to buy the lavender range of toiletries I make. But after a while, and as I got to know her better, I realized that the usual complaints of old age were starting to wear her down, and I recommended the St John's Wort. She was a little sceptical at first, and I think she only bought the first jar just to show that she trusted my judgement. But where she led, others followed, I'm glad to say.' Jasmine laughed. 'They wouldn't dare do anything else! And after that, I got several people coming in and buying it regularly. Still, it keeps us in business,' she added, waving a hand at the cluster of shops outside her window.

Effie, realizing that she had obviously been gifted with a ready-made source of intelligence about the lavender lady, said casually, 'So St John's Wort is good for the elderly, is it? What was it poor Mrs Watkins suffered from? Arthritis?'

'Oh no. Well, yes, she might have had a touch of that,' Jasmine said with a frown. 'And I know she had a heart condition,' she mused, then added hastily, 'not that I had anything to do with treating *that*. As I tell all my customers, I'm not a doctor, or a pharmacist. If anyone has any kind of medical condition, I always tell them to see a GP,' Jasmine said firmly, once more making Effie feel bad for doubting either her professionalism or her credentials. 'No, St John's Wort is basically nature's anti-depressant. And let's face it, most old folks these days are depressed. Just read a newspaper! But this lovely stuff,' Jasmine tapped one of the bottles of pills, 'has far fewer side effects and can act more quickly than the stuff that doctors prescribe on the NHS. In addition to hypericin and hyperforin, it has other naturally occurring substances to help with depression.'

Jasmine indicated one of her diplomas. 'I might have studied chemistry, and have a good deal of respect for modern medicine, but as I also tell all of my customers, naturally occurring chemicals are better than the man-made, manufactured ones any day of the week! And luckily for me, good old Claudia agreed.'

'You sound as if you liked her but found her exasperating in equal measure! I never met her myself,' Effie added craftily, 'but from what Isabel let slip, I get the feeling that her mother was … well … a bit of a martinet?'

Jasmine threw back her head and laughed. 'Oh my word, yes. A total dragon, in fact. But a smart dragon, with a good heart. Well. Goodish,' she added judiciously, but with a twinkle in her eye. 'Mind you, I'm careful not to let my brother hear me praise her. I'm afraid they never did get on. Not that that was surprising. Claudia had a very high opinion of herself and her family, and Clive was never going to be her choice for Ros.'

Effie nodded. None of this was news to her, though, so she carefully steered the conversation back to where she wanted it.

'What else was it about St John's Wort that she liked, do you think?'

'Well, for Claudia, I rather suspect that she used it mainly because she suffered from insomnia. It has other uses too, mind you – it helps with nervousness for instance. Not that *that* was Claudia's problem at all.' Jasmine laughed. 'If ever there was a woman who was sure of herself, and unlikely to suffer from nerves, it was her!' she confided with another grin. 'But like a lot of people, as she got older she found it harder to sleep.'

Effie nodded. 'Perhaps her illness worried her too. She did die because of her heart problems after all. She'd had the condition for some time, I understand?'

'Yes, she did,' Jasmine said with a small frown. 'But I don't think that it affected her *that* much. It didn't seem to curtail her life much. Mostly Claudia pretended it wasn't happening – and she was certainly fit enough for her age, considering. Her attitude was that there was nothing wrong with her, and she intended to live to be a hundred. Which was a good attitude to have – you'd be surprised how often the body believes what the mind is telling it. You wouldn't have the placebo effect otherwise. And to be honest, I was as surprised as could be when I heard that she'd upped and died. She was just the sort of stubborn old trout that you thought *would* live to see her century in, just to prove a point. You know what I mean?'

Effie laughed, and agreed that she did.

'So, do you want some St John's Wort?' Jasmine asked and again there was something in the look she cast over Effie – a sort of professional, gentle concern – that instantly raised her hackles.

Was the fact that she was still in mourning, and often lay awake for long periods at night – really visible on her face?

But before she could speak, Jasmine went on, 'I make all the pills myself out the back in my lab/workshop. It's really quite a simple process when you know how. I gather all the raw materials myself – the actual flower is practically a common weed, and it might surprise you to know just how much of it grows in the wild. You need to know how to extract and distil it properly and safely of course, and get the doses right, but the actual physical manufacturing of the pills themselves needs little more than gelatine to set the liquid extractions, and pill moulds to shape the end product.'

Effie glanced at one of the full bottles, noting that the slightly yellowish pills did indeed look a bit like round pieces of very hard jelly, and shook her head firmly.

'Oh no, thank you. No pills. I'll just take the hand lotion,' she said.

And Toad, who had been getting bored with the waiting – especially as nobody seemed to be interested in stroking him or telling him how gorgeous he was anymore – gave a sudden sharp bark, as if in agreement.

Jasmine laughed and reached down once more to fuss over him, before going behind the counter to get Effie's impulse buy and pop it into a small, white paper bag.

Feeling that she was slowly but surely getting an ever more accurate picture of Claudia Watkins, Effie drove home thoughtfully, fed her dog, and then set to work in the garden. As usual the hours passed happily, as they always did whenever she was in her garden, but as the afternoon lengthened, she went indoors to prepare her usual quick-fix dinner of salad with either fish or sliced lean white meat from her favourite delicatessen.

But that evening, and for the first time in a long while, Effie began to feel restless. She felt that the evening seemed to stretch ahead in a way that unnerved her. The silence of her lovely, comfortable home, seemed heavy and repressive.

Was she beginning to feel lonely?

That thought was a very uncomfortable one, and one she didn't feel up to exploring. Where had her moment of carefree happiness this morning gone?

She turned on the television and found an old episode of *Time Team* being repeated. It had always been one of Michael's favourites, and it had triggered in herself a mild interest in archaeology.

But after ten minutes of it, she found herself unable to concentrate. Finally conceding defeat, she let her mind wander to where it really wanted to go – which was to tomorrow afternoon, and the next vigil at Adderbury with Corwin and the others.

True to his word about research needing to be done both in the daylight as well as in the evening hours, the C-Fits were scheduled to arrive in Adderbury at four o'clock, after meeting at the cricket pavilion at three. Naturally, Lonny and Malc wouldn't be able to make it that early, since they would still be at work. But the retired Jean had no problems with it, neither would Mickey, who seemed to have no compunction about skiving off lectures or classes whenever it suited him. Gisela worked flexi-hours and so had managed to arrange her time to fit it in, and the men would join them later, going straight to Isabel's from their workplace.

And Effie had to admit that she was really looking forward to it. Although, when she tried to analyze why that was, it wasn't so easy to say. Certainly, finding the cold spot on their last vigil had been, if nothing else, interesting. But the long following hours of inactivity had hardly been entertaining. And yes, there was a growing sense of friendship with the rest of the group, especially, perhaps, with Jean Bossington-Smith, with whom Effie felt a growing rapport.

Perhaps it was simply time that she got away from her old routine, and did something totally out of character. And Corwin Fielding was a very warm, intelligent and interesting man to be around.

Whatever the reason, Effie was forced to come to the conclusion that time was chaffing on her now simply because she felt like she finally had something to actually *look forward to*. Something that was novel, exciting and compelling which challenged her and took her out of her comfort zone. *Well* out of her comfort zone, in fact.

And, as she finally took herself to bed and settled down under the duvet, with Toad curled up comfortingly in the small of her back, the thought flitted through the back of her mind that perhaps it was high time that she did something to please herself for a change.

By the time Jean, Effie and Gisela had all arrived at Isabel's house the next day, it was to find that Corwin, not surprisingly, had beaten them to it. It wasn't that he drove his sports car dangerously fast (or that Jean drove her car particularly slowly), it was just that she'd noticed he drove very competently and well.

As the women climbed from Jean's car, Effie noticed his tall figure in the back garden, talking to a white-haired old man who was holding a pair of hedge clippers in his hand. No doubt he was the gardener that Isabel had mentioned before.

When Corwin spotted them congregating on the pavement, he shook the old man's hand and walked quickly back around the side of the house to join them. Today he was dressed in grey slacks and a crisp white shirt, open at the throat and with the cuffs rolled back halfway up his arms. Over his shoulders, he'd looped a plum-coloured sweater, tying the arms around his throat, like a scarf. His smile was wide and welcoming, and Effie smiled briefly in response as he drew level with them.

'I've just been talking to Geoff,' he said unnecessarily. 'As Claudia's most long-term member of staff, he knew her well. I was trying to get his opinion on us being here, but he was being very cagey. If he's ever heard or seen anything amiss since Claudia died, he's definitely not letting on. But then, I got the impression that he thought what we did was a load of old codswallop.'

'He probably doesn't want to upset Isabel by calling us a bunch of weirdos to our face,' Mickey said cheerfully. He was in a particularly good mood because Corwin had let him ride with him in the Jag.

'Probably,' Corwin agreed now, totally unfazed.

No doubt, Effie surmised, he was used to people thinking his chosen career was a bit of a joke, and had probably grown a very thick skin about it, over the years.

'Anyway, he was telling me that he sticks almost exclusively to the gardens and his greenhouse and shed, which is equipped like a small kitchenette by the sounds of it. Complete with a comfy old chair, so no wonder he isn't all that keen to retire.' He grinned. 'But the important thing is that he hardly ever goes inside the house. And when I asked him if he'd ever been here when it starts to get dark, and had noticed a strong scent of lavender, he clearly thought I was going doolally.'

Jean nodded. 'Well, that's only to be expected,' she said complacently.

Effie, impressed by the way all the others seemed to accept such scepticism as a matter of course (and by the way they refused to let it get to them), smiled.

'Besides, there's probably lavender growing all over the garden,' she felt obliged to point out. 'And it's one of those plants that you can get a very strong scent from, just by walking by it – it's very rich in oils, you see. That's why the Victorians used to plant it at path edges, so that the ladies going by it in their huge crinolines brushed against it and released the scent. But it's a little early for it to be flowering just yet,' Effie said at once.

And again he shot her a rather lazy but approving, warm-eyed smile. 'I know – so he told me. He also said that most of the lavender is grown around the kitchen gardens, well, at the back. And that there had never been any in the more formal beds nearer the house, and, more importantly, none at all in the small front garden. So that can't have been what Isabel was smelling earlier.'

'Excellent,' Jean said with satisfaction, scribbling something in her ever-present notebook. 'So whatever it was Isabel experienced, we've definitely ruled out that it could have come from any actual lavender plants in the garden nearby.'

'Correct, boss.' Corwin grinned. 'So, let's go and see if the temperature gauges that Malc left inside the bathroom have been recording that cold spot all night, or if it comes and goes.'

But it quickly transpired that Isabel had a visitor, and so the bathroom and the cold spot would have to wait.

After responding to their knocking, Isabel ushered them straight through to the lounge, where a man of average height in his early fifties, with greying hair and pale blue eyes, rose a little stiffly from a settee to greet them.

'George, this is Mr Fielding. Corwin, George Dix, Mother's solicitor.'

She competently and quickly introduced the rest of them, and Effie felt her hand being taken and held fractionally longer than that of the others. In addition to that, the warmth of his smile and the quick but comprehensive glance that took her in from top to bottom told Effie that Mr George Dix probably considered himself to be something of a lady's man – notwithstanding the wedding ring that he wore.

Beside her, she felt Jean Bossington-Smith stiffen slightly and begin to draw herself up. Effie tensed, expecting the retired teacher to give the legal man a tongue lashing for daring to hint that the C-Fits might actually try to steal the silver, but as she looked at the older woman apprehensively, she saw that Jean's eyes had moved on to Corwin. And slowly, Jean's lips formed into a straight, tight line.

Clearly, although she longed to, Jean wasn't prepared to make a scene in front of their client, thus possibly ruining their chances of being allowed to continue with the investigation. And Effie felt strangely touched by how protective Jean was of Corwin.

'Ah yes. The paranormal investigators,' George Dix said now, his voice smooth and blandly amiable. 'Mr Fielding, I'm currently reading your latest book. After Isabel told me that she'd called you in, I found myself intrigued.'

'I hope you're enjoying it,' Corwin said mildly.

'Oh, I'm only about halfway through. But it's certainly thought provoking,' the legal eagle said politely.

'And I'm about two thirds of the way through cataloguing the house contents,' Isabel said. 'George was just reminding me that I need to cross-reference certain items with Mother's contents insurance.'

There was a slight edge to Isabel's voice that told Effie that she hadn't found the solicitor's visit a particularly pleasant one. And by the way she was hovering, and not sitting down or offering coffee, it was clear that she was anxious that he be on his way.

'Well, I must be getting along,' George said, as if sensing that he was becoming *de trop*. 'Lady Cadmund, as ever, please do let me know if there's anything that I can do to help you. Ladies ...' Again, George's eye lingered longest on Effie.

Isabel, with a slight grimace behind his back, led her mother's legal representative out of the room.

'Ugh, creepy or what?' Gisela whispered loudly. 'Effie, he was positively ogling you.'

'Yeah, gal, I think you pulled there,' Mickey said helpfully.

Effie stifled the urge to slap him down. Although she could put up with most of his more boorish behaviour, sometimes he made her feel really angry. Like now. It was embarrassing enough to be so obviously eyed by such a lecherous old goat without Mickey intimating that she might actually have enjoyed it.

'Cut it out!' Corwin said, a shade harshly, as Effie felt her face beginning to heat with humiliation.

Mickey looked surprised, then a little shamefaced. 'Sorry,' he muttered to Effie.

'Oh, don't worry about it,' she said, forcing a brief smile onto her lips. 'Having to put up with flirting old married men who should know better is just one of those things that we women learn to put up with. Right, ladies?' she added through gritted teeth.

Jean snorted. Gisela giggled.

'OK, let's get to work,' Corwin said crisply, changing the subject.

Which was fine by Effie. The centre of attention had never been a place in which she felt particularly comfortable.

CHAPTER SEVEN

The cold spot, according to the temperature readings that had been relayed every three minutes to Malc's laptop, had come and gone four times in the last twenty-four hours.

Isabel, it was clear, didn't quite know what to make of that, which made two of them, Effie thought wryly, although the others all seemed very upbeat about it.

The men got to work setting up the equipment, and when Malc and Lonny arrived at just gone half past six, Corwin handed out their night-time assignments.

Effie, for some reason, had assumed that everyone would be doing the same thing as they had the last time – but in that she was wrong. Because of the cold spot, Gisela wanted to spend the night in the bathroom to see what she could intuit, which made sense, Effie supposed. But that meant that Claudia's bedroom was now in need of monitoring.

'Of course, if that's what you want,' she said calmly. After all, what else could she say? She was here to ghost-watch, wasn't she?

Corwin nodded encouragement at her, a slight smile that silently but clearly acknowledged her bravery, and Effie felt an absurdly warm sensation flood through her. To cover any visible effects of it, she hastily turned to Malc.

'Malc, I haven't had time to get myself a little digital recorder yet, and I'm still getting used to this new all-singing, all-dancing mobile phone of mine. But I believe we're all supposed to keep one on us and record our own verbal notes and thoughts, as well as any … er … other kinds of noises?'

'No probs, Effie, we've always got loads to spare,' he told her cheerfully. 'Here,' and he rummaged in a large canvas bag and came out with a tiny micro-recorder that barely covered her palm. 'Just switch it on and keep it in your pocket. It's small but it has a powerful battery for its size and it will easily last all night. It also has a very sensitive and powerful mechanism that instantly starts recording the moment a sound is made. It can even record the slightest sounds through a layer of cloth, since some of us tend to keep them in our pockets, so feel free to do the same. Although if something really juicy does happen, you might want to take it out and hold it in your hand, just so that we all get the best record of it possible.'

'Oh, right,' Effie said, slipping the small gadget into her handbag and leaving the clasp open, since her outfit that night didn't have any pockets. Even as she did it, she couldn't help but hope that nothing 'really juicy' happened that she would need to record!

Which was, she had to admit as she thought it, rather contrary of her, not to mention downright lily-livered. And it was certainly unfair to the others, who were all so clearly desperate for some ghostly action. But since it looked as if she was the one designated to stay in Claudia's room that night, she didn't feel particularly guilty about her disloyalty.

She comforted herself with the thought that, when Gisela had stayed there, nothing out of the ordinary had happened. And then had to stop and wonder. If she was thinking like that, was she really the person for this job? Shouldn't she, like the others, be hoping that something 'juicy' did happen? Perhaps, at their next session, she should tell Duncan that she was having doubts about being right for this project.

But she knew what he would say. She was his 'average woman in the street' and what he wanted were her honest opinions and thoughts on what she felt and did. And that her reluctance was all part and parcel of that.

With a small inner sigh, Effie realized that she wasn't going to be able to let herself off the hook that easily. Damn Duncan! He must have known that, once she'd committed herself to something, she would see it through, no matter what.

Michael had always said that quitting was for losers. Besides, she tried to cheer herself up, the bedroom was bound to be a more comfortable all-night spot than a chair in the hallway, right?

'OK then, it won't be fully dark for another three hours or so,' Corwin said, glancing at his watch – a rather nice, if slightly flashy Rolex, Effie noticed. 'So everyone to their positions. When it starts to get dark, either Lonny or me will come around with night-vision gear.'

Everyone nodded and after an uncertain pause, Isabel said that she was going into the living room to watch television. But as she passed the open door, Effie heard her on the telephone, clearly talking to her husband, and reassuring him she wouldn't be absent from home for much longer.

Not wanting to overhear any private or personal marital murmuring, she quickly swept on and all but raced up the stairs.

Up on the landing she paused.

Michael would never have worn a Rolex. The thought startled her, as much for its clarity, as for its irrelevance. He'd always worn a slim, discreet, mechanical Swiss watch that he wound very carefully each night before taking it off and putting it on the bedside table. An Oris, if Effie remembered correctly.

And knowing how much he'd liked to stick to routine, Effie had made sure that he had had it on his wrist when he was buried.

She shook her head, wondering why her subconscious had chosen to throw up that memory now.

Knowing that she couldn't dawdle on the landing forever, she turned and walked slowly towards the door at the end of the corridor. Feeling a bit of a ninny, she found herself hesitating outside Claudia's bedroom door, and then with a small self-derogatory smile, she firmly pushed open the door and took a step inside. Then almost leapt about a foot in the air as a voice right behind her said warmly, 'Well done.'

She found her heart seemed to be lodged somewhere in her throat, and gave a quick, rather inelegant gulp. Then she forced a small smile, turned to face Corwin and said shakily, 'Don't do that!' It came out as half-laugh, half reprimand. 'Creeping up on people in haunted houses should be against the law or something.'

Corwin grinned, and held his hands up with a *mea culpa* shrug. 'Sorry, I didn't do it on purpose, I swear. It's just that I get so used to walking about quietly. It's a habit you get into when you've done as many vigils as I have. You keep noise to a minimum without thinking about it. You'll find yourself doing it too before long,' he predicted.

Effie took a deep breath and nodded. 'Apology accepted.'

'Good. Because I come in peace, I promise. I just wanted to make sure that you were OK with this,' Corwin said, sweeping a hand around to indicate the room as he did so. 'I was worried that I might have rushed things a bit, asking you to jump in at the deep end so quickly. And it belatedly occurred to me that in asking you in front of all the others, I really put you on the spot. You could hardly have said no without feeling like … er …'

'A cowardy cowardy custard?' Effie put in with a quick grin as he grappled to find a more polite way of putting it. And of course he was right. Nothing would have induced her to admit to nerves in front of the others. Especially Mickey, who being Mickey, would never have let her hear the end of it. (And the thought of being the butt of his childish jokes for weeks to come was unthinkable!)

Corwin laughed and leaned more comfortably against the door-frame. 'I have to say, you don't strike me as the cowardy cowardy custard type. But it's still OK if you'd rather stay somewhere else tonight.'

'No, it's fine,' Effie said, looking around her. 'It's just a perfectly pleasant bedroom, and will probably be more comfortable to stay in all night than the hall,' she said firmly.

Corwin nodded. 'Yes, sorry about that. But long draughty uncomfortable nights sort of come with the territory. Actually, this place is a breeze compared to some places we investigated. There was this old railway station once that was due to be demolished. Half-derelict, with smashed windows, graffiti on the walls, you name it. Dead of winter too. Half of us came down with pneumonia. And on top of all that, the sightings of ghostly dancing lights turned out to be just kids mucking about.'

'Oh, I'm not complaining,' Effie assured him.

'I never thought you were,' he said quietly, with a slightly puzzled frown. 'Why do you always put yourself down that way?'

Afraid that she might start to blush with pleasure at the compliment, Effie murmured something vaguely self-derogatory and turned quickly away. The four poster bed had been made and looked neat and crisp, and even as she remembered envying Gisela the opportunity to lie on it in order to catch forty winks, she knew that she herself could never bring herself to use it.

Instead, she eyed the chairs that were placed either side of the big sash window. Made of walnut, with lovely cabriole legs and tapestry-backed material, they had to be early nineteenth century. And whilst they might be worth a small fortune to an antique dealer, she doubted that they'd be particularly comfortable. Claudia had probably put them there to decorate the room, rather than use them.

Then she noticed that there was a rather delightful and fully padded window seat by the main window, and she gave a silent cry of delight and instinctively made her way towards it.

As a child living in a modern council house, Effie had always wanted to live somewhere with a window seat, ever since she'd read about the feature in a children's book, where the eleven-year-old heroine had moved to a large, gloomy house, to live with her grandfather.

Unfortunately, it was the one feature her own home had lacked, so the sight of it here in Claudia's room made her smile.

The day had been another hot one, and the room felt stuffy. Knowing that the weatherman had forecast a particularly muggy and humid night to come, she walked to the sash window behind the window seat and tried to raise it. Either the mechanism was old or it was just stiff, but she couldn't budge it.

'Here, let me,' Corwin offered at once, coming over, and Effie quickly moved to one side to give him room. He grunted a little with the effort of working it loose, but he finally got it free. 'Do you want it open all the way?'

'Yes, please.'

Effie placed her hands on the window sill and leaned out to look across the village rooftops, and for a moment they stood in companionable silence as a blackbird began to sing magnificently in a neighbouring cherry tree.

'Well, I'll leave you to it,' he finally said. 'Don't forget, there's a coffee break at eleven thirty, and another one at two. Usually we bring our own thermos and snacks, but Isabel has insisted we make full use of the kitchen,' he reminded her.

'Lovely,' Effie said.

Corwin nodded, looked as if he was about to say something else, then clearly changed his mind and left. And it was only when he was gone that Effie finally felt able to relax.

Because it was still light, she sat on the much-appreciated window seat and drew her new Kindle out of her bag and found her place in the latest novel she'd been reading, a classic whodunit set in the local area. She'd always loved crime fiction, especially those written in the golden age era of Agatha Christie and Dorothy L. Sayers, although Michael had declared such novels to be a waste of time. He preferred the classics, but Effie had never been able to get into Dickens, Lawrence, or Hardy. No doubt, her rather inadequate working class education at the local comprehensive school had something to do with that.

Early on in her marriage, she had constantly worried that she was never going to be good enough to be Michael's wife. That, at some party or other, she'd shame him by committing some social faux pas that would betray her ignorance about how the well heeled behaved.

But whenever she'd told him that, Michael had only laughed and told her that she worried too much.

As the light began to fade outside, Effie turned up the brightness on her new toy and promised herself that she'd read just until the end of the chapter and then turn it off and concentrate on the business at hand.

And if she'd stopped to think about that, she might have realized that, subconsciously at least, she wasn't expecting anything to happen during the hours of broad daylight. Even given Corwin's assurances that phenomenon weren't restricted to the hours of darkness. So, perhaps it was because of that, or perhaps because she was so engrossed in her favourite form of fiction, that it took a little while to come to Effie's attention that she was actually smelling something.

Something scented and floral and very familiar, in fact.

Lavender.

For a second, Effie simply froze where she was, staring down at printed words that no longer mattered. Then her head shot up and she looked wildly around and about her, an icy sensation spreading its way up her spine and leaving her feeling as if a cold hand was clutched around the base of her neck.

But just one quick, manic, wild-eyed look informed her that the room was totally empty. Of course it was. There was no ghostly figure of an old woman standing by her bed, or lying beside it, which was how Claudia had been found. There was no moaning, or mist, or rattling of chains.

Effie blinked, and her breath shot out of her in a noisy exhale.

Her heart was pounding though, making her feel slightly light-headed.

Automatically, she half-rose, her legs feeling a little jellied at the knees and alien beneath her. *OK, Effie, get a grip,* she told herself firmly. *There's nothing and nobody here.* Although twilight had fallen, the room was still perfectly visible.

OK, what did she do now?

Be calm. Be sensible. Do your job.

She found herself, ridiculously, nodding like one of those toy dogs in the back of car windows. She'd also, all this time, been unknowingly holding her breath, because suddenly she was obliged to take a deep breath.

Along with being so sensible, it would probably be a good idea to breathe as well, girl, a mocking little voice piped up somewhere in the back of her head.

Slowly putting away her Kindle, she forced herself to reason things out. OK, first things first. Had she simply imagined it? That was the most likely explanation, of course. Just because her conscious mind hadn't been thinking about Claudia, or being in the same room where the woman had been found dead, that didn't mean to say that her subconscious mind hadn't been at work. In fact, she would hardly be human if it hadn't been, right?

So perhaps her mind had been playing tricks?

Well, there was obviously one way to find out.

Slowly and carefully she fully exhaled, then closed her mouth firmly, and drew in another breath, deeply and carefully, through her nose.

And there it was. And this time there could be no possible mistake. A strong, undeniable scent of lavender.

Her eyes shot around the room, frantically seeking its source. But there were no bowls of potpourri, no bars of soap or talc or anything else like that in the room. Of course not – she knew from listening to the others that all such sources of possible contamination had long since been removed.

OK. So perhaps someone had secreted a scent bottle somewhere? Perhaps Mickey, playing a joke on her? She wouldn't put it past him, the dozy little…!

But even as she thought it, she just as quickly dismissed it. Although Mickey might consider himself the joker of the group, when it came to what the C-Fits did, to be fair, he seemed to be as serious about it as anyone. Besides, neither he nor any of the others would let Corwin down by playing such a stupid trick. If nothing else, it would lay their findings open to even more question than usual, and she knew how fiercely they were dedicated to doing their job properly.

Isabel then? Could she be behind it – not to cause mischief, but perhaps out of a desperate need to prove to everyone, especially her family, that she hadn't been imagining things? And what better way to do that than to have someone else smell lavender, just as she had?

But how, even if Isabel had put a hidden bottle of lavender perfume in here, had she managed to rig it up to produce scent nearly an hour after Effie had first come into the room?

And then it was as if someone had given her a swift kick in the shins, as she realized that she'd been standing here frozen for what felt like hours, fruitlessly searching for an explanation, when what she'd needed to do all along was blazingly obvious.

Quickly, and with fingers that fumbled only slightly, she reached into her bag for her phone and began to text.

CAN SMELL LAVENDER. COME QUICKLY. She hit the button that would send the text to Corwin, and then realized that she should have sent it to everyone, and wondered why she hadn't.

But it wouldn't matter; she was sure that Corwin would tell the others anyway.

As she stood, waiting, knowing that they'd soon all be here, the feeling of sheer relief that she would no longer be alone abruptly fled as another, far more insidious and horrifying thought hit her.

What if they came, and none of them could smell it?

Hastily she took another deep breath through her nose. Reassuringly, the scent of lavender was as strong as ever.

To her, yes. But what if it turned out she was the only one who could smell it?

For a second, Effie appreciated the irony of what was happening to her. Right from the start, she and Duncan had agreed that, for the most part, ghost sightings relied on the evidence given by ordinary people, whom you either believed or didn't. By their very nature, stories of having seen ghosts were utterly reliant on the witness's credibility. And a lot of people were sceptical. How ironic it was then, to find herself in that very position. If the scent faded and no one else smelt it, why would anyone actually believe her?

After all, she'd volunteered to go ghost hunting, so people could reasonably presume that she must have had some pre-disposition for believing – or at least *wanting* to believe – in such phenomenon. She was recently widowed, so perhaps that had made her emotionally vulnerable and susceptible to thoughts that some sort of afterlife existed.

If she had been hearing someone else tell this very story, would she believe it?

Then the door opened, and her jitteriness dissipated. As expected, all of them had come, if not running exactly, then swiftly and silently. Corwin was first through the door, his eyes darting around and seeking her out.

Without thinking about it, Effie beckoned him over. Behind him,

Gisela, Lonny, Malc, Mickey and Jean followed in rapid succession. And as they approached her, Effie felt another moment of panic as she heard them all begin to sniff the air.

So convinced was she that her mind might have been playing tricks on her, that she almost wilted in relief as various expressions of excitement and elation crossed their faces. Mickey even went so far as to punch the air in triumph.

Clearly, they could all smell it too.

Effie collapsed back onto the window seat, and only then realized that she was trembling a little. Quickly, she folded her hands in her lap and hoped that nobody had noticed.

For several minutes, and still without speaking, the rest of the C-Fits split up and paced the room. This puzzled Effie, who wondered what they were doing, until Corwin reached her side, sniffed, nodded and moved off, then came back again.

'It's clearly strongest right here, right by Effie,' he whispered, and the others, coming over, nodded their agreement.

'Yes,' Jean Bossington-Smith murmured. 'It's definitely more noticeable here.'

'Not by the bed,' Gisela said, a puzzled frown creasing her brows. 'You'd have thought it would be strongest where she died. Phenomenon usually is centred around …' She shook her head in puzzlement, then glanced at Effie. 'Effie, perhaps Claudia is trying to attract your attention specifically.'

Effie blinked. 'Er, I don't think so,' she whispered, her voice barely a croak. That was a truly hideous thought! She was only here as an observer after all. Then, quickly following on from that thought, came another, rather childish one.

Why pick on me?

'Tell us what happened,' Corwin said, his voice firm and no-nonsense.

Effie looked at him blankly, and then became aware that everyone was staring at her intently. Of course. They needed a report – a comprehensive, clear, report.

She rose to her feet and then shifted a little nervously from one foot to the other. 'Well, that's not that much to tell,' she began. 'I smelt lavender, I texted you to come, and that's it.'

Corwin smiled at her patiently. 'Not quite, Effie. Where were you when you first smelt it?' he prompted.

'Right here, reading ...' Effie faltered then shrugged, deciding that she might as well come clean. 'Actually, I was reading a book on my Kindle,' she admitted, abashed.

Jean smiled. 'Sensible. I usually knit.'

Effie smiled her gratitude for the support.

'OK, so you were reading,' Corwin said. 'Then what? Did you hear anything? Catch any sense of movement out of the corner of your eye? Anything like that?'

'No.'

'Did you sense a presence?' Gisela asked. 'Did you feel as if you suddenly weren't alone?'

'No.'

'Did you hear a voice or feel a sudden unexpected emotion for no reason?' Gisela pressed. 'Angry, sad, scared?'

'No.'

'OK. So you were reading, you smelt lavender, then what?' Corwin said quietly. Effie, aware that everyone was eagerly awaiting her pronouncement, felt helplessly inadequate.

'Nothing. I just ... looked up quickly and looked around, but the room was empty. Then I ... yes, I stood up, and took a long deep breath through my nose to confirm that I hadn't imagined it.' She didn't think she needed to mention any of the other wild and fruitless speculations that had washed over her. 'And then I texted you.'

'It's beginning to fade,' Malc said, his words instantly setting the others off into a paroxysm of sniffing.

'Damn, he's right,' Lonny said.

'It's really annoying that we don't have any way of recording smells,' Malc complained. 'But we agree that we all smell it, yes?'

There was a chorus of vociferous agreement, and Jean glanced at her watch, and noted down the time and began scribbling furiously in her notebook.

'Effie, do you mind if I take your recorder?' Malc said. 'I'll get you another one, but I want to run it through the computer for possible EVPs.'

Effie nodded and happily handed over the recorder.

'OK, Gisela, Jean and Lonny, I want you to spend the rest of the night in here. Malc and I will man the monitors,' Corwin began issuing instructions briskly. 'Mickey, you keep an eye on the cold spot in the bathroom. Effie, would you mind taking the hall again?'

Even as he asked it, Effie knew what he was doing. He was removing her from the room and giving her a way out without losing face. Even as part of her wanted to tell him off for assuming that she couldn't handle herself, another part of her wanted to throw herself into his arms and kiss him with gratitude.

And that wayward thought made her turn abruptly away. 'Of course not,' she said, and even to her own ears her voice sounded ridiculously prim and undeniably cool.

As she left, she was sure that she could feel the eyes of the others boring into her back. What were they expecting her to do? Suddenly run screaming off into the night, waving her hands in the air like a mad thing?

'We all think you did very well.' Predictably perhaps, it was Jean who approached her first, at the two a.m. coffee break. The former teacher had come down to start brewing in the kitchen, and after seeing some of the others also come downstairs, Effie decided it would look petty and silly if she stayed out in the hall, like a wall-flower at a party.

'Thanks,' Effie said.

Perhaps something of her disbelief echoed in her voice, because Gisela went up to her and put an arm comfortingly around her. For a moment, Effie froze, then she slowly relaxed, and gave the tall redhead a grateful smile.

'Honestly, we did,' Gisela said. 'You were super-cool and all business. Even Corwin was impressed.' She gave her arm a final squeeze and moved off to rummage in her bag for biscuits.

Corwin, Lonny and Mickey were still upstairs. Malc accepted a mug of tea from Jean and sat down heavily in one of the chairs.

'Smells are buggers,' he said disgustedly. 'There's just simply no way you can prove that they exist. Corwin and me did some research once about certain chemicals soaked in cotton wool, and how some types of molecules can be extracted from the air and analyzed. But in the end, we had to give it up. There were too many variables, and besides, the cost of having a lab do all the tests that would be needed was astronomical.'

'But we all know what we smelt,' Gisela said firmly. 'I just knew this case was going to be a good one.'

Malc grinned. 'Yeah, it'll be a good chapter in Corwin's next book all right. Let's just hope it's only the start of some other, more recordable phenomenon. I can't wait to watch and analyze the camera-feed recordings in Claudia's room.'

Effie, with a start, suddenly realized that, along with other rooms of interest, Claudia's bedroom had been under constant surveillance. And that meant Corwin or also anyone else who happened to be looking at the monitor, would have been able to watch her too. And not only that, but it was all being recorded.

Good grief!

She was going to have to bear that in mind from now on. What if she'd done something hideously embarrassing like pick her nose or scratch her bum?

A hasty mental review of her time in the bedroom reassured her that she had done nothing but sit and read. But it was a close call. From now on, she was going to remember that she had to act with decorum at all times.

Michael would have been appalled if she'd …

Abruptly, Effie thrust the thought away. Michael was … gone.

Mickey chose that moment to breeze in, yawning hugely. 'Nothing,' he said gloomily.

And 'nothing' remained the order of play for the rest of the night, much to Effie's relief, if nobody else's. Eventually, at seven thirty, Isabel got up. Corwin told her about the night's excitement, apologizing and forthrightly admitting that he'd simply got so caught up in the excitement of the moment, that he'd forgotten that she'd wanted to be notified of any events at once, as and when they occurred.

Effie found herself pleased by his honesty, and Isabel seemed to share her approbation, since she took it with good grace. And with evident relief, since she hastily left the room and came back ten minutes later, saying that both her husband and her daughter were on their way over.

'Jeremy has business in Banbury anyway, and is just dropping by, or so he says, to remind himself of what his wife looks like,' Isabel explained laughingly, 'but Ros admits to being out and out curious. Besides, she's dying to meet you all. I hope you can stay and meet them?'

Lonny and Malc had to apologize, since they needed to get back to work, but the others didn't mind. Mickey also had to admit that he had a class at nine and needed to go back to his digs and guzzle coffee in order to say awake throughout the ordeal and would catch a ride back to the pavilion in Malc's van.

But Effie knew that Corwin would be glad of the chance to talk to other members of Claudia's family, if only to help fill out the casefile with more background information, and Effie herself was also curious. Just what *would* Claudia's nearest and dearest make of the C-Fits and the latest manifestation of the lavender lady?

Jeremy Cadmund was clearly a good decade older than his wife, but for someone in his early seventies, he looked fit and healthy, with a robust figure and a definite tan. Of course, Isabel had once told them that she thought of herself as a farmer's wife, and when Effie shook hands with him, she could easily imagine Jeremy driving a tractor, helping to birth lambs, and checking wheat fields for weeds. He had a competent, unflappable down-to-earth persona that Effie found instantly appealing.

His silver hair contrasted sharply with his florid colouring, and his hands were square and slightly callused.

'Hello,' he gave the group a general greeting. 'I understand that you've been having fun in the night?'

The question might have sounded jovial but the gaze he levelled on Corwin was steady and thoughtful. Clearly he didn't know what to make of these odd people that his wife had called in to her old family home.

Corwin, quickly sizing him up, smoothly handed him over to Jean, who began competently running down their scientific methods of research for him. And under her no-nonsense attitude,

Effie could almost see the man's suspicions and unease melt away.

Whilst it was clear to her that he didn't know what to make of his wife's contention that her mother's spirit might not be resting easily, under Jean's tutelage, he quickly came to realize that the C-Fits were harmless. Or at least, that they weren't a predatory bunch of charlatans, who were only interested in trying to part Isabel from any of the family cash.

And indeed, Effie knew that no mention of money had ever been mentioned.

Corwin had made it clear, right from the start, that he didn't expect Isabel to either pay them for their services, nor did they intend to offer any money to Isabel for letting them investigate their mother's house. No money would be changing hands, on either side, and Effie couldn't help but see the sense of this. Whatever accusation anybody might level at the C-Fits, clearly financial wrongdoing could never be one of them.

So when Rosamund Carteret arrived, clearly looking a little apprehensive about what she might find, everyone was sitting at the kitchen table, amiably eating toast and marmalade, with her father listening with rapt attention as Gisela explained to him the finer points of cold spots.

'And I could go up there and feel it now, could I?' he asked somewhat doubtfully, when she'd finished.

'If it's currently there, yes,' Jean said. 'We'd have to check the latest temperature readings.'

'Dad?' Rosamund said, coming around the table to kiss his cheek. She was a tall woman, with thick honey-blonde hair in an artlessly untidy cut, and grey-blue eyes. Her skin wasn't particularly good, and her nose was slightly too big for true beauty, but her face had character.

'What's all this about cold spots?' she demanded, with an uncertain smile.

CHAPTER EIGHT

'And was she as impressed by it as her father?' Duncan asked curiously. They were in his room at St Bedes, and the sounds of the ancient college drifted up through his open window. A mixture of city bells, young voices, traffic and, very intermittently, the sound of the choir practising in the seventeenth century chapel. Although some Dons lived in, Duncan, being married, preferred to keep his domestic life private from his workplace, and so had been designated just a single room by the Bursar. Here he taught the odd (and according to Duncan, inevitably bemused, lazy, or dozy) student and worked on his latest opus behind a large Florentine desk, which had such exquisite inlaid marquetry that his laptop computer looked like an insult, sitting on top of it.

'Not quite,' Effie said, after a moment's thought. 'She seemed to accept what the temperature readings showed, but wasn't anywhere near as excited about it as her mother. Nor was she as quizzical as her father.'

'Sir Jeremy?' Duncan clarified.

'They don't use the title,' Effie corrected him automatically.

'From what you've been saying, I take it that you took to him?'

Effie, sitting in a button-backed leather chair of a lovely deep claret colour, regarded her old friend archly. Surrounded by the college's idea of art – mostly early and unexceptional seventeenth century English landscapes with the odd bit of French post-impressionism thrown in – he looked very much at ease in his setting of faded, shabby, genteel academia.

Once Effie had asked him about the eclectic way the college was decorated, and he'd told her that most of the furnishings, et al, came to them via bequests from the wills of past alumni. Which ranged from absolute treasures worth hundreds of thousands, to downright tat. (Which made sense of the elephant foot that was used as an umbrella stand and took pride of place in the Hall.)

'Yes, I did rather feel as if I could get on with him,' Effie answered Duncan's query thoughtfully. 'He seemed a simple sort of man, and I mean that in a nice way. There didn't seem to be any sort of side to him, if you know what I mean? What you saw was what you got. And he was clearly missing his wife and wishing she'd stop spending so much time at her mother's house, and come back to the farm. And Isabel was clearly happy to have him around. They struck me as one of those close, well-suited couples – not the kind that grow further apart, the longer they're married.'

'Ah,' Duncan said, eyes twinkling. 'One of those rare and happy marriages we sometimes hear about.'

'Don't let Margot catch you talking like that,' Effie said dryly. 'Or she'll probably take a scalpel to you.'

Duncan laughed. 'You're probably right. So, we're all invited to a family barbecue this weekend, are we?' he deftly changed the subject.

And that was the last thing she could cope with right now.

'Yes, but remember, it's being held at Rosamund's place in Aynho – not at the Cadmunds', and all the C-Fits are invited, as are you,' Effie replied lightly to his question. 'From what I could gather from their conversation, Jeremy has a large farmstead up in Northamptonshire somewhere.'

'Yes, I know the Cadmund family slightly,' Duncan said. 'Or rather, I knew the father, Jeremy's old man. He was a big pal of my grandfather.'

Effie nodded. She knew that Duncan's grandfather had lived to be nearly a hundred years old, a taciturn but clever man who'd kept mentally alert right up until his death, and also that he'd played a rather big part in Duncan's life. Duncan had often said that his success in life had been down to his grandfather's influence, for it had been he who had encouraged his academic ambitions, whereas his father had urged him to go into some kind of business.

'If I'm not mistaken, Sir Jeremy had to re-mortgage the family estate a few years ago, when the credit crunch hit,' Duncan mused now. 'You'd be surprised what you hear on the grapevine, even if you aren't particularly listening. And in this place,' he waved a hand at the city beyond his window, 'back-stabbing and malicious gossip are the order of the day. Mind you, a lot of land-rich but cash-poor families had to do the same. And I don't imagine there's the money to be made in farming nowadays that there was thirty years ago. Not after foot and mouth, and the glut of wheat on the open market and what not. Apparently dairy farms are going to the wall at an alarming rate.'

Effie sighed in agreement. Although their client had never said anything, Effie had begun to get the feeling that Isabel's half of her mother's inheritance would come not a moment too soon.

'I think Isabel will be glad to get through probate just so that she can get back home – she's beginning to look really tired and drawn. I think this whole business of her mother and the things going on at the house is getting to her more than she's willing to let on.'

'Yes. Speaking of which,' he tapped his pen on top of his notebook, 'you were about to tell me all about the curious incident of the lavender that ponged in the night-time.'

Effie smiled, appreciating his attempts at levity in misquoting the title of a well-known novel, which in itself had been cadged from a line in a Sherlock Holmes novel, and took a careful breath.

It took her nearly an hour and a half to get it done properly. With Duncan exploring her every thought and reaction, and taking her back and nit picking over every little detail, by the time she'd finished her account of her first real 'experience' of ghost hunting, her throat was dry and her voice was beginning to get raspy.

'And then, the next morning, as I said, Isabel called her husband and daughter to come over. And, reading between the lines, I'm beginning to think that Isabel might have soft-pedalled her family's resistance to us being there. From what Ros let drop, I'm pretty sure that both her uncle and her husband are more or less convinced that our presence in Claudia's house will end in disaster for some unfathomable reason.' Effie sighed. 'But I think that at least Jeremy might be on our side now. He was certainly relieved to find us all so harmless.' Effie smiled. 'And by the way, Rosamund's invitation to her barbecue definitely included you – in fact, she made me promise to ask you especially. I think she wants to pick your brains about your book. She's clearly a little anxious about it, and wants to meet you so that she can see for herself exactly what you're up to. So please, do come and set her mind at rest, will you? Then at least we'll have another family member on our side.'

'Ah. She's scared I'm going to name her mother and bring shame – or worse still, ridicule – on the family escutcheon, is she?'

'Something like that,' Effie said cautiously. 'She assured us that the barbecue-cum-garden-party or whatever it is, is strictly informal, and that the barbecue was just something that she regularly 'threw together' once a month or so for family and mutual friends. But she seemed a little *too* insistent that the C-Fits and her granny's story would fascinate everyone.'

But although Isabel had added her reassurances that they'd all be made very welcome, Effie still felt vaguely discomfited at the thought of attending. Would she fit in? Would she be able to make intelligent conversation, without sounding ridiculous? Or worse, would people somehow learn of her recent widowed status and feel sorry for her? She wasn't quite sure that she could put her finger on why she felt so reluctant. Perhaps, as her friend Penny had more than once intimated, since losing Michael, she was gradually becoming something of a recluse, and needed to get out more and start socializing before she forgot how. And if her ambivalence about attending a probably harmless barbecue was anything to go by, perhaps Penny was right.

Dismissing her vague but growing sense of unease about the upcoming barbecue, Effie gave herself a mental shake and then glanced across at Duncan. 'So, will you be coming?' she asked curiously.

'Wouldn't miss it,' Duncan said at once, and Effie tried not to examine why his answer should bring such a flood of relief sweeping over her. It was not as if she wouldn't have other friends there as well. Jean, Malc and all the others would be there. And Corwin, naturally.

'Meeting the family of the "ghost" will not only give me some good background on their relationships and family dynamic, but I can also allay their fears about being named and shamed in my next masterpiece,' Duncan rumbled on. 'Although if they'd ever bothered to read any of my work, they'd know that I always change the names and identities of my principles, and in some cases, even where they live, if it helps them to keep their anonymity.'

Effie grinned. 'Sorry as I am to dent your mammoth ego, Duncan, but not everyone reads your books, you know,' she said dryly.

'Well, they bloody well ought to,' he grumbled, his Scots accent coming out strongly with his mock-ire. But his eyes were twinkling. 'So, when's the next vigil then?'

'Not before the weekend. Corwin's having to travel to Scotland for a few days, so everything's on hold,' she said.

'Oh? Checking out another possible case for the C-Fits, is he?'

'No.' She glanced out of the window, where a couple of students passing by were arguing about the merits of John Donne's right to be known as the father of metaphysical poetry. 'His girlfriend has a few days off work, so they're taking the opportunity for a mid-week mini-break.'

'Well, that's good, I suppose,' Duncan said cheerfully. 'It'll give you a bit of a breather from it all, not to mention some time to recover from your lavender-scented ordeal,' he added, regarding her steadily.

Effie grimaced briefly. 'It was hardly an ordeal, Duncan, don't exaggerate.'

'OK, if you say so. So, apart from cold spots and being wafted with lavender, has anything else been bothering you?'

Effie glanced at him sharply. 'No. Why do you ask?'

'Nothing! Don't get so defensive.'

'I'm fine,' Effie said firmly.

'Well, all right then,' Duncan said blandly. 'But if you ever want to talk about anything ... Michael, who let's face it, wasn't the easiest of men to live with ... And how you're coping now he's gone ...'

'I'm fine,' Effie repeated flatly.

Extract from the journal of Corwin Fielding:

18 April: We are now experiencing real progress on the Claudia Watkins case. Last night, at a little before 9.50 in the evening, Effie James, who was alone in the bedroom of the subject, scented lavender. When the rest of us entered the room, the scent was still very much discernible, being strongest where Effie had been sitting. The scent of lavender dissipated after about five minutes or so, and although three of the other more experienced team members remained in the room for the rest of the night, the phenomenon did not recur.

Along with the cold spot, which remains a feature in Claudia's bathroom, this case is providing us with some interesting data, and I remain hopeful that something even more exciting may occur soon.

Isabel Cadmund is being very cooperative, and has told us that we can continue our investigations up until the house is actually sold. Since her brother inherits the house only once it has gone through probate, that might be as much as three or four months in the future – if not longer, if he has trouble selling such a large and expensive residence in the current economic downturn.

I am very pleased by Effie's handling of her first experience of paranormal activity, for although she was very pale when we first joined her in Claudia's bedroom, she was composed and able to give a clear and coherent account of the sequence of events. I deemed it wise, however, to remove her from the room for the rest of the night, but she has assured me that she feels perfectly able to carry on attending vigils. This further confirms my growing belief that Effie will prove to be an asset to the team.

Isabel's daughter, Rosamund, has invited the team, along with

Professor Fergusson, to a barbecue at her house this weekend, which will give me a chance to learn more about our subject, and also to allay any fears the family may have about C-Fit's involvement in their mother's case.

I also intend to discuss further with Professor Fergusson the direction his book is likely to take, given these latest developments. And it definitely won't do to have his work published before mine – even though our reader's markets are bound to be very different. And not only do I want to reassure myself as to the quality of his finished manuscript, I must ensure that Effie's input will remain totally anonymous. I don't believe that Effie has the sort of personality that would flourish were she to gain any sort of notoriety from the professor's latest project. If I have to, I will reinforce that point with Professor Fergusson and get his promise to guard her privacy.

Tomorrow, Zoe and I head to the Trossachs and our favourite little inn for some much needed holiday time, and I look forward to …

The next morning Effie felt cross with herself as she stood once more beside Claudia Watkins's grave in the Adderbury churchyard.

What on earth did she expect to gain from coming here a second time?

From his position at her feet, Toad looked up at her, head cocked to one side, as if wondering the same thing.

'I know, I know,' she told him, her voice a mixture of exasperation and amusement. 'Don't tell Duncan I did this,' she warned him with a smile. 'He'll think I'm showing signs of cracking up or something.'

Her pet gave a little snort – as if he'd ever *dream* of betraying her – and started to pull on his extendable lead towards the tree where he'd encountered the squirrel before, leaving his mistress to stare down at Claudia's final resting place in peace.

Seriously, she asked herself with a hefty sigh, just why was she here?

Had that night in the old lady's bedroom, when she'd smelt the lavender so strongly, convinced her that ghosts did in fact exist?

No. She didn't think so. As she'd told Duncan during their intense debriefing session yesterday, she had no idea what it all meant.

When she'd described how she could find no obvious source of the scent in the bedroom, he'd instantly asked her what she thought that had meant. And she knew that she hadn't been able to give him a satisfactory answer, simply because she honestly didn't know what she'd thought.

She still didn't.

On the one hand, she'd grown a little impatient with Duncan when he'd suggested that she might have been imagining it. Or that, nearly twenty-four hours later, she was remembering it wrong. As she had angrily asserted, she *knew* what she had smelt! Moreover, she knew her own mind, and she didn't think it was particularly suggestible. Even so, the inference that she might have smelt lavender only because she'd subconsciously been *expecting* to, left her feel distinctly resentful. Besides, as she'd pointed out, the others had all smelt it too. And when he'd suggested that she might have experienced her first case of mass hysteria, she'd been frankly dismissive. She hadn't felt in the least hysterical, and she certainly didn't believe that Corwin Fielding had been, either.

Even after the psychologist had explained the finer points of the condition, she still didn't believe that they'd all been the victims of some kind of collective folly, with each one reinforcing the other's belief that they could smell lavender.

Besides, Effie thought angrily now, if you couldn't trust your own nose, what could you trust? And she knew what lavender smelt like, damn it!

So what then *had* she thought, Duncan had demanded.

Duncan, sensing her frustration, had further annoyed her by beginning to scribble madly. No doubt, such confusion in his test subject was meat and drink to a psychologist studying the results of his latest experiment.

To Effie, though, such confusion was irritating. Intolerable too, and insulting. For her own peace of mind, she needed to find some rational explanation for what she'd experienced.

And it was probably that need which had brought her back

to Adderbury. But now, standing in a perfectly pleasant country churchyard, staring down at a dead woman's grave as if expecting answers from the hereafter (whilst her pet amused himself by searching for squirrels), she felt utterly ridiculous.

Corwin is probably walking beside some Scottish lake right now, holding hands with Zoe and wondering where to take her for lunch.

The voice that suddenly piped up in the back of her head was mocking and cool, and made her turn sharply from the mound of turf with a small, irritated grunt.

This was getting her nowhere.

Briskly, and feeling angry with herself for being so asinine, she walked back to the churchyard's wrought iron gate and pushed it open, tugging Toad away from his position beneath the squirrel-free tree, and heading back in the direction towards Claudia's house.

She knew that Isabel would probably be in, but she just didn't feel right in dropping in without the rest of the group being present as well. Even for something as a simple chat over a cup of tea and a biscuit. It would have felt … sneaky, somehow. As if she was trying to cut them out, or wangle some kind of advantage for herself behind their back.

No doubt Duncan would have found that logic fascinating, were she ever to tell him about it. Which, of course, she wouldn't. She might have some obligation to tell him everything when it came to ghost hunting, but bearing her soul wasn't what she'd signed up for.

And so, for a moment, she stood on the pavement and contemplated the Rollwright Inn instead. Attached on one side to Claudia's house, it was built of the same local ironstone, but was perhaps a third of the size of the Watkins residence. An attractive creeper, that would no doubt turn a glorious shade of red in the autumn, climbed the walls in a riot of spring-green foliage. An old-fashioned painted sign was suspended from a black iron bracket set more or less square in the middle of the edifice, and depicted a rather crude but charming image of some ancient standing stones that were situated in a nearby village. Hardly on a par with Stonehenge, nevertheless, the depicted modest ring of stones still managed to evoke the rather eerie sense you got when looking at such ancient monuments.

All in all, the inn looked like just the sort of place foreign tourists would love to stay, believing it would provide them with a taste of Merry Olde England. No doubt it would boast a reasonably good kitchen, and day rooms decorated with some genuine, if largely unexceptional antiques. And of course, it was bound to have a well-stocked and expensive bar, furnished with either genuine polished horse brasses, or vernacular pottery.

And it would almost certainly provide the mandatory 'cream tea' in the afternoons.

For a moment, she contemplated going inside and ordering lunch. Then, realizing that they might not welcome her dog on the premises (especially where food was being served) she turned and moved off instead towards where she had parked her car.

She had just crossed the street when, right in front of her, an old lady suddenly appeared beside her garden gate, rather in the manner of Judy, as in a Punch and Judy show, popping up in her booth.

'Sorry, didn't mean to make you jump,' she said cheerfully as Effie muffled a squeak and put a hand to her throat in surprise.

She was about four foot, with hair so white it almost dazzled, and a face that had the deeply wrinkled crevices of someone well into their ninth decade. She also spoke rather loudly, as those who had a slight hearing problem were wont to do, and she was sucking on a mint or some other boiled sweet fiercely, which made her dentures clack in a rather alarming way.

'Couldn't help but noticing you and them others over at old Claudia's house,' this wonderful old lady said. 'Tell me, is it true that you're trying to catch her ghost?'

'Not exactly,' she said warily. 'We've just been called in to record and make a note of anything … er … untoward that might be happening. Or might not,' she felt compelled to add.

The old woman nodded sagely. 'I thought it was something like that. When my niece told me what was going on, I wasn't at all surprised.'

'You weren't?' Effie said, somewhat taken aback.

From her own experiences of village life, she had always known that Isabel would never be able to keep the C-Fits a secret from everyone for any length of time. As anyone who lived in the countryside knew, in a village, everyone seemed to know your business before you did. But she hadn't expected quite such open and ferocious curiosity from the neighbours. But then, she thought, this lovely old bird wasn't exactly your average neighbour, was she?

'No, I told Jenny, I did, that Claudia was just the kind to make trouble even after she was dead and gone.' This remarkable denizen nodded again, her head bobbing up and down emphatically as she sucked savagely on her sweet.

Effie smiled. 'Oh. I see. How clever of you,' she said faintly. Then, 'I take it you knew Claudia well?'

The old lady gave a bark of laughter, so loud and so sudden, that it set Toad off barking as well.

'Course I do. Lived opposite her for near on seventy years, haven't I?' she said bluntly, then glanced down. 'Hello, little fella. He's a lively little thing, isn't he?'

Effie watched as her pet fawned in front of his latest admirer, but suspected that his newest conquest would be too stiff with arthritis or other like ailments, to bother to try and bend down to stroke him.

'Claudia always was a contrary old cuss. So, have you seen her then?' she demanded.

Effie blinked. 'Sorry?'

'Her ghost. Walking the halls, is she?'

'Oh! Oh, no, nothing like that.' Effie was amused to hear herself sounding so shocked.

The old lady sniffed, obviously disappointed by this clearly spontaneously honest answer, then grinned at herself. 'Sorry, forgetting me manners.' She popped a hand, riddled with age spots and covered with distended blue veins, over the gate, and Effie took it gently, being careful not to squeeze too hard.

'Mary Coles.'

'Effie James.'

Mary Coles nodded. 'Don't mind me, duck, I'm a nosy old so-and-so. My husband always said that he couldn't take me anywhere. Which is probably why he seldom did.' And again she burst into laughter.

'So, is there much talk in the village?' Effie asked, not quite sure how to handle this ancient little dynamo. 'I do hope Isabel won't feel too embarrassed by it,' she stressed meaningfully.

But if she hoped that a little gentle censure would help stem the tide of speculation – at least from this quarter – she was doomed to be disappointed.

'Oh, she needn't worry,' Mary said casually, the gentle hint that maybe she should consider Isabel's feelings a little more going totally over her head. 'To be honest, nowadays folk are too busy working all the hours God sends to care about what their neighbours are up to. Not like it would have been in the old days. A real nine-day wonder it would have been back then. No, it's only the old brigade, like me, who are all agog and chatting about it amongst ourselves.'

Effie nodded and sighed, wondering how best to extricate herself without causing offence. Because, genuine British eccentric though she may be, Effie had no intention of indulging Mary Coles's curiosity at Isabel's expense. Unfortunately, no escape plan came readily to mind.

'So, who do you think bumped her off then?' this remarkable woman said next, tilting her head to one side, rather like a curious robin, as she regarded Effie with bright, sparkling brown eyes.

'What?' Effie squeaked in alarm.

And it was only when Mary laughed again that it began to occur to her that the old bird was having far too much fun for Effie's liking. The little faker was clearly quite happy to lead her on, and was being highly entertained in the process.

'Well, I reckon if ghosts are going to walk, it stands to reason that they have to have a good reason for doing it,' Mary averred now firmly. 'Mind you, with Claudia, she might have come back just so that she could go on arguing with her family. I never knew such a contentious woman as that one.'

Effie smiled weakly. 'Oh dear. Was she really as bad as all that?' she asked helplessly, whilst wondering what the old woman was going to come out with next.

'You don't believe me?' Mary asked. 'Then let me tell you, just a week or so before she passed, I heard her having a humdinger of a row with some man or other. I'm always out in the garden, see, and since we've been having such fine weather recently, I'm getting a head start on me weeding. And what with the village being so quiet like, during the day, sound tends to carry, so it does. And old Claudia was really giving someone a tongue lashing, I can tell you. Now then.' And she nodded her white head savagely and took the opportunity to pop another sweet into her mouth.

'Really? Who was it, do you know?' Effie, in spite of her misgivings, found herself asking eagerly.

'Couldn't see him,' Mary said with such frank and open disgust that Effie almost laughed herself. 'They was in the back garden, see,' the old lady continued morosely. 'And although the sound carried across the road, I couldn't see 'em. But Claudia was in fine fettle. At one point, she even warned the young fella that she was going to get the police on to him.'

Effie blinked. Now really that was too much. Just how gullible did this old lady think she was?

'The police? Really?' she echoed sceptically.

Mary grinned at her unashamedly. 'You think I'm lying. I swear, so swipe me Bob, she was threatening all sorts,' she promised. 'Started telling him that she had friends in high places who would soon "fix his hash". That's her exact words. She had a real turn of phrase, when it suited her, did our Claudia. Mind you, she probably did. Have friends in high places, I mean,' she clarified, when Effie looked at her blankly. 'When old Claudie said she was going to do something, you could always bet your last penny that she meant it. And she had the clout and the backbone to follow through as well. She never was one for issuing idle threats, you had to give her that.'

Effie eyed her doubtfully. Although Mary sounded coherent enough, she supposed it was possible that she was suffering from some form of dementia.

'Course, I hung around, to try and see who he was,' Mary swept on, mercifully unaware of Effie's thoughts, 'but I had to go in and use the damned loo. Nowadays, I have to go more and more often. Damn doctors. And wouldn't you know it, when I got back out again, it was all quiet, and the fella must have taken himself off. But I reckon it was that solicitor she had. Never did like him. Or maybe that grandson-in-law of hers – Claudia couldn't stick him, either. She never did like her Ros's choice, but in the last year or so, she was really getting a downer on him. Not sure what he did to deserve it, but I'm with Claudie on that one. That fella's a little too good looking and a little too sharp for his own good. Know what I mean?'

Effie decided it was probably best simply to indulge her, so she nodded, doing her best to look sage and wise.

'Or maybe it was her gardener that she was arguing with,' Effie offered. 'I know she had some sort of fixed idea that he should retire, didn't she?'

'Oh no, it weren't Geoff,' Mary denied confidently. 'I *know* his voice. Besides, he's got an old man's voice. The other fella, the one Claudia was giving what for, he had a younger voice.'

Effie nodded. Then, giving Toad's lead a little tug, she said shamelessly, 'Well, I must be getting back. My dog is going to want his dinner.'

And Toad, bless him, reacting to that magic word – dinner – began barking excitedly and straining on the lead to get going.

But as Effie began to move away, Mary Coles shot her a last, knowing look. 'Well, if you ever do spot Claudia's ghost, come over and fetch me, will you? I can't move as fast as I used to, but for something like that I'll go like a rocket. Yes, I will.'

Effie, promising to do just that, hurried quickly away, but by the time she'd got back to her car, she was beginning to laugh out loud. Sometimes, just when life seemed set on getting you down, some unexpected little bonus like Mary Coles came your way, just in the nick of time, to give you some perspective and cheer you up.

Driving home, Effie defiantly tuned the radio to a channel that only played sixties music, and sang along with The Kinks, who were deploring the taxman and lazing about on a sunny afternoon.

No doubt Michael would have preferred that she listen to Classic FM.

Leaning forward, Effie turned the radio up a little louder.

CHAPTER NINE

Duncan called around to pick Effie up at just gone eleven, on a gloriously bright and sunny Saturday morning. One of his many indulgences – along with fine cognac, first editions and leggy blondes – were classic cars, and had he inherited millions, he'd no doubt have accumulated a fleet of beautiful automobiles by now. Since he had to live on an Oxford Don's salary, however (amply supplemented by his book sales though it was), he confined himself to one new purchase every decade or so, and was currently in possession of a breath-taking Bentley, circa 1952, in racing car green.

As she slipped into the original cream leathered interior, complete with its mahogany dashboard and retrofitted art-deco clock, she wished she wasn't still feeling so nervous about the upcoming party.

Her morning hadn't started out well, and it had taken her nearly an hour and a half to choose her outfit. Had Michael been there, he'd have been pacing the floor with impatience. What's more, he would have easily been able to help her pick out something that would be just right for the occasion without having to think about it.

But Effie had stood in front of her wardrobe for what seemed like ages with her mind a dithering blank – if such a thing was possible. As a child, her working class parents hadn't been able to afford much in the way of clothes, and growing up, Effie hadn't exactly had much to choose from by way of outfits, so choosing what to wear had never been much of an issue.

After her marriage, however, Michael had made it clear that he expected his wife to dress well. And so she had quickly learned a lot more about fashion, which shops she should buy from and what looked smart, both in the work environment at her husband's office, and in a social environment.

But knowing what to wear for, say, a night out at the theatre followed by a late supper, and an informal barbecue held in someone's garden, wasn't, she had quickly come to realize, the same thing. And, once she'd thought about it, she had to concede that she'd never attended a barbecue with Michael in all their years together.

He'd not been a barbecue-in-someone's-back-yard sort of man.

But surely, she'd reasoned, a summer dress/summer hat combination would be too garden party-ish. Right? It was not as if she was going for tea at Buckingham Palace! Far too formal! But on the other hand, jeans had to be a definite no-no, too, since it went too far in the other direction. Which only seemed to leave a skirt and jacket combination – but that just seemed too business-like.

The trouble was, she didn't really know Rosamund, or her family, that well. Nor did she know what type of house she lived in, and so she didn't feel confident in being able to accurately guess just what Ros would consider to be a 'casual' occasion. Did she really mean *casual*, casual, in which case practically any presentable slacks and blouse would do? Or did she mean dress-up casual, in which case only designer label slacks and blouses would do?

Perhaps Michael's favourite stand-by, dark trouser suits, were best after all? How ironic that would be, just when she was beginning to dislike wearing them all the time.

And what about jewellery? Diamonds were hardly appropriate, or pearls, but discreet gold accessories should be all right, shouldn't they?

Her make-up she'd kept to her usual, discreet minimum.

She'd solved the shoe problem by firmly reaching for a pair of silver-grey sandals that were almost totally flat, and putting them on and then going downstairs before she could start agonizing over whether or not she should have worn something with heels.

But surely not? After all, puncturing holes in your hostess's lawn was hardly likely to endear you to her, was it? Unless she wanted her lawn aerated that is!

Finally, she managed to laugh at herself, and felt better.

Even so, when she'd walked out of her house to get into the newly-arrived Bentley, Duncan had earned himself a totally unearned black look when he greeted her with, 'Hello, gorgeous, you look as refined as ever.'

'What's that supposed to mean?' she demanded edgily, once she slipped into the passenger seat and was fastening her seatbelt.

Duncan slipped the stately old car into gear and shot her an amused look. 'Got up out of the wrong side of the bed, did we?'

Effie had the grace to look a little shamefaced. 'Sorry. I'm just feeling a bit out of sorts, that's all,' she mumbled, by way of apology.

'You always did get the jitters when having to deal with a whole bunch of strangers en masse.'

'I don't!'

'Yes, you do. I remember when Michael first introduced you to us at that party at the Cadwalladers, you clung on to him like a frightened limpet.'

'Sod off, Duncan,' she said sweetly.

He laughed. 'That's the spirit,' he said. 'It's better to be mad than scared.'

'You can be really aggravating at times, did you know that?'

'So I've been told,' he acknowledged cheerfully. 'I do hope they're going to serve booze at this party. It'd be ghastly if it turns out to be one of those affairs where they serve only fancy mineral water or elderflower cordial or something equally awful.'

'It'll serve you right if they do. Besides, you're driving,' Effie reminded him primly.

Duncan sighed elaborately. 'So I am.'

Aynho was a pretty village perched on a hill overlooking water meadows, and boasted a very fine, big, palladian-looking mansion that they drove past three times before eventually managing to find Rosamund's place. Tucked up behind a very steep and narrow back lane, it was a large, unassuming house that had probably been built some time in the 1950s. Two recent and very well done extensions tripled the floor space and blended in seamlessly with the original structure. Luckily, the garden had been sufficiently large enough in the first place to accommodate the expansion without looking silly, and as Duncan nabbed a prime parking space on a nearby grass verge, Effie checked her image in the side mirror.

She could see Corwin's Jag parked further down the road, and as she slung her silver, chain-mail effect handbag over one shoulder, she took a deep breath.

'Once more into the lion's den, eh?' Duncan drawled blandly beside her.

'Sod off, Duncan,' she repeated affably, but when he offered her an elbow, she quickly slipped her hand through it. After all, having a presentable man on your arm when walking into any social arena still had some benefits. And today, her old friend was wearing cream slacks and some sort of polo shirt in powder blue, with a jaunty Panama hat on his head that somehow succeeded in making him look more debonair than daft.

Michael had also possessed that same sort of effortless, careless panache, and Effie found herself hoping that she didn't let the side down, and that her make-up held up during what was clearly going to be a hot day.

The sounds of light classical music guided them through a small front garden and around to a side entrance, where an arched trellis, trailing some lovely morning glory, let them out into a large, formal area. Here, the traditional square lawn was very much a centre point, and was surrounded by mixed borders on three sides, with open French doors leading into the house itself on the fourth. About twenty or so people stood around, holding various sorts of drinks – which most definitely included wine – and chatted. Several men were also grouped on the paved patio area in front of the house, from which smoke and the appetising scent of roasting meat emanated.

'Behave.' Effie just had time to admonish him before Rosamund, spotting them from across the expanse of lawn, suddenly said something to the woman she'd been talking to, and began to head over.

'Hello, Effie, isn't it?' Rosamund greeted them with a smile. She was wearing, Effie was so glad to note, a similar outfit to hers, although her slacks were deep maroon in colour, and her top was more of a man's style shirt in pale pink. A gold chain glittered around her throat, and several gold bangles chimed delicately on her wrist as she impatiently shooed a fly away from her face.

'Yes, hello again,' Effie said. 'Rosamund, this is Professor Fergusson.'

'Call me Duncan, please,' Duncan said instantly, shamelessly bringing out his most melodious Highlands accent and deliberately lowering the timbre of his voice an octave. He reached out and shook her hand heartily. And held on to it for a good five seconds longer than he needed to. 'I've been looking forward to meeting you ever since Effie relayed your invitation. It was so kind of you to invite me. You have a charming garden and lovely home.'

As poor Margot had once confided to Effie, her husband had a way of making any woman he spoke to instantly believe that she was the centre of his attention, and was genuinely interested in every word that she said. Which was probably a good thing in a psychologist, who needed to encourage people to talk. Unfortunately, it was also flattering in a way that mere flirting could never match.

And Effie watched as Rosamund now inevitably blushed with the pleasure of meeting this charming and attractive man. No doubt she'd been expecting an Oxford Don and a professor, at that, to be some dried up, pedantic old stick, instead of this obvious silver fox of a man.

'Oh, well, thank you. I'm so glad you could make it,' she all but gushed.

'I hope you don't mind, but I haven't bought any flowers,' Duncan swept on. 'I simply refuse to turn up with a generic bunch of blooms that might or might not please my hostess. So please tell me now, so that next time we meet I don't have to arrive so shockingly empty handed – what are your favourites?'

Rosamund blushed again. 'If I said carnations, would you think me hopelessly plebeian? But I just love their rich, dense scent.'

'Not at all. Carnations show taste and tell me that you're a lady who knows her own mind, and has no silly qualms about trusting her own judgement,' Duncan said grandly. 'You'd be amazed how many women, when asked that question, feel obliged to say roses. Or orchids.'

Effie managed to keep from rolling her eyes. Really, she knew Duncan was determined to get Isabel's family on side, but wasn't he laying it on a bit thick? What if Rosamund saw through him?

But one quick look at Rosamund's shining face told her that wasn't likely to happen any time soon.

'You must come and meet my husband,' she said, and then, very much as an afterthought, included Effie in this invitation by smiling at her. 'He's been really keen to meet you, ever since we heard you were involved with this thing with Granny. Though I should warn you in advance, he thinks Mum's rather lost her head over all this … er … paranormal ghost business,' she added, waving a hand helplessly in the air.

As Duncan fulsomely predicted that all would be well, and she had no need to worry, Effie silently wandered after the two of them towards the patio. There, a tall, well barbered man with thick dark hair and brown eyes was standing sipping at a glass of pale lager, whilst desultorily watching an older man turn some sausages on the grill.

'Clive, this is Professor Fergusson, the man who's writing the book. And Effie James, a member of the team working at Grandmother's house,' Ros introduced. 'My husband, Clive.'

Clive Carteret looked over at them and smiled briefly. She knew from what Isabel had already said about him, that her son-in-law had not long turned forty, but Effie noted that he appeared much younger than his years. Wearing tight-fitting designer jeans in a fashionably washed-out looking blue, with a Lacoste shirt in pale lemon, he looked tanned and fit – and was undeniably good-looking.

But Effie immediately decided that his muscles probably came from regular trips to the gym, rather than trips around his building sites and hard manual labour. For although his company might be responsible for throwing up houses, she doubted that this man knew how to so much as lay a brick or plaster a wall. There was something so very well barbered and aloof about him that told her he was more at home with a spreadsheet than a cement mixer.

'Oh right. So how goes all the ghost-busting?' he asked sardonically.

Effie forced herself to smile politely and murmur something vague, now well on her way to understanding how much patience the others must have in order to regularly put up with such off-hand scorn. Such scepticism was beginning to annoy and weary even her with its dreary and wearying predictability, and she was just an unbiased observer!

'Oh, Effie's very new to all that,' Duncan slipped in smoothly. 'In fact, she's only doing it as a favour to me.' He went on to explain things further, during which time Rosamund brought them drinks, an orange juice for Effie, and a glass of red wine for Duncan.

And as Duncan continued to state his case under Clive Carteret's increasingly amused but far less antagonistic eye, Effie glanced around, perking up when she spotted Jean and Malc chatting to an affluent-looking, middle-aged couple over by a budding lilac tree. The woman, especially, seemed fascinated by the conversation, and Effie smiled, remembering how Malc had predicted that most people at the barbecue *would* be intrigued and interested in talking about ghosts. It was one of those subjects, he'd assured her, that would liven up even the dullest event, since nearly everybody had a ghost story to tell, or alternatively would relish the chance to do a bit of debunking. Either way, he'd told her with a wink, the C-Fits wouldn't be considered boring.

'Hello, Effie.'

Effie jumped, nearly spilling a little of her juice as Corwin suddenly appeared in front of her. She looked up to smile at him, then found her eyes instantly sliding past him as Zoe Younger pressed closer against his side.

Today, the young weather presenter was wearing a white summer dress with a tight-fitting bodice and flowing skirt that swirled just below her knee every time she took a step. Her hair was swept back in an elegant French pleat, and she wore a single diamond-drop pendant on a silver chain around her neck. She was wearing white sandals with a tall but wedged heel.

'Hello, Corwin. Zoe,' Effie greeted them cordially. 'Rosamund and Duncan you already know. And this is Clive, Rosamund's husband.'

'Just call me Ros, please, everyone,' Ros said.

Clive's eyes lit up at the sight of Zoe's youthful summery presence and slowly reached out to shake her hand. With some reluctance, he then turned to Corwin and slowly looked him up and down. And as he did so, Effie got the distinct feeling that Clive Carteret was used to being one of the better looking and better dressed men wherever he went, and she strongly suspected that he was less than pleased with the competition that Corwin clearly offered.

Dressed in plain black trousers and a crisp white shirt, there was nothing obviously eye-catching about the leader of the C-Fits, but nevertheless, Effie could tell that many of the people around them were watching him curiously. It was not that he had an air of theatricality so much, as that he just carried with him an aura that he was important. And interesting. It made you wonder who he was. And left you wanting to find out more.

'Zoe, you look very familiar,' Clive was saying smoothly, and as Zoe began, with obvious pleasure to tell him why she might seem so, Effie began to feel distinctly *de trop*. Murmuring something about refreshing her drink, she gladly slipped away, heading towards the safety of Jean and Malc, and their spellbound companions.

'Hey, girl, the grub smells good,' Malc greeted her cheerfully. 'This is Janice and Pete. Friends of Ros's. Effie, you arrived just in time. I was just about to tell them about the cold spot we found …'

With a smile of relief, Effie let herself be swept away by Malc's account of their last vigil, and was not at all surprised to learn that her friend was definitely something of a raconteur.

Jean took the opportunity to move closer to her and glanced around. 'So, how are you?' she asked quietly.

'Fine.' Effie smiled. 'You?'

'Looking forward to the next vigil,' Jean responded predictably.

'So what's he like? Rosamund's husband?' Jean asked, looking across to the patio. 'We haven't met him yet.'

'We hardly exchanged two words. Why?'

Jean smiled knowingly. 'I've been here nearly an hour, and you'd be amazed at the things you can pick up, just drifting about and listening. It seems that he hasn't been making any secret of the fact that he thinks his mother-in-law has made a serious mistake in calling us in.'

'Oh, well,' Effie said a shade helplessly. 'You can't expect everyone to understand or accept what we do.'

She used the 'we' without thinking about it, but Jean didn't fail to pick up on it, and smiled approvingly.

'There's being sceptical, and then there's being anti,' the former schoolteacher pointed out, a shade grimly. 'And from what I can make out, he's definitely the latter. And he wasn't any too happy with his wife for inviting us to this shindig, either, I gather.'

'Oh no. I don't like to think we're causing any marital trouble,' Effie said, casting a concerned glance Ros's way.

And the fact that Ros seemed to be paying rapt attention to something that Duncan was saying didn't make her feel any more sanguine. She did so hope that Duncan wasn't going to be too naughty. She didn't think that Ros was particularly his type, but she didn't for one moment doubt that he would be happy to take anything that might be offered. And if there were already fractures in the Carteret marriage …

Jean sighed. 'No, I don't like making trouble, either,' she admitted.

'Well, with a bit of luck, Duncan and Corwin between them will succeed in winning Clive over. And once he sees that we're not going to be a nuisance, with a bit of luck, he'll come around.'

'Well, that's what we're here for,' Jean said with a slightly wicked smile. 'To soothe, reassure, entertain and pass muster. Which is why we persuaded Mickey not to come.'

Effie had to laugh. Jean, although much better at ignoring Mickey's more annoying habits than she was, clearly had her limits. And this proof that she wasn't the only one who could find that young man very trying at times, bolstered her spirits a little.

'This sort of thing would probably be too boring for him anyway,' she said diplomatically, glancing around at the largely middle-aged and sedate crowd. She hadn't seen Isabel yet, but she had said that she and Jeremy might be a bit late.

'Exactly. Oh, there's Gisela and Debbie.' Jean waved briefly to the tall redhead and her short, dark-haired companion.

'Debbie?' Effie said. 'Is she another C-Fit member?' She knew, from listening to the others, that there were another half dozen or so people who irregularly attended some vigils, as and when the mood took them. These had an interest in the subject, but lacked the core group's commitment.

'No, that's her partner,' Jean said. 'They've been together for nearly seven years now. Debbie's a physiotherapist. She might be five feet, but she can haul around grown men almost twice her size, believe me. I've seen her do it. She works at the John Radcliffe Hospital. Come on over, I'll introduce you.'

Effie nodded amiably, and moved off in Jean's wake.

At one o'clock, the men declared the meat to be cooked to their satisfaction and an orderly queue began to form. Burgers, hot dogs and chicken legs were born away on plates, and a salad bar, set up to one side, began to do brisk business.

Effie, happy to stick to the salad, found herself standing in a shady spot, alone for once and more than happy to take a break from talking about ghosts, her 'work' for Duncan, and explaining how her unbiased, man-in-the-street mission was supposed to work.

For the last hour she'd had to either defend her neutral status, or listen to others either argue the case for ghosts, or fend off equally determined arguments against their existence. But as Malc had promised, nobody she had spoken to seemed bored by the topic.

Now, as she rested gratefully in the shade, half-hidden by an overgrown, white-blooming spiraea bush, she speared a rocket leaf on her fork, listening whilst others talked for a change.

And right now, two women who were helping themselves to potato salad and coleslaw, were happily chatting away in front of her. Both were middle-aged and comfortably plump, and Effie pegged them as near neighbours, invited to the 'do' in the cause of good neighbourly relations, rather than because they were lifelong friends of the Carterets.

'I notice Ros isn't wearing any of her grandmother's jewels today,' the darker haired one said to the other, who promptly snorted.

'Talk about having the luck of the Irish. I wish my granny had left me a handful of baubles when she passed away, bless her.'

'I know. It is a bit sickening, isn't it? Especially when she doesn't even need it. That husband of hers is making money hand over fist.'

Effie couldn't bring herself to eat any more of her salad now and, glancing around for something to distract her, spotted Gisela and Debbie by the mobile bar on the patio. They made such a striking couple, being as they were, so physically very different. Gisela, almost giraffe-like, with her striking red colouring, and the physiotherapist, being short, dark and fit.

She'd had no idea that their 'sensitive' had been gay and now wondered, a little sadly, if someone else, someone far more attuned than she was to other people, would have picked up, long ago, on the fact that she was. Probably, she acknowledged with a small sigh. She really had lost any social skills that she might once have had.

How had she let it happen? Did other women who lost their husbands unexpectedly, retreat into such a tight shell that the outside world passed them by without their noticing?

'Of course, jewellery doesn't make up for everything, does it?' the fairer haired woman in front of her said abruptly to her friend, who in return shot her a quick, questioning look.

Effie shrank back a bit further in the spiraea, wishing Ros's so-called friends would move away and find somewhere else to talk. This was becoming so embarrassing.

'What do you mean?'

'Well, it's obvious that they're in trouble, isn't it?' the darker woman said. Then, leaning a little closer to her friend, lowered her voice – but unfortunately not quite enough for Effie not to hear, 'Everyone knows that Ros wants kids and that *he* doesn't.'

Effie went hot, then cold, then felt abruptly sick. This was intolerable. She simply couldn't stand here a moment longer, listening to this. In fact, her legs were beginning to feel distinctly weak.

'Really? Why on earth not?' Then before her friend could answer, proceeded to do so herself. 'One of those selfish types, is he? Doesn't want the smooth running of his domestic life interrupted with kids?'

'Either that, or he's one of those jealous, controlling types. You know, he wants to be the centre of her world, and thinks that having kids will only provide him with competition. I don't understand men like that.'

Effie swallowed hard. She had to get out of here. Any minute she was going to … to … well, either be sick or pass out or do something equally embarrassing.

Just why on earth had she agreed to come here this afternoon? What had made her think she was ready? She'd always had a bad feeling about this party, and she should have had the courage to just listen to her instincts and make her excuses not to come.

She glanced around desperately, looking for Jean. If she could just catch her eye …

'Apparently, the old lady, Ros's grandmother, the one who left her all the bling, wasn't helping matters any in that department, either. According to Miranda, she'd been encouraging Ros to divorce him for years.'

'Well, you can hardly blame her for that, can you? She probably wanted grandchildren, poor thing. I've got three myself, and wouldn't be without them.'

Effie bit back a whimper. She couldn't see Jean or Malc anywhere, and the only other members of the C-Fits nearby were Corwin and Zoe. And she couldn't hope for rescue there. Even if she did manage to catch their attention and indicate she needed rescuing, she didn't think Zoe would bother. It was becoming more and more clear with each time they met, that the younger girl simply didn't like her.

Effie wondered if it could possibly be true that the weather girl actually thought of her as some sort of threat. But that was absurd….

'I haven't got any myself yet,' the conversation in front of her went painfully and remorselessly on, taking on a rather nightmarish quality now. 'None of my three seem serious yet about settling down. Oh, poor Ros. If I were her, I'd get pregnant whether he liked it or not. There's nothing like carrying a child ...'

That's it, Effie thought. I simply can't stand this a moment longer. And then, just as she was about to step boldly out of the shrubbery and push past the two gossiping women, help came from an unexpected quarter.

Ros herself suddenly appeared, smiling widely and bearing a tray full of delicious little mini nibbles of the sweet variety.

'Babs, Nancy, you have to try these mini-cheesecakes and tell me what you think.' Her eyes flitted past them to Effie, abruptly cutting short her hopes that she'd gone unseen. 'Careful mind, they're really moreish. I haven't been able to eat just one ever since I got the recipe.'

As the two women hastily took one each, Ros turned and pointed towards the far end of the garden. 'I think Vince and Ewan are looking for you.'

'They probably think we're going to go and get them more beers,' the dark haired woman said with a laugh. 'That's husbands for you.'

'Lazy swines, both of them,' her friend agreed, but together the two women ambled away.

'It's OK, you can come out now,' Ros said with a brief smile, and Effie, feeling foolish, drifted free of the shrubbery. 'Are you all right? You look very pale,' her hostess said, and Effie shook her head.

Quickly, Ros took her arm and looking around, neatly and unobtrusively led her to the nearest chair – one of those ubiquitous, white moulded plastic chairs that seemed to multiply at garden parties. Set up in the shade of a neighbour's over-hanging cherry tree, it was just what she needed.

Thankfully Effie sank down and Ros pulled up another chair to sit beside her. Her hostess smiled and raised a glass at a passing friend, and Effie was relieved to realize that nobody was staring at them. And that thanks to Ros's quick thinking, she hadn't disgraced herself after all.

'Bit too much sun? Or was it the punch?' Ros asked sympathetically. 'I told Clive not to make it so strong.'

Effie laughed hollowly. 'Actually it was neither,' she said, and then could have kicked herself. Why hadn't she just said something rueful and pretended to be a little squiffy? As an explanation it was by far preferable to the truth.

And for a brief, hysterical moment, Effie wondered what Ros would say if she did just blurt out the truth. That her distress had been caused because two women had been talking about the joys of having children, when she herself couldn't conceive.

It had been quite early in their marriage when Effie became aware of her problem. She'd always wanted a family, and Michael had agreed that, given the age difference, it would probably be a good idea for them to have a baby sooner, rather than later. He didn't, he'd said with a smile, want to be in his dotage whilst dandling a baby on his knee.

And Effie had eagerly agreed. She'd stopped taking contraception right away and began to watch the calendar carefully, at first fully confident that it wouldn't take long. After all, they were both fit and healthy people.

But nothing had happened.

After a year, Michael, rather thin-lipped, had taken the decision to have some tests done. Effie could still remember the look on his face the day he came home with the results, to tell her that he had checked out fine. It was a mixture of relief, guilt, and worry. Relief, of course, because no man's ego or libido could easily cope with the idea of infertility. Guilt, she also understood, because after feeling triumph at having had his manhood proved beyond doubt, it was now obvious that the fault must lie with her, and that, somewhere deep inside, he was glad that it did.

And worry, of course, over how she would cope with this knowledge.

In the circumstances, she'd always thought that she had coped rather well. She'd had tests of her own done, of course – far more extensive and intrusive tests than those that Michael had had to endure. And when the sympathetic doctors had told her that there was nothing to be done – no surgical procedures that would help, and that IVF would be pointless, she'd told everyone that she would be fine.

Her parents had been supportive but bitterly upset, of course. As their only child, they'd been relying on her to produce grandchildren. But her mother especially had been worried about her, and had kept a very close eye on her for years afterwards.

The doctors had recommended counselling, but she'd not felt comfortable with that. And Michael had treated her like a china doll for nearly a year before she'd finally persuaded him she was not made of glass.

No matter how brittle she had felt at the time. And sometimes, still did.

But then, as you have to do after life had given you a knock, she'd managed to shrug it off and get on with things. What other choice was there? So she'd assured both herself and Michael that she was fine, and that, since there would be no children, she'd simply devote herself to her career instead.

So she'd taken some night classes in architecture, the better to understand her husband's business and what he did. She'd also gone on to take the top secretarial courses on offer, and thus became qualified to become not only her husband's secretary but also his PA.

They'd discussed adoption, of course, but in the end, had decided against it. Because Effie knew, deep in her heart, that Michael, if he couldn't have children of his own, wouldn't want to raise someone else's. There had always been a sort of fastidiousness to his nature that she found both irritating and, in some profound way that she'd never fully understood, also endearing.

Even though the injury had been done to her, it left her feeling as if she was the one who needed to take care of *him.*

Gradually, over the years, the fact that she was barren got pushed to the background of her life. And whenever it raised its ugly head, she simply told herself repeatedly that it didn't matter. After all, the world was so grossly over-populated already, wasn't it? Nowadays, women hardly needed to be mothers in order to justify themselves or their place in the world. Right? Michael had never made her feel less of a woman because of it. Not once had he ever indicated that he felt cheated or robbed in marrying her.

Which had only served to make her love him more.

And after nearly twenty years now of living with it – and especially since losing Michael – she'd thought that the fact that she couldn't have children was all done and dusted. Irrelevant. Something that didn't even impinge on her existence any more.

But it only took two complacent women, gossiping spitefully about their friend and neighbour, to show her how wrong she was.

'Effie?'

Effie quickly looked up as Jean Bossington-Smith drew a chair up on the other side of her. And as she did so, she noticed the ex-schoolteacher glance at Ros questioningly, and could only wonder what their hostess was signalling back.

Really, this wouldn't do. She had to pull herself together and fast.

'Hello, Jean. I think I've been overdoing it a bit,' she said, with a slightly wobbly smile.

'Yes, I'm feeling a bit faded myself,' Jean responded quickly. Which was obviously a lie. The older woman looked as indomitable and indestructible as ever.

'I'd better go and see if Clive's managed to avoid incinerating the chops again, like he did last year,' Ros said diplomatically, and got up to see to the rest of her guests.

Effie slowly shook her head.

'What's wrong?' Jean asked softly. 'You look, if you'll pardon the expression, as if you've seen a ghost.'

And in spite of herself, Effie had to laugh. And then, to her horror, she heard herself say, 'Oh Jean, I can be such a liability sometimes.'

'Rubbish,' Jean said bracingly.

Effie smiled weakly and slowly leaned back in the chair. Thankfully, the awful light-headedness had gone, and even the weak feeling in her knees was beginning to wear off. She still felt slightly sick though, and suddenly realizing that she was still holding on to her plate of salad as if her life depended on it, deposited it gently on the ground beneath her chair.

Somewhere behind her, she heard Zoe laugh happily, and heard Corwin's voice say something laconic in response. All around her, people were eating and drinking and having a nice time.

'Jean, I've been meaning to ask you. Just how did you come to join the C-Fits?' Effie asked. What she needed now was some ordinary conversation, something to take her mind off what a fool she'd nearly made of herself. And Jean, bless her, seemed to understand her need for normalcy.

'Oh, it was nothing dramatic, I'm sorry to say,' she began dryly. 'So if you're hoping I'm going to regale you with some gothic story of seeing something nasty in the woodshed, I'm afraid you're in for a disappointment.'

Effie smiled. 'You don't have to tell me if you'd rather not.'

'Oh, I don't mind,' Jean said amiably. 'I suppose it all began with my mother. Now that sounds a bit dramatic – I didn't mean it to. I had a very normal childhood! Anyway, I knew I'd always wanted to be a teacher, so when I finished my A-Levels and got my degree, I went straight on to teacher training college. One day I went home in the summer vacation for a bit of a family get-together – you know what I mean. A proper cooked Sunday lunch and a bit of cosseting. So I arrived with a pile of dirty washing, and looked forward to some of Mum's apple pie.'

'Sounds lovely.'

'Oh, it was. I used the washing machine, and gobbled up the roast beef and Yorkshire pud, and all that – just good, normal stuff. But I noticed that Mum seemed a bit … off.' Jean gave a brief shrug. 'Sort of distracted and a bit shamefaced. And I noticed that Dad would sometimes look at her and grin, like he always did when he knew something that I didn't. So, naturally, I demanded to be let in on the joke. And that's when Dad said that Mum had seen a ghost.'

Effie shifted in her chair a little, in order to watch her more closely. 'Really? And what did you say to that?'

Jean smiled. 'What you'd expect me to say, I suppose. What anyone would say. I demanded to know the details. She didn't really want to say at first – I suppose she felt a bit silly. But in the end I persuaded her to come out with it, as you do. And it seems that Mum had gone to my nan's grave to lay flowers and tidy up, as she did every fortnight or so. And when she'd got up from clipping the grass, she saw a man, about two rows down, standing by another grave. Naturally, she'd simply assumed that he was another relative, making a visit to his own loved one. But, and this is where Dad began to smile even more like a loon, Mum swears that, when she bent down to pick up the dead flowers and then looked up again, he had vanished.'

'Ah,' Effie said. 'And he couldn't have just walked off? Or went behind a tree or something?'

'Mum said not. She said the churchyard was deserted and that there were no trees or anything nearby. And that, for the man to have just walked away and vanish without her catching sight of him, he'd have had to sprint as if he'd been rocket-propelled.'

'So what did she do?' Effie asked, beginning to get drawn into the tale. Which was just what she needed, of course.

'Well, after looking around her for a while and trying to catch a glimpse of him and failing, she went over to the grave where he'd been.'

'And?'

'It was the grave of a woman, with one of those older stones that have lovely old-fashioned inscriptions on them. Apparently she'd been a "spinster of the parish" who'd died at the age of twenty-one.'

'Oh no. I hate it when they die so young,' Effie said.

Jean nodded. 'I know. Me too. Anyway, Mum came home and told Dad, who laughed at her, of course. And then Mum laughed too. After she told *me* all about it, we just let the subject drop. I could see Mum was embarrassed by it. But she continued to be sort of thoughtful and distracted all that weekend.'

'And what did you do?' Effie pressed.

Jean looked at her, one eyebrow slowly rising. 'I did nothing, of course. Except go back to college, then spend the next forty years teaching all manner of children all kinds of things about world geography.'

Effie laughed. 'Sorry, Jean, I was being rather fatuous, wasn't I?'

What had she expected? That Jean would have instantly done some research on the occupant of the grave, found out all about her, and discovered that some lovesick swain had romantically died of a broken heart after losing her? And who now, according to local legend, was seen visiting her grave and grieving, before vanishing into thin air?

But that sort of thing only happened in Gothic novels. Not in real life.

'I know, it's all very unsatisfactory.' Jean's eyes twinkled as she regarded her. 'But actually, that's where it all began for me. For all the years I worked at various schools, I often thought about that story, and the more I thought about it, the more it intrigued me. Because I knew Mum wasn't lying – why would she? There was nothing in it for her. And if she'd been one of those sort of people who like to make things up in order to be the centre of attention, she would have made the story far more elaborate. Besides, I just knew that she wasn't like that. And she *had* been genuinely puzzled and even slightly annoyed about it. More importantly, I reasoned, how *exactly* could she have been mistaken in what she'd seen? It's not as if there was an obvious explanation for it. I even went to the churchyard myself once, going through the same routine as Mum had. And it was just like she said. There was no way anyone could have gone out of sight so quickly, even running flat out. It only takes two or three seconds to bend down and pick up some dead flowers, after all. No matter how slowly you do it!'

'I can see how puzzling that must have been,' Effie agreed.

'Hmmm,' Jean said briskly. 'But there wasn't much I could do about it, was there?' she added with a wry smile. 'After all, that sort of interest in ghosts and the paranormal wasn't something that I could openly admit to in my line of work. If my colleagues didn't start looking at me cross-eyed, you could bet that the headteacher would have something to say about it. Not to mention the parents! And as for what the children themselves would have made of it,' Jean laughed with a mock shudder, 'the little monsters would have made my life a misery. Miss Spooky Smith! Forget it!'

Both women laughed.

'No, it was only *after* I'd retired that I was finally free and able to indulge my curiosity in ghosts,' Jean continued. 'So I did some research on the subject. Some of it was fascinating, but some of it downright daft in my opinion. But I *did* come across Corwin's books and articles and when I learned that he was local, I wrote to him, explaining my interest. I didn't really expect a response from him. My credentials, as it were, were hardly impressive, were they? But to my surprise, he invited me on a vigil, and I met Malc and Lonny and three others who have now since left. Gisela and Mickey joined after I did. And that was that. I've been with the C-Fits ever since. And a grand bunch they are.'

'Have you ever regretted it?' Effie asked curiously.

'Not once,' she said quickly and definitely. 'It's given me something fascinating to get my teeth into, and stopped me from becoming a lonely old crone. Besides, Corwin's a dedicated researcher and it makes me feel useful again to be able to help him. And Malc and Lonny are like me, genuinely curious about what might be out there to discover.'

She didn't mention Mickey, but Effie had the feeling that she was hoping that Mickey's somewhat wearing enthusiasm would soon fade, as had the enthusiasm of others before him, and that he might drift away from the group before his studies were over.

Or was she the only one hoping that, and she was projecting her own wishful thinking onto others, she wondered with a wry sigh.

'And Gisela?' she asked carefully.

Jean looked at her thoughtfully. 'Gisela is a lovely girl.'

Effie nodded, but couldn't bring herself to actually ask the retired schoolteacher whether or not she believed Gisela to be an authentic 'sensitive'. That would have been impolitic.

'And does Zoe believe in ghosts?' Effie heard herself ask, and then wished she hadn't.

Zoe Younger was strictly none of her business.

'She says she does,' Jean said blandly, starting to rise to her feet. 'And she's certainly very supportive of Corwin's career. He does, after all, earn a very good living from the books and television,' she added, somewhat ambiguously.

Once on her feet, Jean stretched discreetly and glanced around. The garden was beginning to look crowded, and as the wine flowed more copiously, the noise level began to rise. Effie, now that she was beginning to feel better, supposed she should once more join the fray.

Luckily, when she stood up, she felt fine.

She was about to suggest to Jean that they go and find Ros, so that Effie could thank her for her kindness, when a large, rather fleshy man with a mop of shaggy blonde hair that was fast turning salt-and-pepper, moved up towards them.

'Hello. Someone pointed out you two ladies as belonging to this ghost hunting bunch staking out my mother's house. I'd like a quick word, if you don't mind,' he added, a shade aggressively, Effie thought with some dismay.

Beside him, a very thin woman with short, reddish-brown hair and wide hazel eyes regarded them with a look that also verged on vague hostility.

Effie's heart sank a bit. The last thing she needed now was more aggravation.

'Monty Watkins.' The big man thrust out his hand and took Jean's hand in what looked like a crushing grip. 'This is my wife Celia. So what sort of nonsense exactly has poor old Izzie been filling your minds with, hmmm?'

CHAPTER TEN

Effie felt Jean tense beside her, and had to bite back a smile. She rather thought that Claudia's son and heir was about to discover that this conversation wasn't going to go quite as he might have expected.

'Isabel?' Jean said with exquisite politeness. 'Yes, what a very fine lady she is. She *is* your sister, I take it?' Her tone indicated quite clearly that she had severe doubts about whether such a boor as Monty could possibly claim kinship with such a paragon, and as Effie watched, she could see Monty Watkins's spine slowly straighten up and come to attention.

And she didn't blame him. Jean hadn't been a schoolteacher for forty years without learning how to put real steel in her voice. The look on her face, calm, slightly supercilious and politely curious, was enough to make anyone quail.

No doubt the middle-aged man in front of her was being instantly transported back to his schooldays, when teacher definitely knew best, and misbehaved or rude boys had better watch their Ps and Qs.

'Er, yes, my little sister,' he mumbled, reddening slightly.

Jean nodded. 'Lady Cadmund has been most gracious in letting us investigate your grandmother's house for detectable phenomenon,' she deigned to say, with a wintry smile. 'So far we've found two instances that call for further research, though we are hopeful of finding more.'

'Oh. Right,' Monty said, his voice clearly sounding as baffled as he now looked.

'Oh, for pity's sake.' It was, predictably, his wife Celia who spoke, her voice impatient and slightly high-pitched. And it was immediately clear to Effie, that whilst her spouse might have been reduced to the consistency of a wet lettuce leaf by Jean, she wasn't made of such lily-livered stuff. 'You're talking about some ridiculous cold air in the bathroom, and smelling lavender. It's hardly anything to write home about it, is it? Isabel's been going on and on about it until we're all sick and tired of hearing it. Aren't we, Monty?'

Even given the fact that the woman was clearly irritated, there was something whining and insistent in her tone that instantly grated on Effie's nerves. And her voice seemed pitched slightly too high to sit easily on someone with such a sour appearance.

And Effie found herself, unexpectedly, feeling suddenly sorry for Isabel's big brother.

Clearly, Celia wasn't going to be intimidated by an older woman with better manners than her own, and had no difficulty in making her displeasure clear. In fact, Effie could well imagine that Celia had probably been a horror at school as well, and had probably delighted in thwarting her teachers and acting up. Something that Jean sensed too, since she barely glanced at her, choosing instead to keep her stern eye on Monty.

Celia looked to be a good few years younger than her husband, and was obviously attempting to look even younger still. She was stick-thin, with the body of one dedicated to exercise and dieting, and was wearing a trouser suit in mint green that had probably cost a mint as well. Her short hair had been cut in a stylish bob, and careful highlights occasionally caught the sun. Her make-up was thickly but expertly applied and she had a big, sparkling ring on nearly every finger of every hand. Precious gemstones sparkled whenever she moved them. Her eyes were narrowed in growing temper.

'I really don't know what got into Izzie, asking strangers to come prodding and poking into our private family business. I told her no good would come of it. Especially when it's quite clear to everyone that it's just Izzie making a silly fuss, like she always does.'

'You don't think there could be something in it?' Effie put in, more to stop the flow of censure than because she was interested in anything the woman might have to say.

'Of course not! It's all rubbish,' Celia predictably shot back.

'You don't believe that your mother-in-law may not be resting in peace, Mrs Watkins?' Jean asked casually.

Celia surprised them all by suddenly smiling. Even if a shade grimly. 'Now don't go putting words in my mouth. If anyone were likely to carrying on causing trouble even after they were dead and gone, then it would be my mother-in-law Claudia.'

That was becoming so common a refrain that Effie barely paid it any attention. So the recently deceased old woman had had a strong, pugnacious personality. So what? Did everyone really think that you needed to be particularly bloody-minded in order to be able to come back as a ghost?

In which case, she could take it for granted that she was unlikely to come across any gentle spooks with a sweet nature! Effie, aware that she was letting her whimsical thoughts get away from her again, abruptly forced herself to focus on the conversation going on around her.

'But not even I think that Claudia would be able to cheat death,' Celia swept on. 'Which probably came as a real shock to the old bat! So no, I don't think there's "anything spooky" going on,' she said, using her fingers to make little quote marks in the air. 'I think Izzie's just been imagining things and is putting two and two together and coming up with five, as usual. Either that or she's just trying to delay probate just to spite us.'

'Now hang on, Celia,' Monty said sharply. 'I've told you before, these things always take time. It's nothing to do with Isabel how long it takes. It's that old buffer of Mum's solicitor who is dragging his feet for some reason.'

His wife shot him a quick, fulminating glance, and Jean caught Effie's eye. Quickly, both women looked away so as not to burst into embarrassed laughter, because Effie had no doubt that they were both thinking the same thing. Clearly Monty's wife was so keen to get her hands on her late mother-in-law's money that having to wait for it was beginning to seriously chaff.

'Oh, don't mind me,' Celia said, with a laugh so false it was almost painful to hear. Clearly she'd had second thoughts about arguing in front of the hired help, as it were. 'I'm off to find a drink. Monty, do you want another Pimms?' she offered aggressively.

'Yes, thanks, old girl,' Monty said, more, Effie thought, to get rid of her, then because he wanted a top up.

When she was gone, he smiled at them both a shade uneasily. 'Don't mind Celia. She's had a lot to put up with over the years, you know. Mother was never an easy sort to get along with.'

Effie wasn't at all convinced that Celia had had a particularly hard life, but wasn't about to say so. 'Her relationship with your mother was a bit strained, I take it,' she contented herself with saying diplomatically instead.

'Like I said, Mother had her little ways, you know. And the older people get, the more, er, difficult, they can become, don't you find? And she could be … insensitive at times,' Monty admitted stiffly. 'But look, I really do want to know how much longer you people are going to be … well, doing whatever it is that you're doing.'

'Why?' Jean asked bluntly. 'Is there a problem we should know about?'

Such a frontal and blunt attack clearly took the other man by surprise, because for a moment, he just boggled at Jean like a goldfish. Finally he managed to gulp and pull himself together.

'What? No, not really. Of course not – I mean, why should there be?' he blustered. 'Everything's all above board and all that.'

And Effie felt her heart skip a little beat at that. Why had he put it like that? That everything was above board? When someone said that, it immediately made you wonder why it wouldn't be. And also served to put the suspicion in your mind that the person saying it didn't actually believe it, either. So just what was it that Monty Watkins had in the back of his mind? What did he think *might* be wrong?

An old lady with a known heart condition dies. Alone, at night.

A very wealthy woman, a sardonic voice piped up in the back of her mind.

And one member of the family goes against everyone's wishes

and calls in a paranormal research team, because she's been having dreams where her dead mother is trying to tell her something. And odd, inexplicable things have started to happen.

So was there more than just greed behind Monty and Celia Watkins's desire to have the house sold and the inheritances dished out as soon as possible? Were they in fact scared that the C-Fits might stumble on something else, some other truth about the Watkins family, that didn't involve ghosts?

Oh, don't be ridiculous, Effie told herself, seeing all too well where her wild conjecturing was taking her. It was just too silly even to contemplate. She was beginning to let her imagination run riot. She was not, for pity's sake, in some grown-up version of an episode of *Scooby-Doo*, where villains masquerading as ghosts went about, using a haunting as a cover for some other nefarious business!

But if she were, she'd rather like to be Daphne! The impish, childish voice in the back of her mind almost made her laugh out loud. Then, the desire to giggle abruptly passed as another thought followed quickly on.

If anyone in the C-Fits were qualified to be the beautiful, glamorous Daphne, it would be Zoe. Not her.

'We just want to get the place shipshape as soon as possible so that we can sell it,' Monty continued stoutly, his harsh voice mercifully breaking into her increasingly out of control thoughts. 'And we don't want any silly rumours about it being haunted getting around. Such things can affect property prices, you know,' he said huffily. 'People can be so silly about that sort of thing.'

And to be fair, Effie supposed he might have a point there. 'You haven't considered living in the house yourself then?' she asked him, genuinely curious now. 'It's such a fine place, after all. And your wife struck me as the kind of lady who would appreciate quality,' she added, a shade mischievously.

Beside her, she heard Jean muffle a snort.

'Celia would rather … Er, neither Celia nor I would feel quite right about living in Mother's old house,' Monty began stiffly. 'Too many memories, and that sort of thing,' he added gruffly. 'No, give us a modern build any day. Eco efficient and what not. Got to be green in this day and age, haven't you?'

At this, even Effie's eyes widened a little in disbelief. If this man gave a hoot about saving the environment, she was the sugar plum fairy.

So again – why didn't he want to live in his mother's house? Was he, in spite of all his bluster, scared of ghosts after all? Had he or his awful wife done something that would make his mother want to come back and haunt him?

'Well, you really need to speak to Corwin about how long we'll be running our investigations,' Jean said, pointing towards where Corwin and Zoe were now standing in the middle of the lawn, chatting to a couple around their own age. 'He's the head of our organization.'

'Oh, right,' Monty said, and with barely a grunt goodbye, he began to march purposefully across towards them.

'Now don't you feel a bit guilty, passing him on to Corwin?' Effie asked Jean, her voice rich with suppressed laughter.

'Not a bit of it,' Jean said crisply. 'Corwin will soon sort the old windbag out. And if he doesn't, Zoe will quickly wrap him around her little finger. What a ghastly person he is! And that wife of his is no better. You ask me, they're well matched, those two.'

'Now, now,' Effie said, ever the peacemaker. 'Oh, look, there's Isabel and Jeremy. Let's go and say hello.'

The barbecue began to wind down around six o'clock, and the C-Fits regrouped in a neighbouring village where the pub had come highly recommended. Sited on the Oxford canal, with the sun slanting through some weeping willow trees, Effie could easily see why. The wooden tables with affixed benches were grouped in a large, attractive garden, and on the khaki-coloured water of the canal, a flotilla of disinterested mallards swam past. Malc threw them a few crisps from his packet, which went largely ignored.

'So, I think that all went very well,' Duncan said now contentedly. 'They're a very nice couple. Isabel and Jeremy, I mean,' he clarified.

'We didn't think you meant Monty and Celia,' Zoe said waspishly, and everyone laughed.

'At least we were able to put most of their minds at ease,' Corwin said, sipping from a half pint of cider. He was leaning back in his chair, his face tipped up to catch the last rays of the evening sun, and he looked as boneless and indolent as a cat. 'I think Clive Carteret was convinced that we were a bunch of con artists out to fleece the family coffers. I had to tell him a number of times, and in front of witnesses, that the C-Fits didn't charge for our services.'

'That one,' Gisela said darkly, 'is only interested in one thing. Money. His aura is … Ugh!' She shuddered theatrically.

'Well, his company builds houses,' Debbie said mockingly, reaching across and taking her lover's hand in a teasing grip. 'Throw 'em up fast and cheap, then sell 'em for a mini-fortune. That's his mantra. And everyone knows that houses in Oxford and the surrounding area are now as expensive as property in London. Which means there's a fortune to be made in real estate right now. So what else did you expect him to be interested in?'

'I'm just saying – he's got a really dark aura,' Gisela said pertly. 'I tried to warn him that he needed to start thinking about karma and all that, but I don't think he could have cared less.'

'No, he wouldn't,' said Malc, and something in his tone made everyone turn and look at him curiously. Noticing, he gave a self-effacing smile and a shrug. 'Sorry, but in our trade, you get to hear things.'

'Oh, yes. *You're* a builder too, aren't you?' Duncan said. 'Ever work for Clive's company?'

'No, I'm glad to say,' Malc said shortly. 'Luckily the construction industry's picking up – everyone wants new, affordable housing – so us tradesmen can now pick and choose who we work for.'

'And you don't want to work for Mr Carteret?' Jean put in curiously.

Malc shook his head firmly. 'No, I heard on the grapevine that he's supposed to be a bit of a sod to work for. Doesn't give a toss for health and safety, and he isn't exactly clamouring to pay good wages, either. But most of all, I just don't like the rumours that are going around about him.'

'Now you can't say something as good and juicy as that and then leave it there,' Lonny teased him. 'Just what sort of rumours?'

Malc held up his hand, and rubbed his fingers together in a gesture that was instantly recognizable. 'His business runs on back-handers, doesn't it?'

'Don't they all?' Corwin put in, a shade cynically.

'Sure, a bit of that sometimes goes on,' Malc said. 'Not surprising really. Councils have to build a certain amount of houses to meet government quotas but local residents don't want them in their back yard – typical NIMBY-ism. It stands to reason, something's gotta give. But our Mr Carteret is a master of it – and some say he doesn't just stoop to bribes, either, but is willing to do whatever it takes. Blackmail, a bit of intimidation even, or so I've heard.' He paused to take a gulp of his beer as everyone looked at him in dismay. 'Mind you, nothing's ever been proved or gone to court, anyway. So it could be that it's just his rivals bad-mouthing him. Let's just say that he always manages to find a way of gaining planning permission that other contractors can't, if you know what I mean. Take this latest proposal of his, to build that small estate a couple of miles from Adderbury. Practically on green belt. If there wasn't something very dodgy going on there, then I'm a monkey's uncle.'

Effie frowned. 'Didn't someone say that Claudia was very angry about that?'

'She probably was,' Jean said. 'From what we know about her, it was the sort of thing that would probably rile her. Old people don't like change, and the idea of having so many new houses built within sight of her lovely old house would have been bound to upset her.'

'And it couldn't help that it was her own grandson-in-law who was busily shovelling council members and planning officers into his back pocket,' Lonny mused.

For a moment everyone was silent, and then Gisela sighed. 'See. I told you he had a dark aura.'

'Another round?' Duncan asked mildly, adroitly drawing a line under the subject. 'Effie, let me get you something a bit stronger than bitter lemon. You're not driving, after all.'

Effie shot her old friend a knowing look. Was he really trying that oldest of old chestnuts on her, and trying to get her squiffy? If so, what on earth did he think was going to happen? That he would drive her home, and she'd be so intoxicated that the poor lonely widow would turn to him for comfort and a little physical intimacy?

As if!

'No, thanks, Duncan,' she said, giving him a gimlet glance.

Duncan's lips twitched and he sighed softly, silently acknowledging his culpability. And, typical of Duncan, looked both hangdog and contrite but fully confident that his charm would let him get away with it.

And it was only then that Effie, looking away, realized that Corwin was watching them closely. And that he'd clearly understood the silent by-play between them.

Or had he *misunderstood* it?

The thought that he might have, made her feel slightly sick. Did he think she might have been actually encouraging the hopeless reprobate?

For a startled second, as her eyes met his, she felt herself go pale. Then, before she had time to register any contempt or amusement that might be on his face, she turned quickly to Jean, her heart thumping uneasily in her chest.

'Jean was telling me earlier just why she joined the C-Fits,' she heard herself burble. 'But what about the rest of you? Gisela, I understand why you would be interested, but what's everyone else's story?' she asked, a shade desperately.

Hopefully, with someone else doing all the talking, she could start piecing back together what remained of her equilibrium.

'Corwin, why don't you tell her why you formed the C-Fits?' Jean said, unknowingly coming to her aid. 'And explain to the professor just why you got into the paranormal field in the first place.'

'Yes, you got a good literary degree, didn't you?' Duncan rejoined the conversation, as he returned with drinks. 'Presumably you could have done any number of things. Journalism, for instance?'

Corwin took a sip from his glass, then shrugged. 'Sure, why not? It's no big secret. But I should warn you, I have no blinding revelations to offer. Nearly everyone who works in this field has a similar story.'

But even as he spoke, Effie could sense the others stirring with interest, even though they must have heard it all before.

'"We plough the fields and scatter", perhaps?' Jean put in dryly.

'That's the one,' Corwin said, snapping his fingers with a smile. 'Never sang it before or since,' he confirmed without contrition, making the boss sigh elaborately and mutter underneath her breath something about falling education standards.

And Effie noticed that everyone had fallen silent and were listening intently, whilst Duncan was watching everyone else avidly, clearly having put his psychologist's hat on.

'Anyway, I'd just picked up another book,' Corwin took up the narrative again, 'when something moved over by the font. Naturally it caught my eye, and I looked up and saw this old man standing there, watching me. I could see him clearly – just like I can see any one of you now. He was wearing a black cassock and had a dog collar, so I just smiled vaguely at him and went on gathering more hymnals. The only thing that struck me at the time was that he wasn't the same vicar who'd given the service. But I didn't really think much of it. It wasn't as if I was in church often, and for all I knew, there was always a back-up vicar around, just in case.'

Effie smiled at the childish logic, and once again she heard Jean sigh heavily, making everyone else smile.

'So anyway,' Corwin said, giving Jean a wide grin, 'I took the books back to the vicar who was up at the front helping Brian bag the food up, deposited the pile on the front pew and went back for more. And the other vicar was gone – presumably out the door and off to wherever it was vicars went, whenever they weren't vicaring.'

Jean shook her head. 'You do that on purpose – don't think I don't know! Make up words, willy-nilly. It's a good job you don't do that in your books. Your publishers would soon haul you over the coals for it.'

'Yes, boss,' Corwin said meekly.

'Please, go on with your story,' Effie said quietly. 'That can't be all there is to it, obviously.'

'No,' Corwin said quietly. 'Well, after we'd finished in the church, Brian and me were invited back by the vicar's wife for some squash and cake – all very Enid Blyton. But, naturally, we didn't say no, since it was *chocolate* cake. So we all traipsed back to the vicarage, and when we went into this little parlour, I noticed all these photographs of past vicars that were hung up on the walls. And one of them was so old it was one of those sepia ones. And the man depicted in it was … Guess who?'

Zoe laughed softly. 'We hardly deserve a medal for guessing that, Corwin! Who else could it be?'

Corwin shrugged elaborately. 'Exactly. Well, I went over for a closer look, thinking I'd maybe got it wrong, but it was definitely him. I asked the vicar's wife who he was, and she pointed to the dates on the bottom of the photograph – and told me he'd been the vicar there during the First World War and had died in 1920. Of influenza.'

'That's not surprising. Millions died of the flu epidemic that swept through Europe after the Great War,' Jean put in, ever the teacher. 'In fact, more people died of the flu than in the war itself.'

'Couldn't you have seen a photograph of him somewhere before you went into the church?' Duncan asked, clearly determined to play devil's advocate. 'Not necessarily recently, but perhaps some time before, in a history lesson perhaps? And you'd forgotten about it until then, when your subconscious made the connection. Or you might even have come across a likeness of him in an old newspaper article, which you barely registered at the time. You'd be surprised how some things, especially images of people for instance, can stick in the memory and then suddenly resurface, seemingly out of the blue.'

Corwin looked at Duncan levelly and again shrugged. 'Of course it's possible,' he admitted readily enough. 'Though very unlikely. I wasn't much into history until well into my teens. When I was older, I researched him, naturally, and the reverend gentlemen concerned hadn't ever done anything noteworthy, so I can't see why he should have made any mark on local history. Or do anything to get his photograph taken by the local press. In fact, when I Googled him, very little came up. And I can assure you, I wasn't the kind of kid who went about reading old newspaper articles. Not when I was twelve, anyway.'

'And you're sure it was the same man that you saw in the church?' Effie asked.

Corwin nodded across at her. 'Positive. At the time,' he added, then grinned at Duncan. 'Of course, I'm sure the professor can tell you how time can warp your memory about certain events. And memories tend to fade. So naturally, as time passed, I could only become less and less sure about what it was that I'd actually seen. But that's a common problem we often come across when talking to witnesses who are telling us about events that happened many years ago. I can only say that the incident was so striking, *so real*, and so convincing to me *at the time* that when I grew up, there was never any doubt about what I wanted to do with my life.'

'And so far your career in the paranormal has been very good to you,' Duncan put in neutrally.

Which made Effie feel like kicking his shins under the table.

Not that Corwin needed defending, because the next moment he smiled just as neutrally back at the professor. 'Thankfully, just like you, Duncan, I can write a book that many people will pay to read. Which is more than enough to cover my bills, and allow me to continue my research.'

Effie promptly put a hand up to her mouth to hide a grin.

A hit. A palpable hit.

Beside her, and ever a good sport, Duncan began to grin widely. 'Touché. Oh, Margot had surgery today,' he said casually. And then, as everyone did an appalled double-take, added quickly, 'That is, she's the surgeon, she's not being operated on.'

'Margot's a heart surgeon at the John Radcliffe,' Effie quickly put in.

'Oh, I see,' Zoe said, as everyone wilted with relief. 'And, Effie, we all thought we'd get to meet Mr James at last. I know that Corwin especially was looking forward to it.' She cocked her head slightly to one side as she regarded Effie. 'Did he have to work as well?'

And as everyone looked her way, Effie felt the earth lurch beneath her feet.

They didn't know.

She swallowed hard as her mind did a little flip. How was it possible that they didn't know? Surely Duncan must have told them?

She turned to look at him, but it was only when he suddenly reached across and grabbed her hand in his in a hard, bracing grip that she realized that she must look a sight. She knew she must have gone deadly pale, because she'd felt the blood drain from her face. And no doubt some sort of gormless, clueless expression must be written clearly on her features for Duncan to look suddenly so concerned.

For a moment – just for one wild, insane moment – she wanted to pretend that, indeed, Michael had just been working, and was thus too busy to come with her that afternoon. And that, even now, he was back in his study at home, working over blueprints and waiting for her to come home.

But of course, the lie would be pointless. Even though some dark, atavistic part of her was telling her that it might be a good idea to just run with it. That it might be best, all around, if these people continued to think that she was happily married, and went home each day to a loving partner.

But of course, Duncan knew the truth, and …

'Effie are you all right?' It was Jean who asked the question first, her voice sharp with concern.

'Yes, Effie, you've gone awfully pale,' Gisela put in worriedly.

Effie took a deep, shaky breath. 'Yes, I'm fine,' she heard herself lie, and forced some sort of a smile onto her face.

She turned to look at Zoe first, since she was the one who'd asked the question, and for some reason, found that she was seeking out Corwin's face instead.

He was watching her intently, his green eyes darkening notably.

And then his eyes slowly drifted down.

When Effie, too, looked down to see just what it was that he found so fascinating, she noticed that Duncan was still holding her hand in support and encouragement.

Gently, but firmly, she pulled it away. And to Zoe, she said quietly but clearly, 'I'm afraid I lost my husband last year.'

CHAPTER ELEVEN

Later, after Duncan had dropped her off back home and gone back to his long-suffering wife, Effie lay in bed thinking.

About murder.

And she was thinking about murder, she freely acknowledged to herself, because it was better and safer than thinking about other things.

Like the look of pity in Corwin's eyes when he realized that she was a recent widow. The concerted rush of sympathy from the others, and the approving nod from Duncan, as if she'd finally passed some sort of test, and deserved a brownie point.

All of which made her squirm, for various different reasons.

So, all things considered, it was much easier to lie in her bed and contemplate murder instead. And Claudia Watkins's murder, specifically, since that was clearly what her subconscious had been mulling over. And probably had been for some time now, if the ease with which she was able to contemplate it now was anything to go by.

With a snort at her folly, Effie turned over in the double bed that still felt so weirdly empty without Michael's solid presence beside her, and determinedly closed her eyes. Only having to open them again moments later.

The thought simply wouldn't go away, teasing and tormenting her, and just daring her to bring it out in the open and seriously think about it. And as she lay, sleepless and uneasy, tossing and turning, she supposed that, as a mental exercise, it beat counting sheep.

So, OK, Effie thought wearily. *Let's play a game of "Indulge Effie's Paranoia".* What, exactly, did she have to go on? Well, Claudia Watkins had been a rich, cantankerous old soul, who argued with her family and staff, and no doubt had thought of herself as the local queen bee. And OK, so a lot of people had benefited from her death. Her son and his discontented wife got the house and half the fortune. Effie had no trouble in believing that Celia had made it very clear to her husband just how very much she was looking forward to getting her hands on it all.

But that hardly meant that Monty would murder his own mother, did it?

And Isabel and her husband might be in financial trouble too. Perhaps they might even have been facing the very real possibility of losing the family farm, and land that had been in Jeremy's family for generations. That might really sting. But could she honestly see either Isabel or Jeremy killing Claudia in order to hold on to their way of life?

The odious Clive Carteret might well be a ruthless businessman, and guilty of any amount of sharp practices. What's more, he'd been known to be at cross purposes with his grandmother-in-law over a proposal to build houses perilously close to her beloved home. And, possibly too, over the issue of whether or not he and Ros were ever going to give her grandchildren.

But it was a big step up from bribing council officials or planning officers, to murder.

And would Ros kill a grandmother that she was clearly fond of just to inherit a few baubles? Even if those baubles might – if sold – net her hundreds of thousands of pounds, and struck envy and malice into the hearts of her neighbours?

And don't forget the gardener, the mocking voice in the back of her head reminded her.

Oh yes. Mustn't forget poor old Geoff, who might have been forced to retire, if the old lady had gone on living. Now there was a motive for you!

With a grunt, Effie turned over in the bed again and Toad, who had been nestled into the small of her back, gave an elaborate, long-suffering sigh and repositioned himself with a small grunt of his own.

'Sorry, little lad,' Effie apologized softly.

And then frowned. A little niggle at the back of her mind was warning her that she'd forgotten someone. But who … Oh yes, the family solicitor. Effie remembered, as a little girl, her grandmother loving to watch those old Hollywood black and white movies made in the thirties, where rich relatives were often bumped off by the crooked family lawyer. Who, if she was remembering her cinematic plots correctly, had all been bilking the family estate for years, usually misappropriating funds and spending the ill-gotten gains on peroxide doxies and trips to Las Vegas.

Now, granted, she hadn't really taken to the somewhat oily Mr George Dix. But that hardly meant she could just go about impugning his character, either. Although, at the barbecue, Monty *had* intimated that, in his opinion, the solicitor was dragging his feet over probate. Mind you, he was hardly a reliable source of information!

Still, it was true that Claudia had at least been threatening to take her financial and business affairs elsewhere. And there might have been something behind that other than just her normal awkwardness and the delight she seemed to have taken in riling people. What if she had genuinely come to suspect something untoward about her once-trusted legal adviser?

Well, for sure, *she'd* never be able to find out anything about it if that were the case, Effie thought with a wry smile. She hadn't knocked around the world a bit for forty years without learning that professional bodies took care of themselves. Be they doctors, solicitors or Oxford Dons. And she certainly had no remit or excuse to go prodding about in Claudia's financial affairs.

Suddenly Effie began to giggle. At least Claudia hadn't employed a butler, so she knew that he didn't do it!

Slowly her mirth diminished and she felt a little tired, but when she tried to close her eyes and sleep, the events at the pub came flooding back over her again, and her heart began to race.

When she'd asked Duncan, on the drive back, why he hadn't

told Corwin that she was a widow, he'd said, quite reasonably, that he hadn't considered it to be any of Corwin's business. Nor, he'd reminded her gently, was it up to him to go spreading around details about her private and personal life to all and sundry that she might not want discussed.

She'd hardly been able to argue with that, had she? Even though she was getting more and more suspicious that Duncan was playing the arch manipulator again. She was already convinced that he'd asked her to join the C-Fits, not so much because he truly needed her to help to research his book, but because he wanted her to get out and about and meeting new people and having new experiences.

Which might be psychologically sound and a very good idea and all that, but it didn't mean that she appreciated being moved around like a pawn in a game of chess.

So she certainly didn't put it past her old friend to have deliberately kept quiet about her recent loss, knowing full well that at some point, she'd be forced to tackle the issue head on. And thus, face her demons?

Damn him.

Once again, she was sitting in that pub garden, her heart pounding, aware that Corwin Fielding …

No. No, no and again no. It was simply too humiliating to think about her growing attraction for him and she quickly and gratefully turned her thoughts back to murder.

That was *much* easier to deal with.

So, OK, she thought patiently. Let's just say, for the sake of argument, that Claudia *had* been murdered. That someone, for some reason, had decided to bump her off. And, if she was going to be *that* silly, Effie supposed crossly, she might as well go the whole hog and add the happenings at the house to the mix.

So. Suppose Claudia Watkins *was* trying to warn Isabel of this fact. (And as Gisela would more dramatically have probably put it, that was why her poor restless spirit was wondering around seeking justice.) Which would account for the reason why Isabel had begun having bad dreams.

Now at this point, Duncan would almost certainly point out

that it was perfectly possible that Isabel too, might have had just the same kind of doubts as Effie was having now about the manner of her mother's death. And that subconsciously, the dreams were her way of trying to work them out.

Why not? It made sense. Of a sort.

For the moment, she would ignore the cold spot in the bathroom and the scent of lavender. Since she didn't, as yet, have any rational explanations for them, it was pointless speculating about it.

OK. So, just for the sake of not having to resort to counting sheep, why not take it as a given that someone killed Claudia? And that the events at the house are somehow related. After all, Effie thought reasonably, perhaps that wasn't quite so wild a thought as all that. People *did* get murdered every day, somewhere in the world, didn't they? You only had to watch the news or read a newspaper to concede that. And rich people were killed for their money too. She could think, off-hand, of a number of modern cases where that had happened.

So, if Claudia *had* been murdered, Effie mused, indulging herself for the moment, there was surely one blindingly obvious question that she should now be asking herself. Namely – *how*? And perhaps, as a good addendum to that – *how had they got away with it so successfully*?

Ah yes, Effie, how indeed, she asked herself with a wry grin. For the facts were plain enough. Claudia had been an elderly lady with a known heart condition. And she had been found, by her daily help, collapsed beside her bed. Presumably, the daily had had a key to let herself in with, and the house had been securely locked up?

Effie didn't know. She could always find out, she supposed, since Isabel would be bound to know. But of course, she couldn't possibly ask her! Effie groaned. Some Miss Marple she would make! This was madness. She rolled over onto her side, once more apologized to her dog, and closed her eyes grumpily.

Of course, she could probably find out by asking someone else, the thought popped into her head helpfully. Everyone in the village would know all the gory details by now. Jasmine at the herbalist shop for instance, not to mention the nosy old lady with a taste for sweets.

OK, just suppose for argument's sake, that the house had been securely locked up for the night. Clearly there could have been no obvious signs of a break-in or someone would have noticed and called the police. So what did this prove? Nothing. The family probably all had sets of spare keys. And Claudia might well have been the kind who liked to sleep with her windows open, for fresh air. And unless the house had a burglar alarm (which Effie didn't think it did) then presumably, anyone reasonably agile and determined enough could have been able to sneak in, do the deed, and sneak out again without leaving any suspicious evidence behind.

But what deed exactly had they done? Claudia hadn't been bludgeoned, or shot, or stabbed. Colonel Mustard hadn't taken a lead pipe to her in the library.

Effie sighed and giggled again.

But still, the game she was playing was better than lying awake, obsessing about other things.

OK. So if Claudia *had* been killed, there was only one way it could have been done. Obviously. It had to be poison. The old lady must have been poisoned.

Effie was aware that, because her doctor had seen Claudia shortly before her death, that no post mortem had been deemed necessary. Indeed, her GP had presumably signed the death certificate without a single qualm. And why not? Claudia was in her eighties with a failing heart, and had clearly died of heart failure.

Unless she hadn't – unless someone had truly contrived to poison her.

Effie stared up at the ceiling and frowned. What did she know about poison? Nothing. What did she know about how a GP went about assessing cause of death? Nothing. What did she know about what tell-tale signs there might have been on the body if foul play had been employed? Again – nothing. If Claudia had been smothered by a pillow for instance, rather than poisoned, would there necessarily have been any bruising to alert a doctor that all was not well? Claudia was an old and, for all her cantankerous ways, probably a rather frail woman. She could have been overcome without putting up too much of a fight, surely?

Just thinking about all the possibilities was making Effie's head swim. What's more it was pointless. And becoming more and more silly.

Although she hated taking sleeping tablets, Effie finally admitted defeat, sat up and put on the lamp. Then she reached into the bedside table drawer for a small brown bottle and spilled two pills into the palm of her hand. Although her own GP had prescribed them for her after Michael died, she'd rarely used them, and the bottle was still half full.

Feeling a little shamefaced, she trotted to the bathroom, popped the pills into her mouth, turned on the cold tap, bent over and filled her mouth with water and swallowed. Relieved that they didn't stick in the back of her throat (she'd always had a little trouble swallowing pills), she went back to bed and lay back down in the darkness, waiting for them to work.

But even as she finally began to drift off to sleep, her mind was still obviously working furiously away. Because her last coherent thought was that, although she might not know much about how heart conditions worked, and what might cause death without any obvious signs, there was someone she could ask who would know all about it.

Someone, moreover, who was a GP herself, and would thus have a good insight into what Claudia's own doctor would have been thinking and doing.

Her friend, Penny Harris.

Extract from the journal of Corwin Fielding:

23 April: The barbecue at Aynho was a qualified success. At least we managed to win over most of Isabel's family to the idea of our continuing investigation into Claudia's case, with the possible exception of Monty Watkins and his wife Celia, and perhaps Clive Carteret. However, Rosamund was clearly pleased that we had made such a good impression on the friends and neighbours, and Malc even got an invitation from one of them, a Mr Tony Inkerman, to check out a deserted and derelict barn on his land that, local legend had it, was haunted. Naturally, Malc agreed that we'd be interested, although he told me afterwards that Tony himself had never 'experienced' anything in the barn, since he hardly ever went there. But when Malc managed to draw him out a bit more, Mr Inkerman admitted that, back in his father's day (c1940-55) a tramp had been found dead in the barn, presumably having died from old age, drink-related problems, or hypothermia. This clearly needs more research, and I'll ask Gisela if she would like to go there one evening and see what she can intuit.

After the barbecue, Professor Fergusson, Effie and the rest of us went to a pub for a drink, and during the course of the evening, we discovered that Effie has been recently widowed. Naturally, we were all very shocked and saddened by this news.

It also worries me slightly, as people who are grieving and still in mourning have obviously heightened emotional baggage to deal with, and aren't ideal candidates for the sort of work that we do at C-Fits. In fact, had I known this from the start, I might not have accepted Effie so readily into the team. Which is something that I suspect Professor Fergusson may well have been aware of. Although I have no proof that he deliberately kept this circumstance about Effie's recent loss from me, I do have my suspicions.

I also noticed that the professor seemed to be very attentive towards Effie. Although I believe I detected a certain amount of coolness and wariness on Effie's part that makes me think that she doesn't particularly welcome this.

Needless to say, we're all now concerned about Effie. Both Jean and Gisela especially have become very friendly with her, and will, of course, do their best to look after her when she's with us on vigils.

Lonny did take me aside after we left the pub and asked me if I thought that it was a good idea for a recently widowed person to be joining our team, echoing my own doubts about this. And I had to admit to him that I didn't think it was ideal, either.

But to be fair, so far, Effie hasn't exhibited any obvious signs of distress or of being under strain whilst with us. In fact, had Zoe not inadvertently uncovered the truth, I doubt that either I, or any of the others, would ever have guessed that Effie had recently undergone such a trauma.

What's more, she clearly has no intention of trying to use the C-Fits for her own personal agenda. But if, for instance, she were ever to approach Gisela and ask her to try and make contact with her deceased husband, then, naturally, I'd have to reconsider our position. At the very least it would be a massive conflict of interest and, to my mind, grossly unethical to undertake any investigation that involved a member of the team personally. But I really don't think that situation is likely to arise. There is an aloofness about Effie that is quite striking, and which tells me that she would be very unlikely indeed to want to involve anyone in her private life – especially relative strangers, such as ourselves. She also seems to me to be the type of person who keeps her emotions tightly under control.

Nevertheless, whilst I will do my best to make sure that Effie doesn't come to any harm, either physical, mental or emotional, whilst she's with us, neither is it fair that we be held responsible for her well-being.

At some point, I am going to have to have a talk with her about whether or not she really feels ready, given the circumstances, to carry on with us in our investigations. And if she decides to leave us, it will be very disappointing but understandable. We've all grown to like Effie very much, and under normal circumstances, I believe she could become a very valuable and respected member of our team.

But if she is certain that she wants to carry on, and convinces me that she is not putting herself under unnecessary pressure by taking on this new project at this particular time in her life, then I really can't see any good reason for asking her to leave.

I shall of course, have to discuss this further with the others, but I'm pretty sure that their joint thinking on this will run along pretty much the same lines.

But from now on, I shall be watching her closely.

'Are you serious?' Penny Harris asked, arrested in the act of stuffing a daffodil into one of Effie's best cut-crystal vases, and staring at her over a fistful of wallflowers.

Effie had invited her friend over for lunch, and whilst the Quiche Lorraine was cooking, she had lured her outside to help her pick some flowers for the table, hoping to lull her sharp-witted friend into a sense of false security before she started probing her for information. So far she'd managed to steer the conversation towards causes of death in the elderly and now on to what GPs were supposed to do if they had any suspicions about a patient's sudden demise.

But clearly she hadn't been as subtle as she'd thought.

'What?' she said now, all wide-eyed innocence.

'Don't give me all that "who, me?" nonsense, Effie James,' Penny said, arching one dark eyebrow ferociously. 'I know you too well. What's with all the questions? And don't try and fob me off with the excuse that we're just talking generally. Or that you're just being curious. It's clear you've got something specific in mind.'

'I don't know what you mean,' Effie said with a grin, and making no further attempt at concealment. Because clearly she'd been rumbled. Not that she'd ever expected to get away with it for long – Penny was far too smart for that. Besides, as she'd quickly discovered, it simply wasn't possible to get the specific answers to the questions she needed, without making it clear which way her mind was running.

'My eye, you don't!' Penny said, stuffing more daffodils willy-nilly into the vase, making Effie wince and surreptitiously rearrange them into a more pleasing alignment. 'Talking about heart conditions in general, you might have got away with.

And even, at a push, how often we GPs have had to sign death certificates. But when you start talking about poison …'

'I was only saying that isn't it interesting and a little scary, how so many garden plants are poisonous,' Effie said, her smile widening even further at her friend's sceptical look. 'And they are, aren't they?'

Penny shook her head, and reached for a bright red tulip. As Effie watched nervously, her friend eyed the vase and plonked it down at the back, not only where it couldn't be seen but where its large blowsy petals would soon open and get crushed.

'You might just as well come out and tell me what this is all about. I'm not feeding you any more information until you do,' Penny warned her as Effie rescued the tulip and put it in pride of place front and centre, where it deserved to be. 'And then you can feed me. That quiche smells like it's done and I'm starving. And if I'm going to have my brains picked without being paid for my expert time, I expect at least to be given a glass of wine with my lunch.'

'Deal,' Effie said quickly.

Soon the two women were seated at the table, eating their salad and drinking the promised wine, as Effie told her all about Claudia Watkins. Since she'd sworn to be discreet, she didn't go into details about the C-Fits or Corwin's investigation, which Penny didn't like at all. Naturally, she was more interested in ghost hunting than in old ladies dying of heart attacks.

But once she had finished explaining the circumstances of Claudia's death, Penny grew more serious and thoughtful.

'You think she might have been murdered, don't you?' her friend said flatly, making Effie look at her nervously.

The last thing she wanted was for her friends to start thinking she'd gone off her rocker. She already had Duncan keeping an underhanded eye on her mental state. She definitely didn't want another friend – and a GP friend at that – to start looking at her funny.

If she wasn't careful, she might find herself sectioned!

'Pen, I never said, that,' she began cautiously, but Penny held her hand up and stopped her before she could carry on.

'You don't have to be so defensive, Effie,' she said gently. 'I'm not going to tell you that you're being stupid or over-imaginative. I'm not Michael.'

'*What?*'

'Sorry,' Pen said at once, looking contrite. 'But he did tend to put you down … no, sorry, forget I said that,' she said and waved her wine glass gently in the air as a means of calling pax. 'Let's concentrate on your old lady, shall we?'

'She's not mine,' Effie said, choosing to ignore her friend's comment on her late husband. She'd become adept at avoiding thinking about things that upset her, finding it was by far the best way to get along. And she wasn't about to change the habit of a lifetime now.

'So, run me through the suspects and why it's led you to

thinking of foul play,' Penny said briskly.

So Effie did, listing all her suspects, motives and making light of her night spent playing Sherlock Holmes instead of sleeping. And she was genuinely glad to get someone with a mind like Penny's on board. Logical, clever, experienced and able to cut through all the extraneous stuff and get to the heart of the matter – if ever someone could show her how woolly-minded she was being, it was Pen.

'Hmmm. Well, it's intriguing, I agree,' Penny said, surprising her somewhat.

She'd expected her friend to be much more dismissive of her theories. 'But I don't quite see how I can help. I don't know what sort of heart condition Claudia had, so I can't tell you how likely or unlikely it is that she would have died suddenly. But if her GP signed off on it, I can promise you that he or she thought it was all clear-cut and above board.'

Effie nodded. 'Yes, I thought as much,' she agreed mildly. She hadn't exactly expected Pen to criticize her unknown colleague, after all. 'But, given the tremendous amount of pressure you doctors are under nowadays, what with so many patients to see and all the paperwork, and the pressure on you to keep people out of A & E and what have you. Isn't it just possible that … well …' Effie trailed off, trying to find a tactful way of putting it.

'You mean could the old lady's doctor have missed something due to being so tired or overworked? Or that he or she had simply been in too much of a hurry to get on to the next case, so they just signed off on it without bothering to be too diligent?' Penny asked dryly, then shrugged. 'Sure it's possible. But it's still unlikely.'

'And if she'd been smothered with a pillow, say, would there have been many outward signs of it?' Effie persisted.

Penny smiled around a forkful of iceberg lettuce. 'Probably. You've been watching too much television, Effie,' she warned her. 'It's harder to get away with murder than you might suppose.' Then she chewed, swallowed, speared a piece of cucumber, and added thoughtfully, 'Cyanosis would have been present, but then if the old lady had a heart condition, blueness to the lips wouldn't have been unexpected. But there would still have been a redness at certain points on the face. And no matter how old or frail you were, if you have your air supply cut off, you're going to struggle like crazy, so there would bound to be *some* bruising. And even if the bruises hadn't had time to become apparent at the time the doctor was called out, you could be sure that they would come out afterwards – overnight or one or two days later maybe. And by then the undertaker would have noticed and he would have called the police out pretty sharpish,' Penny added firmly. 'On the whole, morticians are a sharp and canny bunch, since they've seen it all. I had a friend in that business once and the tales he could tell ...' Penny caught her friend's horrified expression and abruptly stopped. 'No. Sorry!' she said with a shamefaced grin. 'On the whole, Effie, as entertaining as it might be to think that you've wandered into an Agatha Christie novel, I still think that it's highly unlikely that your old lady was murdered.'

Effie nodded with a sigh. 'Yes, that's what I thought too, deep down.'

Penny speared a tomato, then frowned at it. 'Mind you, having said all that, what you said just now about how many common or garden plants are poisonous, reminds me. Your old lady with a heart condition – the chances are that she was on some form of cardiac glycosides.'

'If you say so,' Effie said.

'Digitalasmin, digitoxin, digitalis, digitonin, gitoxin and gitalonin, that sort of thing,' Penny tossed off the complicated words with ease. 'What does that remind you of?'

'A big bowl of alphabet soup?'

Penny grinned. 'And if I were to say scrophulariaceae?'

'I'd say bless you and pass you a tissue.'

'Come on, Effie, think! What's growing in profusion on your back wall near the greenhouse?'

'Foxgloves,' Effie said promptly, then blinked. 'Of course. You get digi ... whatsits from foxgloves, don't you? I remember that, because a friend of Michael's had an irregular heart beat and he took ... digoxin, was it?'

Penny nodded. 'Exactly. The chances are your old lady was taking something provided by the good old foxglove. And like most medication, it's imperative that she had just the right dose. Too much, and the medicine becomes poison. Of course, that's only speculation,' she added primly.

But Effie had no patience with speculation right then. 'So if she were on some kind of digitalis, and she was somehow fed more of it, say from foxgloves, then it would cause her heart to stop?' she persisted.

'Whoa! Hold on a minute, not so fast.' Penny grinned at her. 'First of all, it's not as easy as all that. You can't just go into your back garden, pick some foxgloves leaves and then mush it down into paste and turn it into a liquid by pouring boiling water on it! Nobody in his or her right mind would drink it! For a start, it would taste foul! Nor could you just sprinkle the leaves into a salad and try to get it into somebody's system that way. The raw plant is an emetic.'

'A what-ic?'

'It would make you sick, and thus eject the poison before it could take effect,' Penny said succinctly.

'Oh,' Effie said, wishing she hadn't had a second slice of quiche.

'No, it would have to be distilled and refined,' Penny mused. 'That way, during digestion it would produce aglycones and a sugar. The aglycones would then affect the heart muscles, slowing the heart down. And acceleration of the heart ahead of this sometimes leads to it being wrongly said to increase the heart rate.'

Effie swallowed. 'Er, Penny, if you don't mind, I'd rather not have a medical lecture just now. Fascinating as it all is, mind.'

'Oh, sorry. I do that sometimes – go off on a tangent. I keep forgetting that not everybody speaks medicalese. Drives Patrick wild.'

Effie's sympathies, for once, were with Penny's other half. 'So, if I've got this right,' she set out clearly, 'Claudia was almost certainly taking some kind of digitalis-based heart pills. And if someone was able to distil and refine some plant material from any old foxglove growing in their garden, they'd be able to produce a poison capable of killing her?'

'Yes,' Penny said cautiously. 'But it would take some doing. You'd have to have some prior experience of that sort of thing or do your homework pretty thoroughly. You'd need to gain a fairly good knowledge of both chemistry, botany, and the distilling process – it wouldn't be something you could just do on the spur of the moment. You can't just make these things up as you go along! But even supposing you could make the stuff, and ended up with a little bottle of clear liquid, you'd still have to find a way of slipping it to the old lady,' Penny pointed out, 'and in a way that wouldn't make her suspicious. You couldn't just pour a bit in a cup of tea for instance. I'm no expert, but I'm pretty sure it would still be detectable to the taste. Your old lady would just spit it out, perhaps thinking the milk was off or something. I'm not so sure about food, though,' Penny mused, but by now Effie was barely listening to her. 'If you mixed it in with something really pungent, say curry, or …'

Her friend's words had by now receded into a vague hum as Effie sat staring down at her plate.

Because it had just occurred to her that she knew someone who would have had no trouble at all in making up such a concoction.

She would even have had the perfect method of delivering it too, and without incurring any risk to herself. What's more, Claudia would ingest it in a way that nobody would ever question or even think about – including Claudia herself.

The trouble was, the person Effie had in mind wasn't even on the list of potential murderers because she had no reason at all for wanting Claudia Watkins dead.

Did she?

CHAPTER TWELVE

Jasmine Carteret looked up as the bell over her shop door tinkled cheerily, and a bright smile crossed her face as she recognized Effie.

'Hello. Lily of the valley soap, wasn't it? How was it? No problems, I hope?'

'Oh no,' Effie said at once. She hadn't, in fact, used her purchases from Jasmine's shop yet, and now she wasn't sure that she ever would.

She entered rather nervously, and glanced around. 'I was looking for a birthday present for a friend,' she began with her pre-prepared lie. 'One of her favourite scents is sweet peas, but you never seem to see anything made out of them in the shops.'

'No, you won't,' Jasmine agreed. 'It's a very hard scent to replicate, perfume wise, and because it's so delicate, it doesn't translate so well into soaps and talcs, either.'

'Ah, that would explain it.' Effie nodded. 'And I don't suppose you have, er … managed to produce anything yourself?' she waffled on, wondering how on earth she was going to question this woman without Jasmine realizing what she was doing. It was all very well to acknowledge that Jasmine Carteret had both the know-how and the means of poisoning someone. It was another thing entirely to actually set about trying to determine whether or not she had.

'Oh no, I'm afraid not.' Jasmine laughed.

Today she was wearing a flowing caftan in crimson and emerald green, and when she laughed, her double chin wobbled alarmingly. With her bright friendly eyes and easy smile, she looked as harmless as a big, somnolent tabby cat.

'Much as I appreciate the vote of confidence in me, I'm not *that* good,' she said with a grin. 'We may have been taught the basics by Mum, and I've been in the business for twenty years now, but that doesn't mean that I can just conjure up whatever I might feel like. I'm not a world-class chemist – or an alchemist, come to that! Worse luck.' She sighed. 'Mind you, I suppose a thin, milk-like lotion might just be doable,' she carried on thoughtfully. 'And like you said, a lot of people *do* like the scent of sweet peas, so there'd probably be a good call for it. If—'

But the economical viability of a possible new range for the herbalist didn't interest Effie much. In fact, she was hardly listening at all now, for one thing that Jasmine had just said had reached out and grabbed her by the throat.

'We?' she echoed, interrupting her rudely in mid-flow. And when Jasmine broke off and looked at her, clearly puzzled, she said sharply, 'You said that "we" were taught by your mother?'

'That's right. Mum ran a shop much like this one in Harrogate when we were young,' Jasmine said. 'We grew up helping her out, mostly making the stock rather than serving in the shop.'

'I see, yes,' Effie said, a shade impatiently. 'When you say "we", you meant…?'

'Me and my brother Clive,' Jasmine clarified, sounding more than a little perplexed now. Whilst she was clearly the sort of person who was open and friendly and probably saw nothing wrong in happily chatting away about anything and everything, Effie was clearly making even Jasmine wonder where she was going with this.

Effie tried to relax a little. 'But he obviously didn't go into the family business, like you did?' She forced her voice to become light, and merely casually curious.

'Oh no. He quickly saw that there wasn't enough money to be made as a small independent trader.' Jasmine laughed. 'Even as a boy, Clive was more interested in the commercial and economical side of the business. Which suited me just fine – I was always more about making things. Which is why you've got me intrigued now about sweet peas.'

But Effie had no interest in sweet peas right then.

'But your brother helped out in the production side too?' she mused, and as Jasmine looked at her, clearly becoming more puzzled than ever, said hastily, 'The last time I was here you were telling me about how the St John's Wort pills were made. With gelatin and pill moulds? I found it all so fascinating. So I suppose that Clive would know how to do that too, would he?'

'Oh yes. Sometimes, if I've got a really big run of pills on, he'll still come over and give me a hand out back,' Jasmine said. 'Mind you, I don't ask him that often. He grumbles about it for days afterwards. Says I should expand and pay someone else to do the grunt work. I tell him he's missing the point, and that the real pleasure about running a small business like this is to be hands on. I don't *want* to be a big, money-worshipping corporation! But there's not much use arguing with him. I'm afraid my brother is wedded to Mammon.'

Effie smiled, and spotting an attractive glass jar filled with colourful bath salts, tied up around the lid with a beautifully executed ribbon bow, she quickly purchased it for her imaginary friend's birthday and after a few more minutes of idle chatter, made her excuses and left the shop.

But behind her, Jasmine watched her go with a thoughtful and still faintly puzzled look on her face.

Effie wandered slowly across the village green, her mind racing. On the one hand, her conversation with Jasmine seemed to have bolstered her hypothesis about the way that Claudia Watkins might have died. And yet, she didn't see how it really mattered. It was all pointless speculation, after all, wasn't it?

What had started out as a game, designed to help her pass a bad night, didn't really amount to anything. How could it?

Briefly, very briefly, she flirted with the idea of going to the police. But just a few moments' thought about that quickly had her changing her mind. After all, Claudia's death had never even been regarded as suspicious. Her own doctor had been satisfied, and had signed off on her death certificate without a qualm. And Effie wasn't even a member of the family. So just supposing that she went to the police station and told them that she was part of a team investigating a possible 'haunting' in the house where an elderly lady had recently died. Right from the moment that she opened her mouth, she'd be held in derision. Or regarded as a crackpot. Or worse! And she doubted very much that pointing out how many people had gained by Claudia's death would impress them much, either. After all, family inherited stuff from their deceased relatives all the time. And so what if Clive Carteret would have known how to distil some form of digitalis from foxgloves? And could he have made a batch of fake St John's Wort pills in his sister's laboratory one night when she was out? And, as he had access to the house, he could easily have switched them with Claudia's original bottle. What did any of that actually prove?

No. It sounded fantastic and convoluted, even to Effie.

Just the thought of the look of amusement or impatience on some disinterested police officer's face made her shudder in embarrassment. It was one thing to talk of such things to Penny, but even that had made her feel slightly foolish. And Penny had more or less scoffed at the idea of someone getting away with murder anyway.

It was just that she kept on feeling obliged to do something about it. It was the same instinct you had when you were driving along the road and noticed a car had run into a ditch. It looked deserted, and you *were* almost sure that nobody could possibly be lying injured or hurt inside. That someone else must surely have witnessed the accident and called for help. Even so, you just had to go and check, because you knew that if you didn't, and you later heard some poor soul had lain in the wreck with a broken leg for most of the day, you'd feel wretchedly guilty.

But really, what could she do? Going to the police was out. Going to Isabel with her suspicions would just be cruel, and would probably lead to all sorts of family rifts and ructions that might have some serious ramifications. And Isabel might then ask the C-Fits to stop their investigation and Corwin and the others didn't deserve that.

No. Effie shook her head, and started to walk back towards her car. She was just being silly. She had amused and indulged herself enough, it was time to call it a day and forget …

And then she had a thought that stopped her dead in her tracks. And a wave of horror swept over her. And just like that, doing nothing ceased to be an option.

Mary Coles answered the knock on her door after a short, but – to Effie – frustrating pause.

'Oh hello, love, it's you back again, is it?' the old woman greeted her happily. 'Wanna come in?'

The unexpected and abrupt invitation took Effie by surprise, but she eagerly accepted. Then, as the old lady showed her into a small, crowded but clean little front room, she supposed that Mary was probably glad of any visitors nowadays, regardless of how little she knew them.

Everyone knew that loneliness in the elderly was an ongoing problem, and so it wasn't surprising that Mary spent her days outside by her gate, watching what little there was that went on in the village pass her by, and hoping for some human contact.

'Cup of tea, love?'

'Yes, please,' Effie said, then added guiltily, 'but please don't go to any trouble. Would you like some help in the kitchen?'

'No, you just sit. I'm not so senile or decrepit yet that I can't make a body a cup of tea,' the old lady shot back spiritedly. 'And I made some shortcake. Would you like some?'

Effie didn't – she knew how much butter went into them – but nodded quickly, too intimidated by Mary's ferocious scowl to decline. Instantly, the old lady smiled beatifically and shuffled off.

She was probably only gone five minutes, but to Effie, who was feeling increasingly desperate, it felt more like five hours. But instinct told her that it was no use trying to hurry someone like Mary. She might just shut down completely and go stubbornly silent, just when Effie really needed her to be her usual, garrulous self.

So she sat up and thanked her effusively when she returned with a tray bearing some lovely Spode teacups and saucers, decorated with a bright floral design. She even took two pieces of shortbread and nibbled on one, before letting it join its twin, balancing on the edge of her saucer.

'So,' Mary said, with a bit of a grunt as she lowered herself into the armchair opposite her. 'Has old Claudia been walking the floor again, rattling her chains?'

Effie smiled. 'Don't tease. And no, she hasn't.'

'Pity,' Mary said with a sigh, and picking up her own cup, blew across the top of it before taking a cautious sip. Effie, seeing that her own tea was still steaming away, decided it would be too hot to drink yet, and nervously twisted her hands in her lap.

'So, what can I do for you then? By the way, what's your name again? My memory's not what it was.'

'Oh, sorry. I'm Effie James. I didn't mean to intrude, but there was one thing I needed to know, and I didn't want to bother Isabel with it.'

Now Effie was being somewhat economical with the truth there. She hadn't gone to Isabel seeking information because she wasn't at all confident that she'd have been able to pull it off without their client wondering what it was that Effie was really up to.

'Well, if I can help,' Mary said, with what sounded very much like mock modesty. And when Effie looked across at her, the little old lady was indeed looking at her with a twinkle in her eye that told her she wasn't being fooled for a moment.

'Oh, it's nothing really,' Effie insisted, giving what she hoped came across as a bright, casual smile. 'It's just that I've been looking around for some time for a daily woman to help me out in the house for a few days a week. You'd be surprised how hard it is to find someone suitable nowadays,' she heard herself say, sounding, much to her dismay, like an appalling snob.

'Oh, ah, well, I dunno that I can recommend anyone, either,' Mary Coles said at once, glancing around at the crowded front room complacently. And it wasn't hard to see why – for as stuffed with occasional tables, ornaments and various other knick-knacks as it was, there wasn't a speck of dust to be seen anywhere. 'I always do for myself.'

Effie flushed, feeling absurdly guilty and lazy, even though nowadays she did the bulk of her own housework too!

'Oh no, I didn't really expect that you would know of someone,' Effie demurred quickly. 'But I understood from Isabel that Claudia had a woman who used to come in and do work for her, and I just wondered if, now that she might be out of a job, she might be free. Does she live locally by any chance?'

'Oh, you mean Annie Darville,' Mary said at once. 'Yes, she just lives down the village aways. Carry on down the street,' she pointed vaguely out of the window, 'cross over at the end, as if you're heading to the church, then turn off up Rickyards Lane. Just off there, there's this little nest of houses the council built just after the war. She's in one of them. Can't think of the number right off, but I know she's in the one with the bright plum coloured door. I remember my niece telling me about her husband painting it last summer. She said it was a hideous purple, but then, some people just don't have any taste, do they?' Mary observed with a small sigh. 'Another biscuit?'

Some ten minutes later, Effie finally managed to pry herself free from Mary, and was walking swiftly towards the church. She found the little cul-de-sac of houses easily enough, and one of them did indeed have a rich, plum-coloured front door.

As she opened the garden gate and walked up the path, Effie found herself wondering again just what on earth she was getting herself into. And half of her still wanted to turn tail and run. She had no idea how she was going to go about getting what she needed from a woman she had never met before. The potential for making a fool of herself – not to mention getting summarily ejected from someone's home – had to be sky-high.

But she knew her conscience wouldn't leave her alone if she simply went home and washed her hands of the whole affair now. Because, if by any chance at all, Claudia Watkins's supply of St John's Wort tablets *had* been substituted for something with digitalis in it, then it was imperative that nobody else should take them, lest they fall ill or die as well.

And she could clearly remember Isabel telling her that her mother's supply of the pills had been passed on to her daily help.

And then Effie had another awful thought. What if the poor woman had already started taking them? But if that was the case, they clearly couldn't be doing her any harm, for surely Mary would have said if Annie Darville had been ill recently.

Before she had even lifted her hand to press the doorbell, the door in front of her abruptly opened, catching her totally wrong-footed. So far, she hadn't managed to formulate a plan, whereby she could ask about the St John's Wort without sounding … well … totally out of her mind.

Now, abruptly, and without any warning, she found herself looking at a small, neat, grey-haired woman in her early sixties. Big brown eyes looked at her with a vaguely curious expression.

'Yes? I saw you coming up the path from the window. You don't look the kind to be trying to sell me anything and Jehovah's Witnesses usually come in pairs, don't they?'

'Er, yes, I suppose they do,' Effie agreed faintly. Then added, a shade helplessly, 'You are Annie Darville, I hope? Mary Coles told me where to find you.'

'Yes, I'm Annie. We've not met, have we?'

'Oh no. I'm a … er … friend of Isabel. Claudia Watkins's daughter? I was hoping you might have time to have a quick word?'

'Yes, I know Izzie,' Annie said, turning to one side. 'Please, come on through.' Evidently, she had decided Effie looked harmless, and the mention of mutual acquaintances had probably been enough to reassure her.

Effie was therefore shown into a large room, with big double-glazed windows framing a view out across the neighbouring estate. Unlike Mary Coles's room, there wasn't a knick-knack in sight. No doubt a woman who dusted other people's ornaments for a living didn't want to come home and do it all over again. A dark grey, wall-to-wall carpet (which presumably hid the dirt well) housed a large, somewhat lumpy sofa and two matching armchairs.

'Please, take a seat.'

'Thank you. My name's Effie James,' Effie began, sitting down and wondering just how on earth she was supposed to set about steering the conversation to this woman's supply of medication.

But when she looked across at her, Annie Darville suddenly

smiled. It lit up her neat, unremarkable features like a firework going off.

'Oh, you're one of the ghost people!' she said with obvious pleasure. 'We've seen you around, coming and going.'

'Yes,' Effie confirmed. And then had to give a mental double take. She had just admitted to that without a moment's thought or qualm. But if someone had told her, just a month ago, that that would be the case, she'd have thought they'd gone mad.

Then again, if someone had told her a month ago that today, she'd find herself actively investigating a possible murder case, she'd have thought that *she* was the one who had gone mad.

Either way, it just went to show how your life could just suddenly change, without so much as a by your leave or any prior warning.

'I was hoping to run into one of you people,' Annie further surprised her by saying complacently. 'We're all so eaten up with curiosity! Would you like a cup of tea?'

'Oh, no, thank you. Mary made me one just twenty minutes or so ago and I'm still full.'

Annie nodded. 'She's a bit of a character, our Mary, isn't she?'

'Yes.'

For a moment there was one of those awkward silences whereby neither party had any idea quite what to say next. Effie, because she still didn't know how to broach the subject that was uppermost in her thoughts, and her hostess because Annie had no idea what had brought Effie to her door.

'So, I was just wondering, what are your thoughts about Claudia?' Effie heard herself say. 'I mean, everyone who knew her has been telling us that she was a very … well, strong-minded sort of woman.'

Annie smiled faintly. 'That she was a bit of a tartar, you mean?'

Effie shrugged, not sure how to respond to that, since she wasn't sure how well Annie had got on with her former employer. If she hadn't much liked Claudia, then agreeing that Claudia had sounded an awful sort of person to work for, might well help her establish some sort of rapport. But if, on the other hand, Annie had been fond of her, or still felt loyal, then it would only antagonize her.

'I never met her,' Effie temporised. 'Which is why I was hoping that someone who knew her well might … er … clarify a few points for me. Always supposing you don't mind talking about her, that is. I understand that you were the one to find her?' she added gently. 'That must have been so shocking and distressing for you, so if you don't want reminding of it, I do understand.'

Annie nodded and took a deep breath. 'It's all right. There's no need to dance around with me. I'm not made of china. And Mrs Watkins might not have been the easiest of my ladies, but she was real quality, you know what I mean?'

And with that simple statement, Effie suddenly felt herself to be on much surer ground. She could sense that this unremarkable woman had probably felt an odd sort of pride in working for someone that the rest of the village still regarded with respect – even if it was of the grudging variety.

'Yes, I do. And I've been thinking much the same thing. From what I've learned about her, she must have been a very strong woman, a woman with an iron will. I do wish I'd known her.'

Annie nodded. For a moment, her lips wobbled a bit, and her eyes became suspiciously bright. Then she visibly pulled herself together. 'I was with her for nearly thirty years. Can you imagine? Started doing for her when my kids were young. It feels odd, I can tell you, not to be going up to the house every morning and getting her breakfast.'

'I can imagine. You were fond of her?' Effie said, with genuine sympathy.

'Yes, I was – though some might have wondered why. A lot of people didn't like her, see. I say that they just didn't understand her. Mind you, it took some doing. Understanding her, I mean. She had a heart of gold about some things. But she could get fixed ideas too, about the oddest of things, and then nothing would budge her.'

'Like her gardener having to retire?'

Annie gave a brief grin. 'Yes. Poor old Geoff. Mind you, he was like me – he knew how to handle her. He just kept on turning up and doing the work no matter what she said, and she kept paying him, because she hated to feel beholden to anyone. It was writ in stone with her that if you did a good and honest day's work, you got a good and honest day's wage. Of course, she would swear each time that it would be the last time that she would knuckle under, and if he kept on coming, she'd just ignore him and not pay him a penny more. Of course, we all knew she wouldn't be able to do it.'

Annie shook her head and sighed. 'Not that she was soft or anything. And sometimes she *did* mean exactly what she said. She could be tough, and hard headed when she felt riled enough. It was more a question of learning when that was, if you see what I mean.'

'Yes, I think I do,' Effie said. 'There were times when you took her ways with a pinch of salt, and times when you'd better pay attention.'

Annie beamed at her as if she were a particularly bright student in a class of dullards. 'That's it! And I reckon there were one or two people who learned the same lesson, but the hard way,' she added meaningfully.

'Oh?' Effie asked gently.

Annie nodded. 'Like that Vince Bagshott, for instance.'

Effie shook her head. 'I don't know him.'

'No reason why you should. He's one of our local county councillors,' Annie said flatly. 'Mrs Watkins had him round to tea … oh … about two weeks before she died. Nothing unusual in that – Mrs Watkins was very active in the local parish and knew a lot of people on the county council as well. And she didn't like this proposed new housing development over near Bloxham, and she was determined to scupper it, if she could. And she might have done too – she had a lot of power, between you and me,' Annie said, without rancour. 'But then, rich people often do, don't they?' she added matter-of-factly.

Effie nodded.

She was perfectly happy for Annie to talk as much as she liked, since it gave her more time to come up with some kind of excuse to leave with Claudia's bottle of St John's Wort. If the worse came to the worst, she could always 'confide' that she'd been suffering from depression recently, and perhaps Annie would just offer them to her. She seemed kind-hearted enough. The only problem with that was, how could she be sure they'd be Claudia's and not Annie's own supply?

'And Mrs Watkins knew people in high places, as they say,' Annie swept on. 'And what's more, many of them owed her favours. You know what I mean?'

'Yes, she was a woman of some influence, I understand,' Effie said vaguely.

'Hmm. As Mr Bagshott quickly found out.'

'I see,' Effie said, her mind still on the rogue bottle of pills. It wasn't until the silence had lengthened significantly and she noticed that Annie was watching her with a dry kind of patience that she actually took in what the daily woman had just said.

'You mean she actually *threatened* him?' Effie squeaked.

'Oh, now, I couldn't really say that,' Annie temporised judiciously. 'I was in the kitchen, after all, putting a casserole in the oven for her evening meal, so I couldn't make out what was being said. I always left about four o'clock in the afternoon, leaving something in the oven for her, like. And they were in the drawing room. But once or twice I could definitely hear raised voices.'

Annie looked vaguely discomfited, and it didn't take Effie long to realize why. The daily woman didn't want to admit to being deliberately nosy.

'Poor you. That must have given you something of a real dilemma,' Effie sympathized cannily. 'On the one hand, it was none of your business, but on the other, Mrs Watkins was an old lady, and she might have been in need of your help. Obviously, you had to do *something*.'

'Exactly,' Annie nodded with satisfaction. 'So from time to time, I sort of wandered up and down the corridor, outside, like. So that I'd hear her if she called out for me.' Annie paused, and when Effie nodded encouragingly, went on. 'Yes. So, anyway. As it happens, it was Mrs Watkins who was the one doing the tongue-lashing. Telling him off good and proper she was. At one point I heard her say clearly that she knew that her granddaughter's husband had been paying him handsomely, and that if he didn't vote against something or other, then she was going to see to it that Mr Bagshott got kicked off the council.'

'Blimey,' Effie gulped.

'That's what I thought.' Annie nodded, eyes bright with

remembered excitement. 'He left pretty quick after that I can tell you, like a dog with his tail between his legs.'

'I bet. And Mrs Watkins?'

'Oh she was pleased as punch, she was,' Annie said with a smile of her own. 'You could tell she was feeling quite smug, in fact. She kept muttering to herself all the rest of that afternoon that she'd fixed young Clive's hash. She'd really taken against young Ros's husband the last couple of years or so.'

'Yes, I'd heard that,' Effie said. And then a thought rather belatedly occurred to her. Annie was being really very candid, wasn't she? Saying all this to a virtual stranger. For a second, Effie looked at the older woman cautiously. 'I hope you don't mind my asking. But ... why exactly are you telling me all this?'

Annie Darville looked away briefly, her eyelids flickering slightly. 'Oh, no particular reason,' she said casually. And it was clear to Effie that now *she* was the one who was not being quite so candid. 'I just thought that you might be interested, that's all.' Annie glanced down casually at her hands. 'That her *family* might want to know about those final few weeks of hers.'

Effie felt a slight coldness start to churn in her stomach. Was she imagining it, or was Annie Darville trying to intimate something, without coming right out and saying it? Or was she just projecting her own doubts and suspicions onto her?

'I'm not quite sure what you mean by that,' Effie said carefully. If the daily was trying to tell her something, she didn't want to scare her off. On the other hand, before she committed herself, she needed a little more reassurance that she wasn't reading too much into all this.

Annie's eyes went to Effie's face, searched it for a few seconds, then moved casually away again to a spot on the wall just a little to the right of Effie's head.

She sighed slightly, and began to look distinctly pensive. At last, she blurted out, 'It's just that there were such a lot of things bothering her, in the days before she went. So when I heard that things had been happening up at the house, and that Izzie had called in some paranormal people in to see what was what ... Well, I just thought you'd be interested in knowing about it. I mean, in case there's anything to all this haunting business. That's all.'

'Do you believe in ghosts, Annie?' Effie asked gently.

Annie looked surprised. 'Me? Never really thought about it.'

'Hmm,' Effie said. Then, even more carefully added, 'But if you think it's possible that Mrs Watkins's spirit is, well, proving to be rather restless … Forgive me if I've got this wrong. But you seem to have it in mind that there might be a reason for it.'

For a moment, Annie Darville continued to contemplate the carpet at her feet, then she finally looked up. Perhaps she sensed that Effie wasn't going to be judgemental. Or perhaps she simply needed to get off her chest – something that had been plaguing her for weeks. Either way, Effie watched as she stiffened her shoulders, and when the daily woman spoke next, Effie wasn't really surprised that Annie did so with some conviction.

'You know, that old lady might have had a heart condition, but I never heard anybody say that it was anything *really* serious. I certainly never got the impression from her doctor that it was, and you can usually tell, can't you? What's more, I saw Mrs Watkins every day. And apart from getting a little breathless when she walked too far, I'd have said she was fit as a fiddle for her age. Now then!'

Effie caught her breath. Was Annie really telling her what she thought she was telling her?

'So you were surprised when she died so … suddenly?' Effie asked, almost whispering now.

'Surprised?' Annie Darville said quietly but firmly. 'I was downright flabbergasted.'

Effie nodded slowly. Oh well. It was now or never. And now it was Effie's turn to stare at a point just beyond the daily's head.

'Izzie tells me that her mother used to take St John's Wort, to help her sleep?' she began quietly.

'That's right. Mrs Watkins recommended it to me too. Since my kids left, I get down sometimes. Apparently it's good for that sort of thing too,' Annie confirmed. She was clearly a little surprised by the abrupt change of topic, but seemed willing enough to go where Effie led.

'And Izzie tells me that … afterwards … she let you have her mother's supply.'

'Yes, it was nearly full, see,' Annie said. 'She'd only just opened a new bottle the week before and Jasmine puts a hundred in every bottle. It was nice of Izzie to let me have them. She said it was a shame to waste them.'

Effie slowly let her eyes drift across and meet Annie's puzzled gaze.

'And have you taken any of them yourself yet?' she asked, aware that her heart was thumping sickeningly in her chest now.

'No, I'm still using my own,' Annie said. 'I've still got a couple of weeks' worth still left, see, so … ah.' She broke off, her large brown eyes blinking rapidly. 'Oh my,' she added. Then again, going slightly pale now. *'Oh my.'*

For a moment, the two women regarded each other in mutually appalled silence. Then Effie said diffidently, 'Annie, would you mind if I … er … borrowed Claudia's bottle of pills for a bit?'

Annie continued to stare at her blindly for a few seconds, then without another word, got up and a minute or so later returned just as silently, carrying a bottle. It had Jasmine Carteret's instantly recognizable label fixed firmly in the centre.

'Here, take it,' Annie said tonelessly. 'And don't bother to bring it back,' she added bitterly, with a brief shudder.

CHAPTER THIRTEEN

One of the good things about living near Oxford, Effie mused, was that there were no shortages of labs capable of doing a full and complicated analysis of almost any material known to man.

And so, after a quick Google on her new tablet (she was pleased at how quickly she was beginning to get the hang of all her new gadgets!), Effie detoured to one such establishment and dropped off six of the yellow, jelly-like pills Annie had just given her. The person she'd spoken to there had told her that it would be easier (and cheaper) if she had some idea of what it was they were supposed to be looking for, so Effie had simply asked them to be on the look out for any digitalis-based compounds. Which, by her reckoning, most definitely should *not* have been found in St John's Wort pills.

Then, feeling both ridiculous but nevertheless relieved, Effie went home and set to work in her garden with a clear conscience. With a bit of luck, she might even be able to sleep well for once that night.

Of course, she was still almost one hundred per cent sure that the lab results would come back negative, and that all the pills would contain exactly what you'd expect them to contain. And then, at last, she could put this moment of madness behind her once and for all.

But as she weeded and bedded out, Effie was also aware that

tomorrow night there was another vigil scheduled at Claudia's house. And, for the first time since they'd found out that she was a widow, Effie was going to have to face her friends again. Which left her feeling a little nervous and uneasy. But not nearly as much as she might once have expected. What's more, she was actually looking forward to seeing them all again.

That night, she slept well.

Effie was sitting with Isabel and Gisela in the kitchen sipping tea when the men had finally finished setting up the equipment. Even with a lot of it now being left permanently in place, Malc had to spend a good hour on the main laptop computer, satisfying himself that all the monitors were functioning and that all was well.

Tonight Lonny had had to cry off, since one of his children was unwell, and his wife had something of a phobia about meningitis, which meant that any rise in temperature or flu-like symptoms in one of their brood set her off panicking.

'OK, we're all set,' Corwin said, as he and the others trooped in. He gratefully accepted a mug of tea from Isabel and glanced around. 'I was going to ask Lonny to do a couple of outside patrols tonight. Mickey, you want to volunteer?'

'Give me a break, Chief, I did it last time.'

'In other words, he thinks it might rain,' Jean said with a smile.

'I don't mind doing it,' Effie said at once.

It was clear that the outside patrols were regarded as a bit of a chore, and she was more than happy to do her fair share of the unpopular jobs. Being Duncan's eyes and ears was no excuse for her to be given more privileges than the others, after all. What's more, if she was going to be a productive member of the team, she needed to start pulling her weight, and experiencing everything about a vigil, both good and bad, would be essential training for her.

And a few turns around the garden at night would be more of a pleasure for her than a chore, anyway. She was sure she'd spotted some night-scented stock growing near the kitchen wall garden, and if the odd cutting or two just happened to find its way into a plastic bag, and thence into her pocket, who would notice?

Like all keen gardeners, Effie wasn't above a bit of botanical larceny.

'Are you sure?' Corwin asked, looking at her closely. 'It's going to get dark tonight – there's not that much of a moon – and it can feel very lonely and isolated when you're outside on your own.'

'Yeah, no need to run before you can walk, Eff,' Malc said. 'You don't have anything to prove to us.'

Jean and Gisela made the same sort of noises, and Effie sighed elaborately.

'Come on, it's not as if we're in outer Mongolia,' she laughed. 'And I'll have my mobile phone on me. If anything worries me, I'll just call for the cavalry.'

'Be sure that you do then,' Corwin said crisply. 'And make sure that you take a digital recorder with you and leave it running. It'll be too dark and inconvenient to take written notes. And be sure to do a commentary on anything that you see or hear that strikes you as at all interesting.'

'Yes, Chief,' Effie said smartly, giving him a brisk salute.

Mickey grinned and gave her the thumbs up. Effie pretended not to notice. Corwin shook his head at her, but she could tell he was pleased, both that she'd volunteered for the job and that she was being such a sport about it.

'OK, then. A patrol every four hours then, please, starting at ten tonight. Last one at six in the morning. And when you're not outside, would you mind taking the hall spot again?'

Effie nodded. 'Not a problem.'

'And, obviously, be as quiet and unobtrusive as possible when you come and go. A lot of the cameras tonight are centred on the hall and stairs.'

Malc nodded. 'They're a favourite spot when it comes to catching anomalies on film.'

'Such as that swirling mist tape you showed me the other day,' Effie said. 'Got it. I'll try not to trigger anything off.'

Tonight, Gisela was going to be back in Claudia's bathroom. She was convinced that the cold spot was the source of the restlessness and dissatisfaction that she maintained was becoming more and more obvious. Malc would have to man the monitors alone, since Lonny couldn't relieve him, which left Corwin to stay in Claudia's bedroom, nostrils aquiver, and Jean to alternate between the downstairs rooms.

Isabel said she was having an early night, and by nine, everyone had settled down to their chores. The house fell silent and it began to get dark. And Effie, sitting in her armchair in the hall, waited patiently for the hall clock to strike ten o'clock.

The night was overcast, but there was no sign of the promised rain as she let herself quietly out of the front door and stepped out into the tiny front garden. It was not quite fully dark, and as she set off around the side of the house, she could just about hear the odd bat, squeaking overhead as they set off on their nocturnal hunting.

There was barely a half moon, but whether it was waxing or waning, she was never sure, and as she walked along the neatly mown paths between the informal flowerbeds, she let the small, battery operated torch in her pocket stay where it was. Her night vision allowed her to see far more anyway, and she knew that Corwin preferred light sources to be restricted to a minimum.

The occasional moth flittered about, and occasionally she caught the lovely scent of early honeysuckle, climbing up the perimeter wall. Her circuit eventually took her to the boundary with the Rollwright Inn next door, and in the night air, she could hear the chatter of people and the occasional clatter of cutlery as the odd, late-night diner finished their meal before retiring to the bar.

The sound was vaguely reassuring, although Effie hadn't, in fact, felt in the least bit apprehensive all night. From time to time she would look carefully about her, but there was nothing that struck her in any way odd. No shadows where there shouldn't be any, no white shapes flitting by, no ghostly voices sighing in the breeze. She smiled to herself as she made her way back around the side of the house and once more towards the front door.

The front garden would take about two minutes to look over. After that, she'd be able to go back inside and try not to set off any of Malc's motion sensors as she did so.

It must have been getting on for nearly eleven o'clock, and in the street a car started up and drove away. And with everything seeming so normal, and with her mind more occupied on how she could best regain entry into the house without anyone being disturbed by her movements, it took a moment for her to realize what was happening.

But then, with her next breath, she suddenly became preternaturally aware that the scent of lavender was suddenly all around her, enveloping her. Stronger than she'd smelt it in Claudia's bedroom. *Much stronger.* In fact, it seemed to be all around her, almost choking her. The scent was so strong in the back of her throat now she could almost taste it. And what's more – it felt *warm*. Like someone's breath.

Instantly her head snapped up, and the little cry of surprise that had formed in her mouth came out in a strangled moan as she saw what was directly in front of her.

The mist!

Wafting in the cooler dark night air, it was clearly visible – a pale, white vapour, tinted vaguely orange by the streetlight opposite. It rose in the air, more or less in a straight line, heading up.

Effie gulped, stumbled back and then fumbled frantically in her pocket for her phone. With shaking fingers, she managed to turn it on.

The scent of lavender was still overpowering, but now Effie was distracted by something else. Something new. A sound. She could clearly *hear* something. And this was not one of Malc's beloved EVPs that needed to be amplified by a computer. This was clearly audible to the human ear. A sort of gurgling noise.

Was it really possible that she was hearing some sort of communication attempt from beyond the grave?

Effie froze.

Gurgling?

For a second, her brain seemed to do a sort of side-slip, as it went from unthinking, instinctive, atavistic panic, into a much more prosaic search mode. *Because that gurgling noise sounded somehow familiar.*

And since Effie was sure that she'd never heard a ghost before, just what the hell was it?

By now her brain was definitely clamouring that she'd heard that noise before. What's more, her eyes were telling her that what she was seeing now, wasn't the same as what she had seen on the recording Malc had shown her of the mist in the cellar of the house in Steeple Aston. That had been thick and had moved in a distinct, swirling, dancing motion. Whereas the mist in front of her was paler, almost white, and much thinner, and seemed to be moving up and dissipating in a steady stream. It looked in fact like … steam.

Steam.

Water. Gurgling. *Yes*!

Her brain gave a mental high-five. *That's* what it was that she was hearing – water gurgling, as only water can gurgle when it was confined in some way and trying to get out.

And a second after that breakthrough, Effie realized exactly where she was. In the front garden, right next to the Rollwright Inn. As she looked up, she noticed the drainpipe that ran down the wall. And remembered again, standing in Claudia's bedroom, looking down at the drain below the window.

And then she began to laugh. Indeed, for a few seconds, she could do nothing but lean against the wall, literally gurgling with laughter herself. Finally, realizing that she was still holding the phone in her hand (that, in fact, less than a few seconds had actually passed, although she felt as if she'd just aged ten years) – she speed-dialled Corwin's number.

'Yes?' his whispered answer came softly in her ear.

'I'm outside in the front garden. I've found the lavender lady,' Effie said. OK, she knew it was a bit naughty, but she was feeling so giddy with relief that she wasn't thinking straight. 'She's still here, but you'd better come quick, before she disappears.' And so saying, Effie turned off the phone.

She glanced up at the inn once more, wondering which guest, in which of the rooms facing the street, was at that moment stepping from a bath full of lavender-scented bath water after pulling the plug. Because that was undoubtedly what had just happened.

And now that she came to think of it, it had been a warm night when Effie had first scented lavender in Claudia's room. Corwin had even helped her open the window. Which is why, when the guest had first emptied their bath, the scent of the rising steam had managed to penetrate into the room.

It took only moments for them all to arrive of course – all of them clearly having run as fast as possible, all protocols now firmly out of the window. Perhaps not surprisingly, Corwin and Mickey, being the fittest and fastest, were first to arrive, but Jean and Gisela, and the more portly Malc, were hot on their heels.

Effie held up a hand, and they came to a quick halt. Malc instantly started filming the still visible steam.

'Can you smell it?' Effie asked quietly.

'Yes, it's very strong here,' Corwin said, slowly edging closer.

She could see that he was following the progress of the steam into the sky, and his eyes, which had been alight with interest and eagerness, were slowly dimming.

And she felt her heart break a little for him.

'I think it's bath water from the inn next door,' she said quietly. 'There's a drain just the other side of the hedge. And Claudia's bedroom is right next to where the house joins the inn.'

Corwin nodded wordlessly, his lips now pulled into a tight, thin line. He beckoned to Malc. 'Film over the hedge, if you can. Get a good shot of the drain.'

Malc obliged, managing to get a shot of where the steam was originating, and confirmed that it was indeed coming from the drain. She could clearly hear a collective groan of disappointment from the others behind her. Moreover, since the bath water had now run its course, the steam was evaporating, and the scent of lavender was going with it.

'I'm sorry,' Effie said quietly, making Corwin turn and look at her sharply.

With the streetlight right facing them, he was able to see her face clearly, and she his. The weird effect of the light and shadows gave his face a cavernous aspect, all sharp angles and pale and dark planes. And she couldn't see the cat-green light normally present in his eyes.

'Why? It's not your fault,' he said flatly.

Effie shrugged miserably. 'But you so wanted it to be something more, didn't you? I saw the look on your face as you came running out. And the others were the same. You were hoping … well … to see a ghost.'

Corwin shrugged fatalistically. 'Sure, we were,' he admitted simply. By now the others were all muttering disconsolately among themselves, and Effie winced. 'And yes, it's bitterly disappointing,' he agreed. 'But that doesn't mean that we'll ever give up trying.'

Effie nodded sadly. 'I'm sorry too. About that phone call, I mean. I shouldn't have played that trick on you.'

He frowned. 'What trick?'

'You know. Saying that I'd found the lavender lady. I could have just explained then and there. Not got your hopes up. The truth was that I was so relieved….' She went on to tell him everything that had happened, freely admitting that, for a few moments there, she'd been badly frightened, and that it was the subsequent relief that had led to her lapse of judgement.

'I didn't mean to be cruel,' she finished miserably. 'Getting your hopes up was unforgivable. I'm really sorry.'

Corwin looked at her, and saw she was literally hanging her head in shame.

'Hey, we can take a joke!' he said. 'Besides, it would have taken you too long to explain it anyway. If you'd tried, we'd have wasted valuable time getting out here to see it for ourselves. As it is, we all got to experience it, and more importantly, we've got documentary evidence of the conditions and phenomenon, so I can now write about it with confidence.'

Effie nodded, not really mollified. 'But it's useless, isn't it? For your next book, I mean.'

'Not at all,' Corwin said crisply. 'It'll make a good chapter. Sometimes, accurately reporting and explaining why a ghost sighting or haunting isn't anything of the kind, is just as important as documenting a genuine case.'

'But not as satisfying.'

'Of course not.' He grinned. But in spite of his upbeat pep talk, Effie could sense that he was, inevitably, feeling dispirited and disappointed. 'But then, I did warn you that ninety-nine point nine per cent of the time, these things have a rational explanation,' he pointed out.

Effie nodded. She knew he was right. What's more, she knew it was stupid and irrational to feel so disappointed as well. After all, she didn't really believe in ghosts, and she certainly didn't have the same emotional investment in all of this as her new friends did.

'I just wish I hadn't been the one to discover the truth, that's all,' she said.

'Don't be daft, Eff,' Malc's voice cut across the gloomy atmosphere. 'You done good.'

'Yes, well done, Effie,' Jean said bracingly. 'It may not be what we hoped for, but the truth is always a good thing to discover.'

'And there's still the cold spot,' Gisela said stubbornly. 'I'm more convinced than ever that that cold spot in the bathroom is important.'

'Speaking of which,' Corwin said flatly, 'Mickey, get back and monitor it. Malc, I need you to finish up here. Continue to record the steam and document the moment the scent evaporates. I'm going to go next door and have a quiet word with the management. If they'll agree, I want to write a brief note to each guest who has a room facing the front, asking them if they'd agree to speak to me. If they will, and I can pinpoint who it is who likes lavender so much, I can hopefully get a timetable of their bath times and confirm that each time either Isabel or we smelt lavender, it corresponds to when they'd just taken a bath.'

Effie could only admire, yet again, his determination to be thorough. Not to mention his ability to bounce back after adversity.

'Gisela, nip up to Claudia's room and see if any scent is still detectable in there, then spend the rest of the night in the bathroom. Effie, I need you to finish your patrol, then back to the hall. OK, everyone?'

Everyone nodded and dispersed. But Effie, knowing that she'd finished the first of her patrols, just didn't have the heart to go back inside the house just yet. Instead, she wandered morosely to the front gate and wandered a little way down the pavement towards the village green.

Around her, Adderbury was closing down for the night. House

lights were being extinguished, and even the cats seemed to be heading for hearth and home. She was just about to turn back towards the house, when a shadow detached itself from beneath a horse chestnut tree and a solid, all-too-human figure loomed up in front of her.

'Hello, Mrs James,' Clive Carteret said grimly. 'I'd like a word with you.'

Effie's heart rocketed into her mouth, and she took several stumbling steps backwards before the iron railings of someone's garden boundary halted her. In the eerie orange glow of a nearby streetlight, Effie could see that he'd noted her reaction, and a furious look crossed his face.

'Oh, hello, Mr Carteret,' Effie finally managed to say, her voice, even to her own ears, sounding breathless and tense. 'You gave me a bit of a fright.'

'So I see,' Clive said flatly. 'An occupational hazard, perhaps? So, how is the ghost hunting going? Has Claudia been sending you any interesting ghostly messages via the ouija board?'

'We don't hold séances,' Effie corrected automatically. But her mind was whirling. Why was he here? What did he want? Was she actually in danger – should she scream?

'No? You surprise me. I thought all self-respecting vengeful spirits liked to vent their spleen on such things.'

Effie managed an uncertain smile. She knew that Malc would still be documenting the evidence in Claudia's front garden for some time yet, and so was well within shouting distance. And the thought of having his burly, capable presence coming running if she called for help gave her some much-needed confidence. So even though her heart was still thumping in her chest, and she felt vaguely sick, she also began to calm down. And think.

'And what makes you suppose that your grandmother-in-law's spirit would be feeling vengeful, Mr Carteret?' she asked, glad to hear that her voice had now lost some of its tremulous quality.

'My sister called me yesterday,' Clive said abruptly. 'She told me about your visit to her shop. I have to say, it rather got me thinking.'

Effie swallowed hard. 'Oh?' Try as she might, she was unable to come up with another sentence.

'Yes. She told me that you seemed to be very interested in our childhood.'

'Oh no. We just got chatting, as you do,' Effie demurred weakly.

'Which I thought was more than passing strange,' he carried on, just as if she hadn't spoken. 'So after I pumped her a bit, I began to see exactly which way your mind was leaning. And I didn't like it. Not one bit. You're a clever little bitch, aren't you?' he added softly.

Effie blinked. 'What?' she gasped, feeling a little shocked at the unexpected and explicit insult. *Was he actually admitting to it?* Why? Why be so stupid? And did that mean she'd actually been *right?* No, that couldn't be. This couldn't be happening. Effie had often heard the phrase 'the mind boggled' but until that moment, she'd never really understood what it meant. Because, for a few seconds, it was as if her brain couldn't seem to get itself into any kind of gear. It was as if she could actually feel her mental wheels skidding for some kind of purchase.

'What's the matter, Mrs James, been reading too many whodunits? Too much time on your hands, was that the problem?' he sneered. 'Were you so bored you thought you'd just stick your nose in where it didn't belong and do a spot of private investigating? Very Miss Marple! Well, let me give you a lesson in reality, lady,' he snarled. 'There's not a damn thing that you can prove, got it? Jasmine's not so good with her record keeping. She didn't even notice that some of her stock was gone. And I was careful to wear gloves at all times.'

Effie swallowed hard. 'Are you … Let me just get this straight. You *did* use your sister's lab equipment to make a batch of St John's Wort pills, then? And put some kind of poison in them?'

'Very good, Mrs James,' Clive said mockingly. 'Tell me, I'm curious. Any idea what it might have been?' He sounded almost amused now. Clearly, he was so cock-sure of himself that he regarded her as no kind of a threat whatsoever.

Effie took a slow, deep breath. This was surreal. This conversation was just … beyond her.

'Well, I thought,' she began hesitantly, 'since Claudia had a heart condition … some kind of foxglove derivative?' But even as she spoke, her brain was shrieking at her. *Just what do you think you're doing? Calmly discussing the ins and outs of murder with a madman. Just run, you stupid woman. Run*!

'Oh, now you are *impressing* me,' Clive continued hatefully. 'And you're quite right, of course.'

Effie's feet felt like lead and seemed rooted to the spot, so running was out of the question. What's more, it was as if she was in the grip of some compulsion that wouldn't let her stop asking questions.

'And then, the next time you were at Claudia's house, you swapped them with the harmless pills she got from your sister.'

'Again, you'll never prove it,' Clive said. 'The old cow is dead and buried and nobody suspects a thing. Why should they? And there's no way you'll be able to get an exhumation order. Nobody will believe you if you go around spouting your fantastical-sounding little theories,' Clive taunted. 'That poor Mrs James, they'll say. Losing her husband really shook her up, didn't it? Still, she's at a funny age in life, isn't she? Did you hear the latest? She's now going around with a bunch of loonies looking for ghosts, and saying some poor chap murdered his wife's grandmother. I can hear them laughing at you now.'

Effie went hot, then cold, but said nothing. Because, finally, she understood what this was all about. Clive Carteret was trying to scare her into silence. To play on her insecurities, and perhaps even to threaten her life if she talked.

'Jasmine will never testify against me,' Clive continued remorselessly. 'And Ros will stand by me, which means that Izzie will too. And after I've sued you for defamation and anything else that my solicitors can think of, your name will be mud.

Plus, you won't be such a well-heeled widow anymore.'

Ah, not a threat to her life then, Effie thought, with a mixture of relief and … was that almost amusement? Just a threat to her social standing – and her financial well-being. Which, once upon a time, might really have worried her. But now….

'So I just thought I'd point out where things really stand, before you go and do something we'd both regret,' he finished viciously.

Effie slowly nodded. 'I see.'

Clearly, he didn't know that Izzie had given Claudia's tainted pills to Annie. Why would he? Izzie had told everyone that she'd thrown all her mother's personal things – like toiletries – away. So he was wrongly assuming that any solid evidence against him was now long gone. If he had known how things truly stood, he would not be so damned confident, she thought, beginning to feel angry now.

'Glad that you do,' Clive said. 'So, it's all settled then?'

'Oh yes,' Effie said faintly. 'It's settled. But there's just one thing I'm not so sure of. Did you kill Claudia because of the baby issue? Or because of the money thing?'

Clive laughed. 'Who cares about brats?' he snapped. 'I've told Ros we don't need them and she agrees with me.'

Effie nodded. 'I see. It was that threat Claudia made to the councillor that did it, wasn't it? The one you bribed to vote for your latest housing project?'

'My my, you have been a busy little bee, haven't you? And again, you're quite right of course – that's why the meddlesome old sow had to go. We had a blazing row about it.'

That would be the argument that Mary Coles had overheard, Effie thought.

'Mind you, she'd been getting on my wick for years,' Clive swept on. 'I was never good enough for Ros, never top drawer enough to be counted as a member of her family. I told her straight, I made more money than that late sainted husband of hers ever dreamed of.'

'I don't imagine that impressed her much,' Effie heard herself say dryly.

Clive laughed. 'No, it didn't,' he agreed. 'Nothing about me impressed her, it seems. Not that I cared one whit – she could gnash her teeth about me as much as she liked. Put me down, drip her vitriol into my ear – it was all water off a duck's back to me. But when she threatened my business …'

'You decided she had to go and so you killed her,' Effie finished flatly.

'Like I said,' he repeated, quick as a flash, 'there's no way you'll ever prove any of it. And if you try, my legal team will tie you up in knots. You'll be in court for years. I'll have every last penny off you, and your reputation will be in tatters. I mean it.'

'I believe you,' Effie said.

'Fine. That's it then. Oh, one more thing – I want you and that Scooby-Doo gang of yours out of the house. Tell Izzie that her dear departed mama isn't haunting her after all, and pack up your cameras and gizmos and just go.'

'That's not up to me,' Effie said stubbornly.

Clive merely shook his head, said something foul and turned and walked away.

And Effie simply stood there and watched him go. She felt … curiously unafraid. Mostly numb. A little cold. And vaguely perplexed. What on earth had got into her?

She realized, of course, that she was probably going into shock. A man, after all, had just admitted that he was a cold-blooded, premeditated killer.

That sort of thing just didn't happen. Did it?

Feeling as if her legs were about six feet long, Effie turned and walked unsteadily back to the house. Once there, she made her way to her chair in the hall and slumped down with some relief, pulling her coat closer around her for warmth.

And, in the darkness, she closed her eyes and, after a little while, fell asleep.

When she awoke, it was light. And she remembered clearly everything that had happened last night, but thankfully, now the shock was gone. She had simply slept it off.

Around her the house was beginning to stir.

And Effie finally began to think – clearly, rationally and carefully – very carefully indeed. And after ten minutes, she got up and walked to Claudia's bedroom. There she knocked on the door and walked in.

Corwin Fielding looked up at her curiously from his position in the chair by the window.

'Hello.' He checked his watch. 'Vigil's not quite over yet.'

'I know,' Effie said. 'There's something I need to tell you. But first, you'd better listen to this.'

And so saying, she brought out the digital recorder in her pocket – the sensitive powerful recorder that had been turned on and in her pocket all night. The recorder that had faithfully recorded every word that Clive Carteret had said to her.

In the end, Effie went to the police on her own, but only after a couple of days had passed, since she'd wanted to wait for the results from the lab to come in on the pills that she'd given them for analysis.

Corwin had really wanted to go with her, but she wouldn't let him. It was something that she needed to do on her own – to prove to herself that she was fully capable of looking after herself now. That she didn't need Michael, or anyone else to hold her hand when times got rough.

And she hadn't gone to the police station thinking that they were going to welcome her with open arms. She wasn't *that* naïve. She knew it was going to be tough, and it was.

At first she was shown into an interview room where she talked to someone junior. And after giving her initial statement and then waiting nearly an hour, she'd had to go over it all again with a more senior officer. The questions had become sharper, harsher and more probing as time went on. Occasionally Effie felt as if she herself was coming under suspicion of something. Once or twice she felt as if they were questioning her mental state.

But she stuck calmly and clearly to her narrative.

And at least she was armed not only with a copy of the recording between herself and Clive Carteret (Malc having made several copies for her) but also with the lab test results of the pills given to her by Annie Granville. Which did indeed confirm that a digitalis-based compound had been added to the St John's Wort. And she was reasonably confident that any medical doctor or chemist would agree that it would have been enough to kill, over time, someone with a pre-existing heart condition and someone already taking medication such as digoxin.

After she was all talked out, the detective inspector had then gone on to give her a short and pithy lecture about something called 'chain of evidence'. And how it was going to be tough to prove to a jury that the pills that had tested positive for the poison could, with any certainly, be traced back to Claudia Watkins's medical cabinet. Even with Isabel's and Annie Darville's testimony.

She was then told exactly how difficult it was to get an exhumation order, and how she'd better hope and pray that a forensic pathologist would be able to detect the poison still in the body.

As for the recording, it would be up to the lawyers whether or not it would be admissible in a court of law. Here, Effie had got slightly lost in the maze of what did, or did not, constitute 'entrapment'. And – amazingly – whether or not Clive Carteret's rights had been violated, when he had been recorded without his knowledge.

In the end, although thoroughly exhausted, demoralized and reeling, Effie had left the police station nevertheless reassured that the police would now be doing a thorough investigation into Claudia's death.

Which, she supposed, was a victory of some kind.

It was nearly a week later, when Effie met up with the C-Fits again, in the cricket pavilion near Cumnor. Malc's case of the haunted barn – and whether or not to take it any further – was on the agenda, and when Effie walked in and looked around a shade uncertainly, there was a moment of silence, before Gisela got up and threw her arms around her.

Jean too rose, and pulled up a spare chair, setting it next to her.

'Here she is, the woman of the hour,' Malc said cheerfully as Effie took her seat beside Jean.

'Yeah, Effie. Have we gotta call you Sherlock bloody Holmes now?' Mickey said breezily, and again Effie had to fight back a genuine desire to give his shin a quick kick. 'Crikey, who'd have thought that the old bird was bumped off?'

'Mickey!' Jean said sharply. And Effie felt the tenseness in her shoulders begin to ease.

She was among friends.

'I always felt that Claudia was getting more and more restless,' Gisela put in sadly. 'And no wonder – she was getting more and more frustrated because she couldn't make us understand what she was trying to tell us. That she'd been murdered, poor thing.'

'I can't believe I missed all the action!' Lonny moaned.

'I really wish you'd come to me earlier, Effie, when you first began to suspect the truth,' Corwin said, and suddenly everyone became quiet. Today he was wearing a pair of black denim jeans and a loose, pale green shirt. He was leaning forward on the chair, his arms resting atop his knees and was looking across at her intently. 'It scares me to think of how dangerous it all was. That man might have attacked you.'

Effie nodded guiltily. 'I know. Believe me, I do. And I wasn't being deliberately secretive, I really wasn't,' she swore truthfully. 'I just … actually, it was all so bizarre. And I couldn't help but think that you'd all think I'd lost my marbles if I started burbling about murder plots and poison and what have you.' She felt herself flush in embarrassment. 'I suppose I just didn't want you to laugh at me.'

'We'd never do that,' Jean said flatly.

'She's right, Eff,' Malc said gently. 'In fact, we'd be the last people in the world to stand in judgement. You should know that by now.'

Effie felt like crying, but managed simply to nod.

Corwin must have sensed how close she was to tears, because he leaned closer and covered her hand with his. His fingers felt warm and comforting as they squeezed hers.

'Well, just promise me that from now on, no matter how flimsy, or bizarre or off the wall you might think something to be,' he said firmly, 'you'll share any theories or thoughts you have with me … with all of us,' he corrected quickly. 'All right?'

Effie nodded. 'I promise.'

'Good.' He straightened up and leaned back in his chair. 'Now, before we go on to listen to Malc's initial report on the possible barn haunting, there is one final note I need to make on the lavender lady casefile.'

'Oh?' Jean said. 'I thought that was all concluded.' Naturally, the C-Fits were no longer welcome in Adderbury, since Clive Carteret had twice been called in for questioning. And it was now gradually dawning on the rest of Claudia's family the nightmare that was facing them.

'Not quite,' Corwin said, his green eyes gleaming. 'After checking the final temperature readings that we did, Malc noticed something very interesting about the cold spot. Malc?'

'Yeah.' The builder grinned, taking over the spotlight. 'First off, that cold spot was in the exact place that Claudia Watkins would have stood, every night, when she reached into the cabinet above the sink. Where she kept the bottle of St John's Wort pills.'

'Wow,' Gisela breathed, her eyes wide with awe.

'Yes. And we now know that it's likely Claudia must have taken a number of the pills, before the accumulative effect of the poison killed her,' Corwin pointed out.

'So Claudia was trying to point us in the right direction all along!' Mickey yelled, punching the air in triumph. 'That's why the cold spot wasn't by the bed, where she was found – it was where the murder weapon had been stored.'

'What's more,' Malc said, his face beaming now, 'according to the readings on the temperature gauges, that cold spot disappeared at 11.05 pm, the night we found out about the lavender bath water, and didn't recur again. Which, by my reckoning, must be about the exact same time that Mr big-mouth Clive Carteret was confessing to murdering Claudia.'

Everyone in the group seemed to draw in a collective gasp. Including Effie.

And for a moment, remembering back to that bizarre night, hadn't she felt as if something or some*one* had almost possessed her, guiding and urging her on, forcing her to confront Clive Carteret with a bravery that would normally have been totally alien to her nature?

And just what, Effie found herself wondering a little hysterically, would Professor Duncan Fergusson make of *that* if she should ever be so foolish as to tell him about it?